DARING THE DEFENDER

WITTMORE U: HOCKEY

ANGEL LAWSON

To all the fictional hockey bois that let us play with their minds and bodies.
You're the best.

FOREWORD

Badgers!

Quick Note for new readers: The Wittmore U Hockey series are standalone books focusing on one couple at a time. You do not have to read each book in the series, but characters do show up in each consecutive book and it may be a richer reading experience if you start with book 1, Faking It with the Forward and 2, Guarded by the Goalie.

For returning readers, I'm so happy to be back here with you again, playing with our Wittmore hockey boys. Diving into this world has really helped me find the balance between the chaos goblins rampaging through Forsyth (and my brain) and the slightly more stable guys at Wittmore U who know what consent means and just want to win the girl *and* the trophy.

This book doesn't have any extreme content warnings. There's some light angst, with themes with religion, foster care and adoption.

I hope you enjoy Shelby and Reid's story.

Angel

1

———————

S helby

PROMISE.

I turn the gold band in my fingers, pulling it off to peek at the word delicately engraved on the inside. I twirl it around, running my nail over the letters, a distraction from the conversation around me, or rather, *about* me.

"I'm thinking we'll hold it outside." My mother nods at the glass windows overlooking our large backyard. "Just after Easter. It should be warm but not too hot."

"It's a gorgeous yard." The woman next to her says as she flips through a stack of bridal magazines. That woman being my future mother-in-law, Carol. "But don't you worry about rain?"

Seriously. What about rain? Or worse, the special brand of humidity we have in Texas.

A drop of sweat slides down my back just thinking about it.

"We'll rent a few tents just to be safe, but I'm sure the day will be blessed with perfect weather as they celebrate their engagement." She looks up at me, where I've been perched on the edge of the couch for the last thirty minutes. Her gaze drops down to the ring in my fingers, and I quickly slide it back on. "Natural light is so much more flattering for Shelby's complexion. You know she can look so pale inside."

Ah, there it is, the real reason.

"Look at this dress," Carol says, ignoring my mother's backhanded compliment, and points to the magazine. "Handwoven lace. I had handwoven lace on my wedding dress." She sighs, her voice turning wistful. "I also had a twenty-two-inch waist."

"Luckily, Shelby was graced with my genes and not her father's, and she'll be wearing my dress," Mother notes, smoothing a hand down her flat waist. "It doesn't even need alteration."

"Oh," Carol's eyes dip down to my mother's slim frame, "how wonderful."

My fingers rise to my throat, scratching at the memory of the stiff high-neck collar. When my mother pulled the dress out of the well-preserved box and had me try it on, I'd hoped that maybe it wouldn't fit and maybe, I could get something lighter, more current, but nope. Fit like a glove.

"Did I tell you I stopped by the fabric shop?" Mother steamrolls on. "I picked up these swatches for a dress for the event." From her stack of samples, she holds up the swatches.

"That lavender is gorgeous!" Carol exclaims, looking over at me. "Don't you think, Shelby?"

"It's pretty," I agree, taking in the array of pastels. "Didn't we talk about blue? I showed you that teal that I liked."

Mother wrinkles her nose. "It's a lovely color, dear, but lavender will bring out the green in your eyes."

"David will love you in lavender," Carol assures, patting me on the arm.

"Of course," I nod, feeling myself drifting away. Even though we're here to discuss the upcoming engagement announcement, it seems like they've already moved on to the wedding. In fact, the plans are already set. The dates, the times, the food, and guest lists. It's all organized.

All I have to do is show up, look pretty, and marry the wonderful man down the hall.

Twisting my neck, I try to work out the tight muscle that pulses from the back of my ear down the opposite side of my spine. Pressing my hand to my lower back, I try to massage it out, but the pounding just moves to my temple. Next, it'll spread to my chest. It's not unfamiliar, and there's only one way to deal with it. I shoot to my feet and grab the pot of tea. "Let me go freshen this up."

"That would be lovely, dear." Neither woman looks up from their magazines and color swatches as I leave, stepping into the hallway. I make my way in the direction of my father's deep voice as he entertains David and his father in his study.

The house is massive, with high ceilings and ornate fixtures. My father is the minister of a mega-church called Kingdom here in Texas, and he claims the house is an extension of that ministry. He's popular, a celebrity, really, with his Sunday services broadcast all over the internet and thousands showing up every week to listen to his sermons in person. I've always loved being part of this community, and David, my future husband, grew up here too. His father is the music minister, so we get what it's like to grow up as a preacher's kid. He's older by two years, a senior at a religious college where he's earning a business degree. Once he graduates, he'll take a position at Kingdom, and I'll take my place as his wife.

Since we already knew I wouldn't need a traditional degree, I didn't continue my education, instead devoting myself to service at Kingdom. Currently, I serve with the youth, which is where I got to know David, but just being Nolan Rakestraw's daughter requires a lot of time and attention. There are a dozen events a week at the church. After my brother and my father had a falling out, he wanted to make sure the congregation knew we were still a stable family unit and my presence has been required more than usual. When David is officially on the staff my duties will expand to however he needs me to support him–until I have kids–then I'll focus on raising them.

Like the engagement party and wedding, all the boxes are ticked off.

Which is why I don't know why everything seems so overwhelming all of the sudden. Nothing has changed, well, nothing but one thing. I'd always thought my brother, Axel, would be by my side as I entered this next phase of life. He promised when he went to college he'd come back to work with the family. But something happened between him and my father–a huge falling out, one that I'm not privy to the details of, but I do know that ultimatums were made, and Axel made the decision to live his own life–chase his own dreams.

That's when I started waking up at 3 AM with a thudding heart and unable to go back to sleep.

It's the change I'm uncomfortable with, that's all, and I need to get back on track. Axel has always been a wild card. Fiercely independent and completely focused on his hockey career. It only intensified when he moved East and joined the Wittmore hockey team as their goalie. And if his social media is accurate, my brother has fallen head-over-heels in love.

I smooth the front of my sweater and peek into the cracked door. My eyes land on David first. He's handsome. Hair a shade darker than my own, with pale blue eyes. He sits across from my father, his long legs bent between the chair and the coffee table. I love how tall he is–his body is lithe and strong, from years of disciplined running.

I'd been shocked when he started talking to me during our volunteer hours. All the girls had a crush on him–including the teens we worked with. He's got a warm, welcoming smile and when he turns it on you, it feels like a ray of sunlight. But better than that, he makes me feel steady.

I'd never had a boyfriend before. Father allowed dating, but when every boy you know is a member of his congregation, most wouldn't dare ask. I wasn't one of those rebellious preacher's kids–that was Axel's job. I like following the rules, and deep down it always felt like I was saving myself for someone. Turns out that someone is David Jones.

"We couldn't be happier with this engagement," my father says, and it warms my heart knowing he approves. "I've prayed long and hard that the right person would come into both Shelby and Kingdom's life and to my surprise you were already here."

I smile when the men laugh.

"With you marrying Shelby and joining the ministry, the council wanted to offer you a little start and keep you close to the church." My father lifts a rolled-up sheet of paper and spreads it across the coffee table. "There's a nice piece of land Kingdom owns that will be perfect for your first home. I've had blueprints drawn up and once I give the final approval the contractors are ready to break ground."

First home?

"I'm thinking of a four-bedroom, which will give you room for a few babies." My father winks at Reverend Jones, and a wave of discomfort passes over me. "I've added a few other perks, like a small at-home office for you, a large kitchen for Shelby, a family room, and a great backyard."

The throbbing in my temple starts its slow and steady beat. A decision to hold the party outside was one thing, the swatches, the dress, the dates... all of that is something I can swallow, but building a house without my input?

A sharp pain shoots down my shoulder so hard that I drop the teapot to the floor with a thud. I grab my neck, trying to ease the throbbing pain, and slump against the wall.

What. The. Heck.

"Shelby?" David's voice penetrates, and I look up to see him standing in the doorway, worry creasing his forehead. "What happened?"

"My neck..." I start but don't know how to finish. I glance down at the shards of ceramic and the dark liquid splattered across the floor. "I'll get it," I say, ignoring the pain and automatically shifting back into gear. I force myself down to the floor, crouching, and David does the same. He quickly picks up the pieces of the broken pot. "Go back with the men. I can do this."

"Shelby." His hand grabs my wrist. "What's wrong?"

I don't know how to say the words. I've been taught to obey and what would I say anyway? Confess that everything is moving too fast and feels out of control? Complain about my family giving me the world, the perfect man, an amazing wedding, and now, a lovely home? It's entitled and bratty and ignoring the throbbing that has moved to my temple, I swallow it back.

But I do have one question. "Did you pick this out?"

He frowns. "Pick what out?"

I tug off the ring, turning it so the word 'Promise' catches in the light. "The ring."

David is a lot of things. Smart. Funny. Handsome. Motivated. But most of all he's not a liar. "Well, not exactly. Your father–"

I've heard the proverb about the straw that breaks the camel's back more times in my life than I can count. I never understood what it meant until now.

But this?

This is my straw.

And I think I'm broken.

2
____

R ^{eid}

It's embarrassing to admit how fast I check my phone when a notification comes through. I lunge for it–heart crammed into my throat.

Thank you for ordering from Badger Pizza! Fill out this survey for a discount on your next order!

Well... fuck. I definitely thought that maybe it was her.

Tossing the phone on the table, next to the half-eaten pizza, I unpause my game and continue with the ass-kicking I'm handing out on screen. At least there's no one else home to witness my humiliation. I'd never live it down.

It's my choice to stay home, even though there are a few parties going on around campus. Tonight isn't a night for a single man, especially not one that has a firm 'no serious relationships' policy at the moment.

It's Valentine's Day, and Valentine's Day is a couple's thing and the last thing I want to do is lead someone on. Looking for a relationship is fine. Women should do what they want. See who they want. Fuck who they want. As *much* as they want. Exclusive or not. But me? I've done the monogamous thing–and I'm taking a break.

This is why I'm sitting at home by myself, playing ice hockey video games by myself, while eating a heart-shaped pizza from the joint down on the strip *by myself*. It's ironic, actually, that two of my roommates found serious girlfriends right when my relationship with Darla fell apart. Hell, Axel is the one that taught me the no dates on Valentine's Day rule, but now both he and Reese are in the throes of it–all loved up and blissed out in that new relationship haze, fucking like bunnies, and simply just basking in one another.

While I'm over here shaking it off, trying to get my groove back one co-ed at a time.

Grimacing at the screen, I maneuver my man down the ice, body-checking the other guy into the boards. "Take that!" I shout to the empty house.

After moving my player into position, I'm waiting for the puck to drop when I hear a noise on the porch–a loud thump, followed by light footsteps. Our house, The Manor, is the biggest one in the old mill neighborhoods surrounding the University, and often the location for some pretty epic parties. Add in the fact that four hockey players live here, having visitors or one of the guys on the team drop by isn't unusual. I assume it's either one of them or maybe Jefferson, my only other single roommate out on the porch. I told him not to go out tonight, but history has proven nothing comes between him and getting his dick wet.

I make a few more plays on the game, waiting for him to come in, or for someone to knock, but that never happens. Maybe he's out there making out with some girl.

Or hell, maybe it's a serial killer.

Dropping the controller, I stand and cross over to where we keep our equipment, grabbing a hockey stick in one hand and gripping the knob with the other. Looking out the window at the top of the door, I can't see anything but the shift of a shadow.

"Sack up, dude," I mutter and yank open the door. I step out with the stick raised over my head. "If you're a murderer, you picked the wrong damn house."

I hear the smallest "eep" and look over to the opposite side of the porch. Blinking I take in the person sitting on the swing. It's a girl. Well, a college-aged girl, with her hands up. "Not a murderer. Promise."

"That's what they all say." I exhale and drop the stick. "Jesus, you scared the hell out of me."

"Sorry," she says, eyes flitting down my body, starting with my cut-up t-shirt and then down to the Wittmore sweatpants. When her gaze returns to my face, there's something in there–and not the hot appraisal I expect. Judgment maybe? I don't often feel exposed. I'm a big guy. Fit–although beefier than my roommates, which is what makes me a beast on the ice. I'm strong as hell, and I know women like my body, but this girl? I can't get a read.

"You need something?" I ask, leaning the stick against the door frame. "There's no party tonight, but I hear there's some stuff going on down on Greek row."

"I'm looking for someone," she says, standing, giving me a better look at her. She's a dirty-blonde, with doe-sized eyes. Her skin looks sunkissed, different from the winter pale skin of the girls on campus. Her clothes are modest; a gray skirt that comes down to her knees, and I see a thick sweater peeking out under a jacket that's not quite warm enough for the weather up here. I try not to wrinkle my nose at her shoes, basic black flats. It's pretty well known that I'm into fashion and know my brands, vintage or current. I figure that if everyone is already looking at me on campus because I'm on the hockey team, I may as well give them a full show.

This girl doesn't look or dress like anyone we usually hang out with. Even Twyler's got a sporty vibe, but the girl on the porch is all bundled up and frumpy. "Is Axel here?"

"Ax?" I repeat. "No."

"But he lives here?" she asks, hopefully.

I could lie. Do my friend a solid and get rid of this girl for him, but she looks on the verge of panic so I throw her a bone. "Yeah, he lives here, but he's not home right now."

"Oh thank goodness. I was really worried I had the wrong place." She exhales, visibly relieved and her eyes, the color imperceptible in this light, shine with hope. "Would it be okay if I waited for him to get back? I can stay out here on the porch if it's a problem."

I grimace, rubbing the back of my head. "Look, I gotta be honest with you, sweetheart, Axel's got a girl now–a serious one. So whatever you're wanting from him is a no-go."

That news doesn't deter her. She clears her throat and says, "I just need to talk to him. If he doesn't want me here, I'll go but... it's important."

Fuck. Did he get this chick pregnant? It's hard to tell with that skirt and that jacket. I mean, I know it's not always obvious, but she doesn't look knocked up. She'd have to be early, and Axel and Nadia have been together a few months... and there's zero chance he cheated on her.

Okay, this chick isn't pregnant, but needs to talk to Ax. Maybe it's just a school thing.

"Come on." I jerk my chin at her. "Come inside. My nipples are about to freeze off."

I don't miss her eyes widening and then flicking down to my chest. Is she worried about being alone with me? Whatever. It's her choice. It's also February in New England and these temperatures are no joke. I step inside and she follows.

"There's pizza on the table by the couch," I tell her. "It's probably a little cold now, but it's still good. You want a drink?"

"Sure, that'd be nice." She shrugs off her jacket, assessing the room. "Thank you."

"No problem." I open the refrigerator and grab two beers and a seltzer left over from the last party. I carry them over and set them on the table. "I didn't know what you'd like."

She stares at the two drinks, looking flummoxed, before settling on the seltzer and opening the can. She doesn't drink it though, instead moving to the pizza box and opening the lid. "A heart-shaped pizza?"

I sit on the opposite end of the couch and pick up the controller. "Valentine's Day special."

"Oh, right." Her face falls. "I forgot."

"What? Forgot you had a hot date tonight?" I click the button to resume the game. "Break the heart of some love-lorn guy?"

"What?" Her voice rises two octaves. *"No."*

I look her up and down, better now that the light is brighter and she's shed the jacket. She looks vaguely familiar, so maybe she has been here before. Possibly with Axel. Now that I can see her, it's obvious she's got a good body, curvy, and her tits are nice. Get her out of that matronly skirt, and into something shorter, a little tighter, that shows off those legs and–*fuck*. I just talked myself into a semi. Good job, Reid. I clear my throat. "Hey, just saying. You're cute. Seems like you'd have a boyfriend, or at the very least, someone wanting to be your boyfriend."

Her cheeks turn red, and damn, I like the way that looks on her. Flushed and flustered. I expect her to make a run for it, but she just nods at the game I'm only half playing. "Your team just got scored on."

"Shit." I turn my focus back to the game. "It's just one goal. I can get the score back."

She's quiet next to me as I maneuver my player down the ice, the forward gets a pass past me, and I curse again. Maybe I'm the one that's flustered.

"Your defense needs to block the passing lanes," she says.

"I know what I need to do," I snap. Yet her distraction and admittedly, my frustration, makes me miss the next play and they score again. "Dammit."

"Told you."

I eye the girl next to me. "You think you can do better?"

She shrugs, a coy smirk on her mouth. "Probably."

"Go for it." I hand her the controller, grab a piece of pizza, and lean back. True to her word, she does do better. Her defender is everywhere, blocking plays and slamming guys against the boards. She helps her team get the two points back and I laugh. "So you're a ringer. You play hockey?"

"Gosh, no. Just this game." She frowns in concentration at the screen. "My bro–*friend* taught me."

"Well, he must know his stuff." I sit back, taking a long drag of my beer, and watch. Not the game, but the player. She's perched on the edge of the couch, completely engrossed in the game, her teeth puncturing her bottom lip, making it fat and swollen. From the side, I get a better view and take in the firm swell of her tits and I get the urge to strip off that heavy sweater and see what's underneath.

Who is this girl? Where did she come from? Is she some sexy, video-playing, Valentine's gift sent to my doorstep from Cupid?

And if so, what does that mean?

Nothing, I think. This girl has a strangely innocent vibe and she came here to see Axel, not get hit on by his roommate.

"Yes!" she shouts as the game-ending buzzer sounds from the TV. My team is up by one because of this girl. She holds up her hand in a high-five and I slap it, because even though she made a fool of me, she's fucking cute. She grabs her seltzer and takes a long drink. Her nose scrunches at the taste but it doesn't take away from her grin. "Can I ask you a question?"

"Sure."

"Don't you get cold not wearing a real shirt?" She gestures to my cutoff shirt. "It's freezing outside."

"I run hot," I admit. "Always have. I guess it's the one reason I got into ice hockey. Being cold never bothered me."

"I'm the opposite." She tucks her hands into her sleeves. "My hands are freezing all the time."

I take her by the wrist, engulf it in mine, and pull it to my chest. She watches me, not saying a word as I lay her palm flat on my sternum. I feel a jolt when her fingertips touch my skin–because damn, they're cold, like ice cubes, but I still feel a sense of warmth spread across my skin.

It's the sensation that drives me to reach out and push her hair off her cheek. She looks up at me and I finally see her eyes–a bright greenish-blue. Aquamarine. I'm struck again by the familiarity but instantly distracted by those dark pink lips.

I want to kiss her.

I'm thinking about kissing her.

Yep. I'm *going* to kiss her.

Fuck, I don't even know her name.

Despite the free for all of the last month, I'm not the kind of guy who makes out with a girl without getting her name.

"By the way, what's your na–" I start, but she's up on her knees, body leaning over mine. Her lips aren't cold like her hands–they're warm–*soft*. Moving my hands to her hips, I run them down her sides, pushing that stupid skirt high enough to drag her onto my lap. She falls forward, those cool hands gripping the thin cotton front of my shirt, her hair making a curtain around us, blonde and feather-light. Although she makes the first move, there's a hint of hesitation. I cup the side of her face with my hand and take control, leaning into the kiss, licking at the seam of her lips for a taste.

Big mistake.

Her mouth is hot, and tastes like the berry flavor of the seltzer, she feels good–reckless. My cock thickens, drills unabashedly into her thigh. Fuck, now I want more.

Her.

I want *her*.

"Seriously," I say between kisses, "I'm Reid. What's your name?"

She pulls back, eyes cast down. "Shelby."

I dive back in, a thought niggling at the back of my brain, somewhere deep behind the foggy lust. *Shelby*.

I jerk back. "Did you say Shelby?"

"Yeah." She loops her hands around my neck and places warm kisses along my shoulder.

"Shit. Shit. *Shit*." Now I know why she looks familiar. "He's going to kill me."

Because it wasn't Cupid that sent this girl to my doorstep but some twisted god of chaos, the front door swings open. In a panic, I shove her off, jumping to my feet.

"What the–!"

"I swear I didn't know." I hold my hands out, but he's already coming at me, a ball of rage and fury that no one, not even Reese expects. I brace myself for the impact of Axel's fist slamming into my jaw. All I can think as he makes contact is that I have it coming.

"Axel! Stop!" Shelby screeches, and there are other voices, Nadia and Twyler. My friend comes at me a second time, but I slam my hand out, blocking his fury until Reese grabs him with both hands and drags him off.

"What are you doing?" Nadia asks her boyfriend. Twyler shrugs. Everyone is confused.

He struggles against Reese's grip, eyes filled with betrayal, and he spits out, "What the fuck are you doing with my sister?"

3

———

S helby

"I swear to God," Reid says, touching the spot on his lip where it's already started to swell from Axel's punch. Mine tingle too, feeling equally swollen and abused. "I didn't know who she was until–"

"He didn't," I cut in. Axel hadn't actually seen me kissing his friend. Just that I was on his lap, which, by the way, I'm aware isn't much better. "I didn't tell him who I was."

"You didn't tell him." My brother's attention shifts to me and there's no missing the sarcasm. Oh boy. I'm not afraid of my brother, but I can't have him mad at me. Not when I need him like I do at the moment. "You think that makes it better? You're just sitting on top of guys you don't know all of a sudden?" His expression shifts as if he's finally processed I'm here, in his living room, and not in Texas like I should be. "Shel, do Mom and Dad even know you're here?"

I open my mouth to answer but feel the heat of every eye in the room on me. Reid and Reese, teammates of my brother's that I know of, but have never met. Reese walks back from the freezer and tosses an ice pack to Reid. A wave of guilt hits, knowing that was my fault.

After handing off the ice, Reese stops next to the smaller girl, sliding his arm around her back. She and Nadia haven't stopped staring at me since they walked in. I don't know much about Nadia, but I do know she's Axel's new girlfriend and is the main reason he and my father had a falling out. The reason Axel isn't coming back home after he graduates.

It occurs to me, making the moment even more awkward, that they're all dressed nice–too nice for a weeknight–including my brother.

My eyes slide to the mostly eaten heart-shaped pizza. They were on a Valentine's Date and I blew it all up.

"I can explain," I say, second-guessing coming here and interfering with my brother's life. "But in private. Please?"

Axel runs a hand through his hair, and sighs, before turning to his friends. "Can you give us a second to sort this out?"

"Of course," Nadia agrees but pushes past him. "I'm Nadia, by the way, your brother's girlfriend. It's nice to finally meet you."

"Shelby," I say, taking in the dark-haired girl. "And same."

"That's Twyler and Reese." She nods to the couple over her shoulder. Then she smirks. "You've obviously met Reid."

Reid. When he'd opened the door I'd been so nervous about seeing my brother that I'd barely taken him in. I'm used to big, Texas-sized guys, so that hadn't intimidated me, but the casual way he leaned in the doorway, the hard curve of his exposed biceps and strong forearms took me off guard. His hair isn't arranged in that intentionally messy way, like my brother's. It's pushed back from his forehead, but short on the sides; styled. His eyes are a warm, kind, brown, and his lips a dark pink. I'm going to blame the force of all of that for my temporary insanity.

"Babe," Axel says, cutting his eyes at his girl. His voice is low with warning, but it's not carrying much weight. She confirms this by turning back to him and kissing him on the cheek.

"We'll give you two some space," she tells him.

"Come on, Reid," Twyler says, waving him over, "I'll check out your face and make sure Ax didn't do any real damage."

Axel doesn't look the slightest bit ashamed for Reid's puffy lip, and calls out, "We're not finished," to his friend. Reid just nods, following the others up the stairs without another word. I watch him go, eyeing the hard muscles that make up his back.

I can still feel the heat of his chest on my fingertips.

Taste his tongue on mine.

"Sit," Axel says, breaking me from the memory. I lower into the armchair, not wanting to revisit the scene of my impulsivity. Axel sits there instead, flipping open the box and picking up a piece of cold pizza with his tattooed hand. "You know I'm already on the Rev's shit list," he starts, meaning our father, "so if you have something to say, do it, because you know I have to call Mom."

"Don't," I say, panic licking up my spine, "please."

My tone must sound more pleading than I realize because his expression shifts from annoyance to concern. "Did something happen at home?"

"It's hard to explain."

If anyone can understand what I'm going through it's Axel. He grew up in the same home–knowing what it was like to live by our father's standards, under the constant scrutiny of being a preacher's kid at a megachurch the size of Kingdom. Even so, things were different for him. He was allowed to pursue outside interests like hockey and go three thousand miles away to college. He's covered in tattoos, always dated freely, and barely cooperated with the family rules. I had none of that leeway. Why did our father allow him to do these things when I couldn't? I only have one guess: because he was a boy.

My father regrets it now, having issued an ultimatum to his oldest and losing.

When I heard that Axel pushed back and took a stand against our father, I'd never been more proud, but I was also sad.

"You traveled two thousand miles and showed up on my doorstep, Shel," he says, "I think you can explain to me why you're here."

"You know I got promised to David at Thanksgiving." I ignore his frown of disapproval at the pre-engagement, and continue, pushing through in a rush, "Well, last night the parents got together to plan the engagement party and start organizing the wedding. Mom told Mrs. Jones I'd be wearing her wedding dress, and they'd already picked out the location, flowers and tents, and it just felt like they were planning *their* wedding, not mine. Then when I went to talk to David, I saw Dad revealing blueprints to the home he's having built for us." Hot tears prick my eyes as I admit the truth. "No one asked my opinion on anything, Ax. It's like I'm not even there."

I touch the ring on my finger not telling him that Dad picked this out too. Yes, I'm still wearing it. I *promised,* but it lacks the same luster.

The muscle in the back of Axel's jaw tics, but he doesn't look the slightest bit surprised. "That sucks. Hard. But it's not exactly unexpected. They've always been controlling and you've never had a problem with it before. In fact, you've always been pretty agreeable."

"I know." Again a wave of uncertainty hits me. Did I do the wrong thing by coming here? Should I have stayed? "I'm having a hard time sleeping–sometimes breathing. It feels like the walls are closing in, you know?"

He snorts, but his hand moves absently to his chest like he feels the pressure. "Oh yeah, I know." He studies me. "You never ran away before. That's what this is, right? A runaway."

"I'm twenty, Axel, too old to run away."

But we both know that's exactly what I did. I packed a bag, called an Uber, and used the money I'd saved over the years to get on the first flight to the only person I knew to go to. The only person that had ever rebelled against my parents.

"Did you break things off with David?" he asks, a little too hopefully.

"No." I twist the ring.

He sighs. "I'm assuming they don't know where you are?"

"I left a note for Mom, letting her know that I was going some-where safe, and I just needed some time to sort things out."

"Well, they'd never consider coming to me as being 'safe' so that's probably why they haven't called looking for you." His hands thrust into his hair. "Fuck, Shel, this is going to blow up."

"I know." Disobeying my father is one thing, but messing up this engagement, which will reflect back on him and his church? Unforgivable. "I think I just need a minute–away from the house and all the rules and expectations. Some time to get my head on straight, so I can be the wife David deserves."

"And you figured you'd prove that by sitting in my roommate's lap?"

The casual accusation brings a blistering heat to my cheeks.

"That was just..." Just what? I don't know. Not like me for sure. I've never done anything like it before. *Ever.*

"I'll let it go, *once.* These guys aren't like you, Shel. Reid's one of my best friends but he's..." he searches for the right word and settles on, "...experienced. You're lucky he's also a good guy because there are a lot of men on Wittmore's campus that would take advantage of an innocent girl showing up on their doorstep." He shakes his head and laughs darkly. "Like a lamb to slaughter."

I don't like the description of me being innocent or a lamb, probably because it's a little *too* on the nose, but I'm not in the position to argue. "I'm sorry, and I promise that if you let me stay here–just for a few weeks–until I get my head on straight, I'll stay away from him and anyone else. I'm not looking for trouble." Or a handsome man with strong hands and lips. "I just need a chance to breathe before the whirlwind of the engagement and wedding kick into gear." I look around the living room, at the messy pile of hockey equipment, and the dishes piled across the room in the kitchen sink. "I'll help around the house. Do whatever you–"

He stands and reaches for me, lifts me off the couch, and pulls me into a hug. "Shel, I'm glad you trusted me enough to come to me," he says, resting his head on top of mine.

A thread of tension in my chest unwinds and I know I came to the right person. For what? I'm not sure yet, but at least he'll give me the space to figure it out.

AFTER BRINGING in the suitcase I'd stashed in the bushes next to the porch, and a quiet discussion with Nadia, Axel gives me his room for the night.

"I can't take your room," I say, standing in the hallway. I give Nadia an awkward smile as she hovers at the top of the stairs, a bag slung over her shoulder. I'm booting her too, which is weird on so many levels. If my parents knew I was in a house with unmarried couples sleeping together, they would be livid.

I'm not upset in any way, but I can't help but feel a little immature when I think about what Axel and Nadia do on that bed and how inexperienced I am. My mind wanders back to the couch with Reid. Is it normal to still feel a kiss this long after it happened?

"There's no way you're sleeping in the living room," my brother announces. "Not in a house with four men."

"That couch is disgusting," Nadia's nose wrinkles, "and I have an early shift at the gym tomorrow and should get home, anyway."

"I'll walk you out," Axel says, grabbing Nadia's hand. "And then I'll call home to let them know you're safe."

They leave and I step into my brother's room, taking in the college version of my brother. It's smaller than his room back home, but it's also more personalized. Mom doesn't like clutter and makes us keep our rooms clean and tidy. The decor is mostly hockey-related: a few jerseys and a couple of sticks are mounted to the wall. There's a poster of Axel, dressed in his goalie kit, with the Wittmore Badgers logo underneath. I feel a small surge of pride, knowing my brother is doing so well with the team, but there's also evidence that he's not just here for athletics. Books and papers are stacked on his desk, along with his laptop and a full backpack. Standing in the middle of the room, I'm able to take a deep breath, I think for the first time since leaving Texas. Even though I feel safe here–steadier–I know I haven't solved a single problem that I left behind.

Opening my suitcase I grab my pajamas, happy to get out of the clothes I traveled in all day. The curtains are open and I walk across the room to close them. Axel's house is at the end of a long row that leads toward campus. It's the biggest on the street–the only two-story. Down below, I see movement; Axel and Nadia. He's got her pressed against a car parked out front, her curvy hips pinned beneath his, and they're kissing.

Oh boy, are they kissing.

My cheeks burn just watching them, and not just because it's inappropriate to spy on my brother and his girlfriend making out. It's more because of what I'd done with Reid before. That wasn't what I'm watching now–two people completely consumed by one another. Mouths in synch, bodies close, hands exploring. The way I'd lunged at him had been sloppy, immature.

Axel's hand drops down and his fingers dip beneath the hem of Nadia's skirt. Her legs shift, giving him room, and with my heart–and other body parts–pounding, I abruptly pull the curtains closed and turn away. Is that what he meant by Reid having experience? Because kissing like that? Touching?

Way out of my comfort zone.

David and I are taking things slow–appropriately slow for a promised couple–I think as I pull on the soft shirt and shorts of my pajama set. Which is why my encounter with Reid was so shocking. Who was that girl?

Downstairs, I hear the door open and close, followed by Axel's voice traveling up the stairs. Moving to the door, I press my ear against the surface, trying to hear better. I hear the word, 'Mom,' and 'she's safe,' but the rest is garbled. Frustrated, grabbing my tooth-brush as a decoy, I step out to the hallway and linger near the closed hall bathroom door. Axel's voice carries up the stairs.

"I don't exactly know why she's here, Mom, but I think things got too intense with the wedding planning and she needed a break." He quiets as he listens, then adds, "Maybe it had something to do with Dad arranging a marriage for her when she's not ready." I lean over the banister as if that will help me hear my mom on the other side of the line. "She can stay here as long as she wants." Pause. "Yes, I have roommates. Male roommates." He sighs. "Jesus, Mom, they're not perverts, they're hockey players–successful ones who have too much on the line to mess around with my kid sister." There's another pause, this one a little longer, finally he replies, "If you give her a little bit of space I'm sure she'll come home and end up the doting housewife you always planned for her to be. Shelby is a lot of things, but being defiant isn't one of them."

The last line hurts, slamming hard into my chest. Not because he's wrong–but because he's right. I'm not defiant, not like him. There isn't a rebellious bone in my body. Right now, I'm just... something I can't put my finger on yet, but I feel more scared than anything else.

I hear footsteps and the front door open and close again as he goes out to the porch, effectively cutting me off from the conversation. Resigned, I turn around, and nearly jump out of my skin when I see a figure leaning against the frame of the bathroom doorway.

Reid.

"You scared me," I say, swallowing back a jolt of adrenaline.

"Sorry. I didn't expect you out here." He's shirtless now, having shucked his ripped up one from before. The soft, melted ice pack is clutched in his hand. His bottom lip is puffier than before, but it does nothing to detract from his rugged good looks. I'd been startled at his... well, *everything* when he opened the front door tonight. He's broad. Big. Confident–but in a different way than my father who commands a crowd with ease. This was a lazy swagger, despite the cold and his exposed skin. Unlike Axel, he's not covered in tattoos. Just the number eight on his bicep.

His reddish hair is more copper than true red, shaggy on top, and has a curled layer of fringe at the nape of his hairline. His brown eyes peek out from underneath as he continues, "I thought he may throw both of us out..."

"He's on the phone with our mother. Hopefully, getting me a reprieve." I gesture to his mouth. "Sorry about that."

"For the kiss?" He touches the bruise with a fingertip. "Or for Axel going all big brother?"

"Both," I say firmly, knowing Axel meant what he said. He's not going to let me stay if I disrupt the house–and I don't want him hurting anyone else. He's protective to a fault. I cross my arms over my chest. This does nothing but draw his gaze to the motion. "Neither will happen again."

Except his tongue darts out to touch the bruise on his bottom lip and my stomach flip flops thinking about the way it felt touching mine.

"Look," he says, lifting the ice pack up to his mouth and holding it there for a second, "I'm not gonna get bent out of shape about a hot girl kissing me, but you should have told me you were Axel's sister."

Hot girl? My skin prickles like it's on fire and from the smirk lifting his lips, he knows it. "I'm not available for kissing," I tell him, feeling the reminder of the ring on my finger. "And I didn't want you to call him or anything, giving me a chance to see him before he heard I was here."

"So why *are* you here, Axel's sister. Aren't you getting married or something?"

"My name is Shelby," I reply, a little too primly, then add, "He told you that?"

He nods. "He mentioned it after Thanksgiving. He wasn't too into it."

"Yeah," I laugh, "he's made his views about me being promised to David clear." Axel has been explicit in thinking that I'm too sheltered —too immature–to be ready for marriage. He thinks I need an education and time to experience life. I think that those are all things I want to do with a partner.

But as we know, no one really cares what I think.

"So, did you break it off with this David guy?" he asks.

"We're fine," I assure him. "I just wanted to get away before everything got crazy with the planning. Visit my brother for a while."

I don't know why there's a flicker of annoyance in my chest. Maybe from the fact that his expression makes it obvious he doesn't believe me.

"Well, whatever reason you're here, I don't plan on getting my face busted up again, so try not to climb into my lap again."

My jaw drops and my hands ball into fists at my side. "I-I," I sputter, then settle on, "Maybe you should have a little decorum and wear an actual shirt when you answer the door."

"Maybe." His tongue darts out. "If you can't handle it."

"What? I can handle it." It being him shirtless, which I won't lie, is incredibly distracting. Do all men have a thick thatch of hair like that on their chests? Or the thin line below his belly. Is it soft?

"Mmhmm." His gaze drops and he notes casually, "You're being pretty bossy for a girl whose nipples are saluting me right now."

My arms snap up, crossing over my chest. "Don't look at them!"

He steps toward me, crowding my space. I step back, but just hit the wall. I've got nowhere to run when he bends, mouth close to my ear. "Your brother told your mother the truth. We're a houseful of hockey players who are very focused on the kick-ass season we're having. But he also lied." His breath is warm and I can smell the beer he had earlier. "We're easily distractible. We're horny. *All the time*, and will absolutely take advantage of a naive, little, good girl showing up at our door." He swallows, Adam's apple bobbing. "Standing in the hallway in a thin nightshirt leaving little to the imagination. But here's the thing, you're lucky I'm the one that opened the door, that I'm the one standing out here with you right now, baby sister, because I'm the *nice guy*." He draws back, our eyes meeting. "I can't say the same about everyone else on this campus."

Heart pounding, I couldn't reply if I wanted. My breath is caught in my throat, my senses overwhelmed by him. His spicy, masculine scent, his massive size, and his warnings. Before I regain control of my senses, the door downstairs slams shut and Axel's footsteps are at the base of the staircase.

I glance over and when I look back, Reid's back in his room, quietly shutting the door behind him.

Axel's pushing his hands through his hair when he appears at the top of the staircase. "You're still up." His eyebrows furrow. "What's wrong?"

"Nothing," I say. "I'm just eager to hear what Mom said."

"She's not happy," he admits. "Mostly about how this will look to everyone else, but she's willing to spin this into something that will give you a little time."

"Spin it how?"

"Apparently, you've been sent out here to minister to your wayward brother and talk some sense into me." His eyes roll and a giggle bubbles out, my chest loosening. "It's not funny."

"Isn't it, though?"

"We'll talk about it more in the morning, but she's giving you three weeks. You'll need to be back before the engagement party."

"Okay." I don't tell him that it feels both like a reprieve and a prison sentence. "Thank you, Ax, I really appreciate it."

"You know how I feel," he tells me. "I never wanted this for you in the first place, and if *you* don't want it–let me know."

"I do," I assure him. "I want it. David. The wedding. I just need some space from Mom and Dad and this deranged planning, you know?" He nods, and it's obvious how tired he is. "Tomorrow we'll also talk about where I'm staying. I can't keep your room for a month."

"Agreed." He rubs his chin, and I don't miss how his eyes dart to Reid's room. "I'll come up with something after practice in the morning, which is early as fuck, by the way." I frown at his language, which prompts him to add, "If you're staying here, you gotta get used to how I live, and talk, and everything else."

"It's fine." I lunge at him and wrap my arms around him. "You're a good big brother, you know that?"

"Yeah," he yawns, stretching his arms over his head, "well you're still the pain in the ass little sister."

4

R^{eid}

I'VE WOKEN up with a boner every morning of my life since I hit puberty. It's a sensation as familiar as stepping onto the ice, or the sound of a puck bouncing off the boards. As are the dreams that come with it–deep, ball-squeezing fantasies featuring whatever woman my subconscious conjured up. A few had recurring roles. The older babysitter three doors down showed up after seeing her sunbathe in a bikini in her backyard. My math teacher, Mrs. Walsh, was another, primarily due to the fact she had enormous tits and wore a tight sweater dress every fucking day. There were others; actresses, models, musicians–most recently Ingrid Flockton who seems to be everywhere with her guitar, long legs, and ever present cowboy boots.

But my best friend's little sister?

That's a first.

Shelby's face and body are the last thing I see before the alarm jolts me awake, but it's the memory of her weight, her thighs straddling mine, and the feel of her ass in my hands that has me rolling over and driving my cock painfully into the mattress.

Shelby Rakestraw showing up on our doorstep when I was home, intentionally avoiding females, is some epic-level irony. Showed up *and* kissed me. Some guys would call that luck, but that's not what I felt when Axel sucker-punched me. Or currently, when all the blood in my body has rushed to my balls. I roll over to release some pressure, but that's futile. Gripping the base of my shaft, I cave, and give it a long stroke.

It feels like I'm tempting fate and asking for another busted lip. Unfortunately, Axel can keep me away from his sister, but he can't stop my subconscious from fantasizing. I don't know what it was about her that got me hard two seconds after she climbed in my lap. The innocent good girl vibe? Those pouty, hot, *naive* lips. The feel of her body bearing down on my dick? I'd kept my wits—but if he hadn't walked in, would I have stopped?

An image of me coming on her chest pops into my head and a second later, I groan, unable to stop the clench in my balls and the following orgasm.

Shit. My chest rises and falls as cum spills over my fist.

Axel's right. I need to stay the hell away from Shelby. My goal for the rest of the year—the rest of my life—is for my relationships with women to be easy. And Shelby Rakestraw, for all her innocence, has complicated written all over her.

SYNCING my phone to the speakers, I turn on my morning workout playlist, letting the music fill the weight room.

"Partner up?" Jefferson asks. His eyes are bleary, but he heads straight to the free weights to start his routine.

"Sure." I grimace, feeling the bruise in my jaw. Jeff notices and his eyebrow raises. "Who the heck did you piss off last night? Someone's boyfriend?"

"Not quite." Although it does make me wonder what Shelby's boyfriend or fiance or *whatever* would have thought about last night. "Someone's big brother."

He howls with laughter and my eyes dart across the room at the big brother in question in the middle of a set of pull-ups. His tattoos and cut muscles make him look like a beast. He *is* a beast and I know the busted lip could've been a lot worse.

"Wait," Jeff says, the pieces slowly clicking into place. "Axel?" He blinks. "His sister? The virgin?" His voice lowers. "Did you fuck her?"

I wince, because that virgin thing is just speculation from things Ax has said about his family. "Dude, shut up unless you want a matching bruise." Making sure no one is listening, I add, "No. It was just a miscommunication."

A miscommunication? Is that what happened when she stuck her tongue in my mouth? Yeah, I don't think so.

"Morning." Reese strides into the room, thankfully getting me out of this conversation. He claps his hands together and announces, "Let's get going!"

At the front of the room, our team leader fusses with the tape wrapped around his wrist. We've been friends and roommates for three years, and I'm lucky as hell we ended up on the same team. He's a powerhouse—our center forward—headed to an early pick in the draft. Like me, he dated the same girl for a long time, then entered his slut-phase. Unlike me, his only lasted a few months before he fell hard for our former athletic trainer, Twyler. He's tall, broad-shouldered, has a chiseled jaw like a Marvel superhero, and is an all-around good guy. He's also captain of the team, but it's the attitude that makes Jefferson jokingly call him Captain America. "Coach wants everyone to do a full series using your personalized training program then we'll suit up for some cardio. We're playing Eastman this weekend, and although we're no longer undefeated, we're in contention for the finals."

His statement is followed by a groan, but Reese is right. Eastman is notorious for having unprecedented conditioning. They may not have the best forwards, but they make up for it with sheer stamina, able to keep going long after other teams have exhausted themselves.

"Is anyone else okay with the fact we lost our undefeated status?" Kirby asks, adding weights to the end of a bench press.

"I'm good with it." Murphy lies on the bench underneath, arms stretched over his head, preparing to lift. "I couldn't take another minute of Axel's porn 'stache."

"It started to look like a squirrel was sleeping on his upper lip." Kirby shudders. "Hey, Cap!" Reese looks up. "From now on, can all superstitions need to be voted on by the team?"

Axel drops off the pull-up bar and gives Kirby a dirty look. He wore that mustache the entire time we were undefeated. It was both hilarious and disturbing.

"If we're voting on anything, it needs to be on music selection," Axel says, the ring in his eyebrow glinting in the overhead light. "Who gave Wilder unilateral control?"

"The music gods," I reply, smugly. "I have a gift for making the perfect playlist."

He looks up to the speakers just as the song shifts from something with an electronic beat to something more pop. "You think this garbage is perfect?"

"Hey," Jefferson calls out, "I like this song."

We all roll our eyes. Jefferson has a notorious love of pop music–especially Ingrid Flockton. Which look, every guy, and some girls, of a certain age has had a crush on her. She's about our age and we grew up listening to her. But in the last year, she's grown from teen sensation to legit pop-star and gone from cute to an absolute knockout.

"You know who else likes this song?" Jefferson says, eyeing me. "Darla. I saw her dancing to it last night at the Kappa party."

"Oh yeah?" I say, feigning disinterest in my ex. "Good for her."

He's testing me–waiting to see how I'll respond to the fact my ex was at a frat party on Valentine's Day. Darla and I dated since freshman year, and yeah, we fought a lot–mostly about stupid stuff. She's bossy. I'm more laid back. She's super organized. I'm a mess. I was in it for the long haul, but it turns out she wasn't. Now I'm a single man.

I lift the weight over my head and focus on Ingrid's voice, the song's lyrics are about kicking her ex's ass and taking names. No wonder Darla was dancing last night, probably on my theoretical grave.

I'm mid lift when the music suddenly shuts off.

"Hey!" Jefferson shouts.

When I look over, Axel is next to the speaker, his tattooed arms crossed over his chest. He glares out at the room. "Listen up. I have an announcement to make."

I rack the bar and move to a sitting position, pretty sure I know where this announcement is going.

"My sister, Shelby, is in town for a few weeks. My *younger*, sweet, inexperienced, sister. She'll be staying at the Manor which means she'll be around some." He makes eye contact with every guy in the room. "She's going through some shit back home and the last thing she needs is some horny, cunt-stunned, hockey player messing with her." His green eyes flick to mine, then away. "Understood?"

A chorus of voices agree, even though they don't exactly know who Shelby is or what he's talking about. Sisters are off limits. It's a standard rule. I have my own sisters and get it. Which is why I'm not only a jerk for kissing her last night, but for rubbing one off thinking about her this morning, too.

Reese steps next to Axel. "I expect everyone to be welcoming to Ax's sister and to be a gentleman. Treat her like your own sister–"

"Or I'll break your face," Axel interjects, this time he lets his gaze linger on me and he cracks a grin. "Not your fingers. You need those to win the championship."

Reese claps, tells everyone to finish our reps and get suited up for cardio on the ice. The guys file out of the room, but I hold back and call out to Axel.

"Got a minute?"

He frowns, looking down at my busted lip. "One. What?"

"What did you mean by inexperienced?" It's pretty obvious she's a virgin but...

"I mean, completely inexperienced. I doubt she's ever been kissed." He grimaces. "Not thoroughly. Not by that dweeb, David Jones, that's for sure."

Well, she *hadn't* been, but even with the bruised lip, my lips tingle at the thought of her mouth on mine.

"Shit," I wince. "I'm sorry. I really didn't know."

"I know." He sighs, running his hands through his hair, and his shoulders sag unexpectedly. "It's not what I want for her–this closed off, sheltered life that my parents built for her. I've tried to convince her to want more, but she was raised with these ideals on purity and marriage and she bought into them, hook, line, and sinker."

"What about you?" I ask, pulling off my weight lifting gloves. "Because you're sure as hell nothing like that."

"God no. It just didn't take. I saw through the bullshit immediately, but Shelby? She wants to believe in it, or she always has. That's why it's a surprise she's here." He rubs the back of his neck. "Something in her woke up, but I doubt it will stick. Probably last minute jitters. She can stay for a bit, but it's my plan to return her back home untouched. From there she can figure out what she wants to do with her life, but I'm not letting her get hurt on my watch, or do anything she'll regret."

"That makes sense."

"This is the first time she's done something rebellious, but the thing about living in a house like ours, is that we're raised to think there are severe consequences for our actions. She's not going to wake up with remorse. She's going to feel guilt. The kind that eats you from the inside. She didn't just do something stupid with you, dude, she committed a *sin*, and I have no idea how she's going to react to that."

It's then that I realize how much I've screwed up. Axel isn't just pissed I fooled around with his sister. He's pissed that I took something from her. Something you can only give away once. Fuck, I'm more of a dick than I realized.

No more thinking about Shelby Rakestraw. Starting now.
How hard can it be?

5

S helby

LIKE AXEL SAID, the guys left the house early. Their heavy footsteps and barely concealed whispers echoing down the stairs didn't wake me. I'd already been up for hours.

It started like it always did, caught in the thick of a dream where I was running–*no*–I was being chased through the dark cold night. The street was unfamiliar, but the feeling of gasping for breath, of running, wasn't. That happened every time. In front of me was a set of steps. I threw myself up them, glancing over my shoulder, looking for the person coming for me. I tripped, stumbling forward, falling into something hard. *Someone* warm.

That's when I woke, scared and confused, my cotton pajamas drenched in a cold sweat. Under the tight, suffocating feeling in my chest, my heart pounded, thrumming like it was on the verge of escape.

I lie there until daybreak, waiting for the panic to subside. By the time the boys are moving, and the front door snaps shut, I'm able to breathe again. When I'm sure I'm alone, I get out of bed and peel off the clothes I sweated through the night before. I didn't pack much, needing to make a quick getaway. Grabbing a fresh set of clothes, I carry them, and my toiletry bag, to the bathroom. The bathroom is small, but cleaner than it was the night before, making me think that Axel must have told Reid to tidy up. Reese has his own bathroom attached to his room and as far as I know, the fourth roommate, Jefferson, never came home. There's the distinct scent of something male in the room and a collection of products lining the window sill. I make the water scalding, hot enough to burn off the grime of travel and the sweat from my nightmare, and wonder if I've ruined my life.

Like Axel said, I'm a twenty-year-old who ran away from her parents, her home, and her fiance.

But it actually may be worse. I think I may be a coward.

Case in point; I haven't turned on my phone since I left home. I wanted to make sure no one could find me on the family tracking app, or cave if I got a text or phone call. And now in the light of day, it seems like too much to manage. Reality. Reality seems like too much to manage.

With my hair still wet, I head downstairs. It looks like a bomb has gone off. The pizza, cans and beer bottles are still on the coffee table from last night. The kitchen wasn't clean when I got here, but has accumulated another layer of mess from the guys eating breakfast. I take in the cereal bowls, the empty jug of milk, the dirty dishes in the sink, and the left-out food and a shudder runs up my spine.

I'd always heard the rumor, but I know now that it's a fact: boys are pigs.

I do a quick tour of the downstairs. The main floor has an open kitchen, dining area, and living room. Near the flatscreen and gaming system, are a set of double French doors. The windows are painted over. I try the knob and it opens, leading to a small enclosed porch. It's cool out here, obviously not as insulated from the winter air. There's a ratty but comfortable-looking couch and two mountain bikes hanging on the wall. I step back into the living room and close the door.

My life may be complete chaos right now, but one thing has always made me feel better; getting organized. And clearly, there's no better place to start than this house. If anything, I see it as a gift–something to keep me distracted from the fact I'm avoiding my phone, my fiancé, and my family.

"Where do I even start?" I mutter, assessing the room. I spot the laundry room off the kitchen and head in. Sure enough, there are actual cleaning supplies on the shelves over the washer and dryer. I grab them and notice the speaker over the sink, I press play on the current song list, and a loud, upbeat, pop song fills the room. It's unfamiliar, but with David's father being the music minister and our shared upbringing, we don't listen to a lot of secular music.

Whatever this girl is singing about, she's got a lot of energy and that's exactly what I need right now. Pushing up my sleeves, I fill the sink with hot, soapy water, and get to work.

"You can take my boots, my car, and my heart, but you can't take my words and you sure as fuck won't get my cat..."

The words come out full-throttle as I peer into the oven at the cheese bubbling on top of the casserole. I've had the song on repeat for at least an hour, the lyrics unfurling something tight and hard in my chest.

"Because you–"

"Shelby?"

I jump and spin around, seeing my brother and his three amused roommates behind him.

"Jeez," I take a deep breath, "you scared me."

"We could hear you two houses away." He tosses his bag on the floor, then squints at me. "Wait. Are you crying?"

"No." I brush a fat, hot tear off my cheek. "Yes. It's just... this music. It speaks to me."

"Ah." A guy I've never met but recognize from some of Axel's ChattySnap photos grins as he shuts the door. He's huge. Taller than the other guys, with broad shoulders and shaggy blond hair that feathers away from his defined, chiseled features. "You got flocked."

"What?" I ask, alarmed, cheeks burning. Is this some kind of college euphemism I don't understand? To be fair, I feel like anything this guy says would make me feel like it's sexual.

"Flocked," the guy says. "That's what people call fans of Ingrid Flockton."

Reid rolls his eyes and mutters, "Here we go."

"I'm Jefferson by the way." He smiles again, and the cutest dimple punctures his cheek, and wow. It's like being hit with a thousand watt lightbulb.

"She's just so raw. Her songs say exactly what I feel." Heartbreak. Anger. Desperation. But most of all empowerment.

"Shel," Axel says, his bright eyes pinging around the house, "tell me you didn't clean this whole place."

I shrug. "I needed something to do. And it's a thank you for letting me stay."

Reid sniffs the air and I can't help but look at his bruised lip. "Is something cooking?"

"Oh!" I rush back over to the oven, grabbing the mitts on the way. Stuffing my hands into them I open the door, letting out a gust of heat. "I found enough ingredients to make a casserole. I thought you guys may be hungry after being gone all day."

"Hell yeah, we're hungry," Jefferson says, following me into the kitchen. Reese isn't far behind, opening the cabinet where they keep the dishes.

After I pull the first casserole out of the oven and set it on the counter, I turn for the second, Axel's hand wraps around my wrist. "No one eat a thing. Not one bite." He glares at the guys. Reid has a serving spoon already in the dish on the counter, steam rising from the surface, but pauses. "We'll be right back."

I set down the second one and stumble after him as he pulls me into the laundry room. "I know you're used to doing things like this, but you're not our maid or cook, you got that?"

"I know. But it was good to do something." I was raised to serve. I've been doing it my whole life. It's not a bad thing, but I see the dark glint in my brother's eyes. He doesn't agree. He views it as me giving too much of myself. But what else do I have to give?

"Just know that it's not expected, okay? These animals can clean up after themselves, even if it doesn't always seem like it."

"Got it." I push him toward the kitchen door. "I think you've tortured them long enough."

He grins, and throws his arm around my shoulder as we walk back in the room. "Shelby gets to go first," he says, grabbing the plate out of Jefferson's hand and giving it to me. Reese offers me his fork, and Reid digs into the dish and scoops out a spoonful of chicken and rice.

I take a seat at the table and the guys follow with plates piled high with the casserole.

"Damn this is good," Jefferson says, through a mouthful.

"So, Shelby," Reese starts, his voice pure innocence, "you have anything we need to know about Axel? Embarrassing childhood stories? Awkward family photos?"

"Nice try," Ax says, holding up a forkful of cheesy rice. "I'm an open book. No secrets here."

"Come on, you have to have something on him," Jefferson says, his steel gray eyes imploring. "Something better than his inevitable regret over all those tattoos."

"He's right about being an open book," I comment, taking a sip of water, "probably too much so for the rest of the family."

"Bed wetter?" Jefferson continues. "Got his ass beat for being a smart ass in high school?"

I shake my head, laughing at how desperate they are for dirt on my brother. I think on it and finally concede, "There is the legend about how Axel insisted on playing the camel in the Christmas pageant seven years straight, even when he outgrew the costume and my mother had to have it altered to fit."

"Camels are cool," Axel refutes, looking completely unfazed. "Fight me."

"It has nothing to do with his 'love' of camels," I say, using finger quotes. "The animals in the nativity didn't have to sing, and Axel would do *anything* not to sing."

"Damn straight," he says. "I was the only highschooler in the stable."

"That's not the brag you think it is," Jefferson says, pointing his fork at him.

"What about you?" Reid asks. "What role were you in the program?"

Axel snorts.

I shoot him a glare. "What?"

He rolls his eyes. "Shelby was the only role fit for her–an angel."

"Always the good girl, huh?" Reid says, looking me up and down. "Seems right."

My cheeks burn at the way he says 'good girl,' because it doesn't sound sweet at all. My brother must agree because there's a hard jerk under the table and Reid flinches, cursing under his breath. Axel, fingers wrapped tight around his fork, stares across the table at his friend.

Jefferson and Reese laugh while continuing to shovel food in their mouths. I have no idea what is going on but my brother can't seem to get his attitude in check, but I'm thankful when the conversation shifts to their upcoming schedule.

"We've got an away game tomorrow night," Axel turns to me, "and we won't be home 'til late. Will you be okay here by yourself?"

"I don't need a babysitter," I tell him. "I'll be fine."

"If not, I'm sure Twyler and Nadia would be happy for you to sleep on their couch."

"Or they could come over here?" Reese offers. "Girls like sleep-overs, right?"

"Children like sleepovers." Reid points out, then leans toward me and adds, "Reese has no siblings so he's clueless sometimes."

"Just because you have four sisters, doesn't mean you know everything."

"It means I know a lot," Reid shoots back, digging his fork in the pile of rice. "More than you."

I turn to my brother. "As hard as it is for you to accept it, I'm an adult. I can stay by myself for one night."

He grunts and goes back to his food, just as Jefferson rises, pushing his chair back. With a casual rake of his fingers through his hair, he says, "Nice to meet you, Shelby, and thanks for the awesome dinner." He picks up his plate and carries it to the sink. "I've got a study date over at the Kappa house."

Reese rolls his eyes and says, "You know one day you're going to show up over there and they're going to have changed the locks."

He shrugs. "Then I'll just go in through a window."

"The dishes in the washer are clean," I call out. "Just leave your plate and I'll–"

"You'll do nothing," Axel says. "Leave your plate and we'll take care of it." He looks at Reese and Reid. "That goes for you too."

"I'm on it," Reese agrees, but adds, "when I get back. I'm heading over to Twy's, remember?"

"Right," Ax says.

"You still coming?"

"Yeah, for a little bit." The way he says it, gives me the impression he'd normally stay longer. When he stands he says, "Don't even think about washing these dishes. We'll get them later, okay?"

"Okay."

"Thanks for dinner," he says, dropping his hand on top of my head and ruffling my hair. I jerk away and notice that Jefferson has grabbed his backpack and is already out the door. Axel and Reese head out right after, shrugging on coats and slipping away. Suddenly it's just me and Reid.

"I'm surprised he left me alone with you," I admit.

"I would be too, except he's got something on his mind."

"What?"

"Se–" he swallows. "Nadia. He's in it deep with her."

I nod. "I noticed."

I have noticed and it surprises me. Axel never got close to any girls back home. He had a bit of a reputation, but nothing that would make my parents mad. He was quiet about his relationships, but nothing about how he feels about Nadia seems quiet, which may be why he chose her over my father.

Reid finishes off his meal and stands, taking not only his plate but mine too. "Oh, I can get that."

He isn't swayed, and carries both plates over to the sink. He opens the dishwasher and steam rushes out. Pulling out the top rack, he starts to unload.

"You don't have to do that."

"I don't mind." He dips his fingers in two different glasses, pulling out both in one hand. "When I was growing up, everyone chipped in with clean up."

I move over to help unload, although I'm not sure where everything goes.

"So you have a big family?" I ask.

"Four sisters. Two brothers." He bends, grabbing a stack of plates. He gestures to a cabinet door and I open it, so he can put them inside. "Thanks."

"Your parents have seven kids?" Even the most evangelical in our church tend to stop at five.

"Yep, and they brought it on themselves, too."

"What do you mean?" I ask.

"We're all adopted."

"Oh wow." I grab two glasses off the rack. They're still warm to the touch. "Your parents must be saints."

His lips curve in a grin. "They're good people."

"Well it was just me and Axel growing up, but when your father is the minister of a mega-church it's pretty much like you have one, giant, extended family."

I reach for the silverware caddy, but he shoos me away. "You heard your brother. No cleaning up."

"It's not a big deal."

"Maybe not, but I owe you one."

I frown. "For what?"

He's focused on pulling out all the knives, but tilts his head at me and says, "For stealing your first kiss."

"Tha–tha–" I'm stammering. My cheeks are on fire. Horror creeps up my spine. "That wasn't my first kiss."

"No?" he asks, unphased by my panic. "Because your brother seems to think so."

"Axel doesn't know what he's talking about." I lift my chin. "I have a boyfriend. More than that. I'm promised to him."

He frowns, eyes darting down to where my finger twists the ring. "What does that mean anyway?"

"It means that we're preparing for the next level. We're committed to one another and soon we'll get engaged and then married. The ring is a way to make it clear that we belong to one another."

"So he wears a ring, too?"

"Well, no," I admit, but add quickly, "but men don't wear engagement rings either."

"Huh."

I lean my hip against the counter. "What does that mean?"

"What does what mean?" he asks innocently.

"That 'huh.'"

"Nothing really," he says, those brown eyes slowly dragging from the ring up to my face. "It's just not how I would do it." Our eyes hold and an itchy sensation climbs up my skin. His gaze feels hot. Intimate. Like he's trying to read me like a book. I break contact first, shifting away, and after a beat he goes back to the dishwasher, starting in on the spoons. "So what's he like?"

"David?" He nods and I think about the man back home. "He's kind. Funny. He has ambition and a great singing voice, although that's not his interest. He's majoring in business administration and will work for my father when he graduates."

"Ah, taking Axel's spot in the family business." He gives me a wink. "He sounds like a nice guy."

"He really is."

So nice that suddenly I feel like a huge jerk for avoiding him like this.

"You know..." He cocks an eyebrow. "I didn't hear 'a good kisser' on that list."

I glare at him and shove his shoulder. "Because that's none of your business."

"Fair." He bobs his head good naturedly.

"Speaking of David," a wave of guilt crashes over me, "I should probably go call him."

"Go for it." He points to the sink piled with the dishes from dinner. "I'll finish this."

"Thank you."

Instead of going upstairs, I duck into the little porch and close the door behind me. I pull back the curtain and watch Reid as he washes the dishes. His shoulders are strong and broad, but he looks completely at ease doing the work.

"Okay, Shel," I mutter to myself, "it's time to put on your big girl panties and deal with this."

I sit on the ratty couch, pull out my phone and turn it on for the first time since I left Texas. Dozens of missed texts and phone messages pop up in a flurry. Not ready to deal with it now, I skip the ones from my mom and dad, and open the ones from David.

David: Finished with classes. Can't meet up tonight. Call you later.

David: Tried calling. Where are you?

David: Did you turn off your location?

David: Is this about the ring? Or the house? Because your dad is just looking out for us.

David: Heard from your mom. She said she can't find you either.

David: Call me ASAP

David: Shelby, it's been hours. If this is some kind of game to get my attention, it's immature and desperate.

David: Your mom said you ran away to Wittmore. To stay with your brother? That sounds like a great decision. I don't know what this little rebellion is about but this isn't the way to handle it.

David: ***It's obvious you're ignoring me, but I want to hear your voice.*** ***You owe me that. Call me, please.***

There are also voice messages, but I can't bring myself to listen to them.

All the anxiety and nerves come rushing back. It's no surprise he thinks I'm just being dramatic. I force myself to open a text box and start typing: *David, I'm sorry for leaving without telling anyone. I was feeling overwhelmed by all the engagement and wedding plans. I just need a little time to get my head clear. I'll talk to you soon.*

I turn off the phone again and wait until I hear Reid's footsteps on the stairs and the sound of his bedroom door closing. Only then do I leave the solitude of the little porch and go to bed.

6

———————

R^{eid}

RUNNING into an ex right before a big game is not recommended. If I hadn't forgotten my mouthguard in the locker room, it never would have happened. But I did, and now I'm stuck on the walkway leading to the parking lot where the rest of the team is waiting on the bus, awkwardly looking at the girl that recently dumped me for the first time *since* she dumped me.

Yeah, Darla dumped me over text.

"Hey," I say, hooking my headphones over my neck.

"Hi." Darla doesn't look awkward. Or tense. She looks like a girl who's moved on with her life. Ouch. "Heading to a game?"

"Yeah. Eastman." Apparently now I only speak in one word sentences. Jesus. "Everyone is on the bus. I had to go back to get something out of my locker."

Her lips curve in a knowing smirk, a familiar smirk. Darla has always thought I was a forgetful, hot mess. Which maybe, but who gives a shit?

"I like your shoes," she says, nodding down at the brown and white wingtips I found at a vintage shop downtown. "Very retro."

I loathe the way my body reacts when I see her. It's not even sexual. That would be acceptable, in my opinion. Nope, it's my fucking heart still wanting to know why she tossed all of this away.

"Thanks." I swallow and look around the back of the arena. "Kind of off of your regular path. Were you looking for me?"

I try to keep the hope out of my voice. Fucking hell. What's wrong with me?

"I wanted to tell you I have a box of your things to drop off."

Ah, the belonging exchange. What was that sound? Another nail in the coffin.

"Sure, well, obviously not right now, but just let me know when you have time. I'll swing by and–"

"Or I'll just leave it on your porch," she says, cutting me off. "It's nothing major. Just a few things that got mixed in with mine."

"Right." I clear my throat. "I'll make sure to gather up anything of yours too."

"I think I got everything already." Of course. Darla is efficient. Organized. Which is why I refuse to believe this breakup was spontaneous. "Well, good luck today."

"Thanks." I'm ready to get away, that feeling in my heart has shifted from something happy, to something dark and painful. And before I can control myself I blurt, "So that's it? After all this time, we're just finished? No reasons why? No discussion?"

"Reid, I don't think you want to get into this now–"

"Why? Because you thought it was okay to dump me over text? After all our plans? Everything we–no, *you*–had organized for the two of us?"

"This is why I texted you. I knew you would get emotional."

I balk, jaw dropped, staring at her. A million responses come flooding back but no. "You know what?" I say, more to myself than her. "Thank you."

She blinks, caught off guard for the first time in forever. "For what?"

"Showing me the real you. It saved me a lot of trouble." I step to the side and pass her, pulling my headphones back over my ears. The beat of the song rushes out, and I take a few steady breaths before approaching the bus.

"Everything okay?" Coach Green, our team trainer asks, as I reach the steps.

"Everything's perfect." The words are as fake as my grin. "Just had to grab my mouthguard."

"Atta' boy," he says, slapping me on my back. "You know my rule: Protecting yourself is the first step to a win."

I climb into the bus and take a seat next to Kirby who's focused on his phone. Long after the bus jolts forward, and starts down the road, Coach's words linger. That's what I did wrong with Darla. For the first time in my life I didn't protect myself. I left my weaknesses exposed. Vulnerable.

I'll never let that happen again.

ONE THING about hockey is that it's great for letting go of some frustration.

The bad thing is that things can sometimes go too far.

"What was that, Kramer?" I shout. This guy has been up my ass all night, which was annoying enough, but then he started trash talking.

"I said you suck, Wilder. And that check was weak. Just like your mama over the buffet table."

He's full of shit, because my teeth rattled when I slammed him against the boards, but I'm not in the mood for it tonight. Not after seeing Darla earlier. And definitely not insulting my mother.

I toss my stick and lunge for him, but before my punch lands, I'm dragged backwards.

"Get off," I argue, fighting against my teammate.

"Chill, bro," Jefferson says, his massive arms tight around my upper body. There's a reason he's our enforcer. "He's desperate as fuck *and* he's not worth it."

"But he–"

"He's losing and he's trying to get you to make a mistake." He knocks my helmet. "There are 36 seconds left. Don't let it happen."

I take a deep breath, and steady myself. Jeff's right. There are times I can let the frustration surrounding the game make me better. And other times, worse. I need to be the former. Ignoring Kramer's stupid face, and the crowd's jeers, I take my stick back from Kirby as he skates by, and I get in position for the puck drop.

Murphy wins it, knocking the biscuit back to Axel. Ax takes control, tracks Reese up the ice, and zings it toward him. From there, it's a quick deke to the left and a backhanded shot: nothing but net. Kramer gets to skate off the ice with his tail between his legs and a big fat 'L' on the board.

"Great game, man," Reese knocks his fist against mine on the way from the lockers to the showers. "That pass in the first period was a thing of beauty."

"Yeah, they were tough."

"Another one down," Axel says, dropping his towel and reaching for his pants. "Which makes us one step closer to the finals."

Reese gives him a grunt. After last season where we blew it in the championship, Reese doesn't like to think too far ahead. Or at least he says that. I know for a fact he's got his eye on the prize. And he should. The closer we get to the end of the season the more likely it is we'll get a chance to play in the championship. Our team is on fire. Everyone is clicking.

I rub the towel over my hair, then change back into my suit.

"You look like a 1930s gangster in that suit," Emerson says.

I flip up the collar of my white shirt and lay it over the suit. "Thank you."

"You're so weird," Murphy adds. He's in a standard gray suit that's nice enough, but I'm pretty sure his mom bought it for him after he learned about Coach Bryant's before and after game dress code. He looks nice. My goal is to look remarkable.

I've always been into clothes. I think it goes back to moving from house to house and having to leave my belongings behind more times than I like to remember. Once things stabilized, I started being more specific in my choices. Clothing isn't just something I wear. It's a collection.

"I think you look good," Axel says. "Not many people could pull off a brown suit."

My roommate is covered in tattoos and piercings. His white blonde hair that he bleaches twice a month always looks like he just got out of a fight with an actual badger. Of course he favors individualism.

"You guys hurry up. I want to get back before it's too late." Reese throws his bag over his shoulder and walks out of the locker room, but then pops his head back in a second later. "Hey, Reid, you've got a visitor."

It's idiotic that my first thought is about Darla, but that evaporates as soon as I think it. I tie my shoe, grab my things, and head out the door. My 'visitor' is my dad and younger sister, Veronica.

"Hey," I say, walking over. "I didn't know you were coming."

"We didn't either," Dad grins, "but Ronnie and I decided to hop in the car and surprise you."

Ronnie is fourteen and the youngest of the Wilder kids. She's wearing a Wittmore Hockey jersey, my jersey, the number eight on the sleeve. I lean in and give her a quick hug. "You didn't have to make the drive."

"Nonsense, you know we love watching you play." Dad beams at me. "And you had a great game."

"Eh, just doing what they pay me for."

Dad shakes his head, and I know he thinks I downplay my skills. I know I'm a good player. I'm a kickass beast on the ice, but when it comes to Darryl Wilder I never feel like I measure up. How can I?

"I thought you were going to get in a fight with number seventeen," Ronnie says. "You dropped your stick, but freaking Jefferson had to pull you back."

"Yeah, good thing or I would've ended up in the bin. That was just blowing off a little steam." I laugh at her frown. "Sorry to disappoint your thirst for blood."

"I know you've got to get on the bus," Dad says, "but I wanted to make sure we saw you. Everything going okay?"

"Everything's good." I give him a quick run through of my classes and what we're expecting with the next few games. I keep any mention of Darla or my subsequent slide into Wittmore party boy out of it. My family loved her and everyone was disappointed when we broke up. Like me, they thought she was end game material. "Oh," I say, trying to think of something PG, "we've got a houseguest at the Manor. Axel's sister."

"Hey!" Ronnie sets her hands on her hips. "How come his sister gets to come for a visit and I don't?"

"Because she's over eighteen and doesn't need full-time supervision." I bop her on the nose, simply because I know she hates it. Sure enough, she scowls. "It's just for a few weeks. She's going through something back home and needed a place to crash."

"Oh, well, I hope she finds some peace, although I think it would be hard in a house full of hockey players." Dad gives me a look. "Treat her like you would your sister."

"Don't worry," I tell him. "We already got the big brother speech from Axel."

"Ah, I knew, despite all the tattoos, that kid was smart."

A smart*ass*, but sure.

"Any word from New York?"

"Everything seems to be on track. If we clinch the season and the playoffs, I can't see any reason for the contract not to go through."

I'd signed last spring to secure a spot with the NHL after graduation. Unlike Reese, I didn't feel confident enough to go as a free agent into my senior year. Axel thought he was going back home to work for his father, but there's no doubt the recruiters are in the stands keeping an eye on him. He's not just good–he's the best. Me? I'm good. Steady. A bruiser. But nothing came easy in my life and I wasn't willing to play the odds.

"Great," he reaches out and squeezes my shoulder. "I'm really proud of you, son, you've come such a long way."

And then there's that. My dad is proud. Happy for me, and if I can give that back to him, I'll do whatever it takes.

"Yo, Reid!" A voice echoes down the hallway. "Bus is ready!"

"Is that Jefferson?" Ronnie asks, perking up. She and the rest of the family have met all of my roommates and I'm pretty sure my sister has a crush on Jeff. This is confirmed by the pink glow in her cheeks. "I'm going to go say hi."

She takes off before either of us can respond, leaving me and Dad to walk toward the bus behind her.

"Out of all the guys on the team she likes Jefferson?" I whistle, thinking of my roommates exploits. We've all had fun during our time at Wittmore, but I doubt Jeff has spent the night alone more than a dozen times over the past four years. "You better keep an eye on her."

"You don't have as many kids as we do without having a wild card," he says, glancing over at me. "You look tired. Sure you're okay?"

"Yeah, it's just that busy time of the year." I give him my best reassuring grin. "And away games are tough, but I'm glad you guys came. I appreciate it."

I give him a hug, and drag Ronnie away from Jeff. We get on the bus, everyone pumped from the win, but also tired from the hard work.

Just as the doors close and the driver takes off, Jeff leans over the back of the seat with his phone in his hand. "Party at Gamma Phi tonight. You in?"

I need something to release this feeling in my chest. The pain of losing Darla, of disappointing my family. A hook up may be just the right thing.

"I'm in."

7

S helby

As I TUG at the mountain bike mounted to the wall, my arms strain against the stubborn weight. The thing seems to cling to the hooks like it's afraid of the ground. Just as I'm about to give it another heave, a knock on the front door draws my attention away, and the door swings open.

Nadia and Twyler step in the living room, and I'm instantly struck by how the two girls look nothing alike. They're both pretty and both have dark hair, but Twyler's is pulled back in an efficient ponytail that matches her skinny jeans and worn Wittmore hoodie. Nadia's cut is more stylish, bobbed at the shoulders with blunt bangs and her eye makeup is on point. The Wittmore hockey jersey she's wearing over black leggings is knotted at the waist and stylish boots come up to her knees. I'd never pick these two as having anything in common, but according to my brother they're actually *best* friends.

"A little help?" I call, my arms wobbling under the weight.

"Oh shit," Nadia says, and they both rush over.

Moving to either side of me, we lift the bike off the rack and lower it to the ground.

"Thank you." I brush back my hair. "I thought the guys may come home and find me trapped under a pile of metal."

"What are you doing out here?" Twyler asks, looking around the tiny space.

"Just trying to clean up the porch a bit." I look around the tiny space. "I thought I'd turn it into a temporary bedroom while I'm here." I give Nadia a small grin. "Give Axel back a little privacy."

"That's super sweet of you," Nadia says. "I appreciate it. He will too."

"You'd just rather sleep in his queen sized bed instead of your double," Twyler jokes.

"He takes up too much room and he's so hot at night." She shakes her head. "Like a freaking furnace."

I wince, not sure I want to know about my brother's body heat, but I do notice the jersey she's wearing has my brother's name on the back. Twyler rests her hands on the handlebars of the bike. "I can go put this on the back porch. Is there anything else you need help moving?"

"No, I think I'm good. I'll put my suitcase where the bikes were. I already vacuumed out the couch and a nest of spiders in the corner. I'll just get some clean sheets and maybe a new comforter. But all in all, I think it'll make an okay bed for the next few weeks."

"You sure it won't get too cold?"

"I can take it." I sit on the arm of the couch. "What are you two doing here anyway? Don't tell me Axel made you come check up on me."

"No," Nadia promises, "but we're heading over to the Badger Den to watch the game and thought you may want to come."

"What's the Badger Den?"

"A hockey bar," Twyler says.

"For hockey players or hockey fans?" I ask, not wanting to admit I've never been to a bar.

"Both." Nadia tugs at the hem of her shirt. "They have on all the games and it's the best way to catch the away ones."

I haven't left the Manor since I got here, having spent the first two days getting settled in and avoiding my phone. "I'm not twenty-one."

"Good news! It's eighteen and up," Nadia replies cheerfully.

Okay, so this is happening. "Sure, yeah that sounds fun."

"Although..." Nadia looks me up and down, taking in my sweats and dirty T-shirt.

Twyler mutters, "Oh boy, here we go..."

"What?" I ask, but Nadia thrusts her hand out at me and I grab it.

She yanks me up, saying, "The sweats look is great for moving furniture and cleaning up a nasty porch, but we're going out, Shelby, and going out means dressing up."

"Don't listen to her." Twyler gives me a sympathetic look. "You can wear whatever you want. I do."

"Yes," Nadia rolls her eyes at her friend, "and the whole student body is still trying to figure out how you won Reese Cain's heart."

"Because he's into what's under the clothes–"

"Yeah, I know, babe. We share a wall, remember."

"That's not what I meant! Reese and I connect on a different level. He's into my brain and smarts, not my body." A small smile curves the edges of her mouth. "Okay, he's into my body too."

"I'm not looking for anyone to get into my body," I declare. "I already have a boyfriend."

"Cool," Nadia says, "but there's one thing that's mandatory if we're going to the Badger Den."

"What's that?"

She pulls at the jersey and grins. "You've gotta dress like a fan."

"FINALLY," I say, rushing out of the cold and into the brightly lit, crowded bar. Once inside Nadia peels off her jacket. "You're from Florida aren't you?" She nods. "How do you stand this cold?"

"You get used to it," she says.

"And a lot is about clothing and just being prepared," Twyler adds.

I should have taken the stained hoodie Nadia dug up from the floor of my brother's closet. Instead, I picked the black women's Wittmore v-neck buried in his T-shirt drawer that seemed logical if I was still in Texas, but we're in the North East and I'm struggling to get used to that.

Unzipping my coat, I look down at my shirt, alarmed at the amount of boob showing. I tug up the V for coverage. "If this isn't yours, then whose shirt is it?"

"I'm going to assume it belonged to a puck bunny." She pushes through the crowd and heads straight to the bar. Not sure what to do, I follow and watch as she lifts her hand, getting the bartender's attention.

"What's a puck bunny?"

"You really don't know anything about this world, do you?" Twyler asks, genuinely surprised.

I shake my head. "My father didn't really approve of Axel's interest in hockey. He let him do it, but never supported it. Plus, it's Texas. Everyone is focused on football."

"Puck bunnies are the girls that hang around hockey players. They go to the games and are at all of the parties." Twyler nods at a group of girls decked out in Wittmore swag in a booth across the room. Curiously they're all looking at us. "They're omnipresent."

"So like a fan club?"

The girls share a look and Nadia snorts. "I guess you could call them that." Then she holds up her hands innocently. "And no shade, because although I wasn't a puck bunny, I definitely was a jersey chaser, until your brother entrapped me." She turns to the bartender. "Hey, Mike, it's slammed tonight."

"You know how it is. The better they do, the more fans come out of the woodwork. It doesn't help that we're short handed tonight." He lifts his chin. "What can I get you?"

"Two seltzers and..." she looks at me, eyebrows raised.

"Just a Coke."

"And one Coke." Her head tilts in my direction. "This is Axel's sister, Shelby. She's visiting for a few weeks."

"Ah, thought you looked a little familiar." He busies himself getting the drinks and a moment later slides them over the bar. Nadia grabs them, handing the can to Twyler and a glass to me.

"Jesus," she mutters as a guy bumps into her. "It's freaking packed tonight. Do you see any free tables?"

"There's one," Twyler says, pointing to the back. I follow them, holding my drink to my chest, and darting through the crowd. The table is directly under the big screen and as we slide into the booth, I notice that the game has already started.

The girls are instantly drawn into the game, but all I see is chaos. Everything moves so fast, the guys swarming over the ice. Axel, I can find, since he's the goalie and has on extra pads, but the girls get me up to date on everyone else.

"Reese is number fifteen–and is a forward. He's on a line with Kirby and Emerson."

I have a vague idea about how the game is played from playing the video version with Axel, but seeing it live is different. "He's captain, and hellbent on getting to the playoffs to make up for last season's fiasco."

"What fiasco–" I start to ask, but Nadia continues.

"Jefferson and Reid are on defense..."

I perk up at Reid's name.

"What are their numbers?" I ask, taking a casual sip of my soda. "So I can keep up."

"Jefferson is number twenty-three and Reid number eight." Eight. Like the tattoo on his arm. Twyler watches the screen and her face lights up. "Oh, there he is."

His big frame zips across the ice and I see his last name, Wilder, printed across his shoulders. He plays hard–aggressively. And I watch with fascination as he battles another player for the puck. He wins the skirmish and slaps it up the ice to Reese who knocks it out of the air with his stick, then turns, accelerating in a burst of energy toward the goal.

What follows happens so fast I can't follow it, but Twyler whispers under her breath, "You got it, babe," and a light flicks on behind the goal.

Nadia jumps out of her seat and shouts, "Yes!"

"Did they score?" I ask after the girls settle back down.

"Yep," Twyler grins.

The ref calls intermission and the channel flips to a commercial. I'm taking another swallow of my drink when Nadia turns to me and tosses out, "So, Shelby, what was going on with you and Reid on Valentine's Day?" Surprised at the question, I choke on the liquid, sputtering into a cough. Her eyes widen. "Twy, help her!"

Twyler rests her hand on my back. "Are you okay? Can you breathe?"

"I'm fine," I say weakly, patting my chest. "Just went down the wrong way."

"Are you sure?" Twyler asks, eyes taking me in. "Do you need some water?"

"No really, I'm fine." And embarrassed. I can't even drink a soda and not embarrass myself.

"Thank god." Nadia exhales. "Your brother will kill me if he found out I took you to a bar *and* let you choke to death."

"He's just overprotective."

"Tell me about it. Overprotective is his entire personality." She reaches for my hand and squeezes. "By the way, whatever you say about Reid, or anything else, I won't tell him."

"You may as well tell her," Twyler says, "because she's not going to drop it."

"Nothing was going on. I showed up unannounced, and when I told him I was looking for Axel, he invited me in and one thing led to another." I say this calmly. Casually. Like climbing onto a strange man's lap is something I do regularly. "It looked worse than it was."

"It usually does," Nadia snorts. "Reid's really sweet and has excellent taste in true crime documentaries, but he recently broke up with his girlfriend and has gone a little wild."

"She would know," Twyler adds. "Nadia totally had a lady boner for Reid last fall."

"*Before* your brother." Nadia clarifies, noticing my surprise. "And it wasn't a boner. He just seemed nice and I was testing the water with hockey guys."

"So you guys dated?"

Nadia's eyes widen again. "Oh god no. We went on *a* date. Here, actually, and it went absolutely nowhere. He wasn't over his ex, and I was unfortunately involved in my own toxic situation at the time. We both moved on quickly and just stayed friends."

"Well, that sounds like a story," I say, swirling the ice in my glass. "The toxic relationship part."

"Oh, it is." She nods vigorously but adds, "Unfortunately, due to legal proceedings I'm not supposed to talk about it."

Some of my father's concerns about Axel's dating situation are starting to make a little more sense. But Nadia seems like a good person and it's obvious my brother loves her. Anyway, I have more questions about something, well, *someone* else. "So Reid had a serious girlfriend?"

"Darla. They've dated since freshman year," she says, resting her empty can on the table.

"Reese says they've always been kind of off and on," Twyler adds, "but this one seems permanent."

"She broke up with him," Nadia confides, "and I think that's why he's drowning himself in puck bunnies and sorority girls."

"Total rebound, fuck-boy behavior." I try not to react to Twyler's language, but it's impossible. No girls I know talk like this. She adds, "It's pretty common with these guys. There are a lot of girls around, willing to have no-strings relationships. Reese and I ended up together after his own spiral after a breakup."

"These men do best with a support system," Nadia agrees. "And *a lot* of pussy. I'm here to provide both."

"Nadia!" Twyler admonishes, but this time my cheeks don't turn pink. I can feel it. I'm full red.

Awkwardly, I slide off my chair and croak. "Bathroom?"

"Back corner." Nadia points behind the bar. "I'm going to get another drink. You guys want one?"

"I'm good. The team has an early workout tomorrow," Twyler says, eyes back on the game. "Kirby keeps favoring his left side. I wonder what's going on?"

Nadia follows me as I try to escape, chattering the whole way. "Twyler was the hockey trainer-intern until she and Reese got serious, then she switched over to work with the basketball team. She's very focused on injuries."

"Ah, okay." I nod my head and hustle forward, trying to get some distance between us. "I'll, um, meet you back at the table."

Although a bar bathroom isn't the ideal place to try to calm my nerves, I do my best. Corralled in a stall with marked up metal doors, I take a deep breath. I'm not a prude. I'm not. I'm just... who talks like that? Is that how college women speak? Fuckboys and the p-word. Gosh, maybe I am a prude.

I stay in the stall until a couple of girls come in talking loud and laughing.

"Oh my god, did you see Jeremy?" one says, the rest of her words drowned out by the flush of the toilet. I head to the sink. Two girls duck into the empty stalls but continue to talk.

"You said you weren't going to hook up with him again?"

"I know but..."

"You're weak, Mallory. W.E.A.K."

"His personality is lacking," she admits, "but he's really good in bed. He does this thing with–"

I bolt out the door before I hear *what* Jeremy does with *whatever* he does it with. The bar is still loud and from the sound of the cheers, Wittmore is still leading. The noise, the volume, the alcohol and language... it's starting to get to me. I'm planning on finding the girls and telling them I'm going to head back to the manor when a figure steps between me and the exit. It's a guy with tousled reddish hair and a lazy grin.

"Excuse me," I say, attempting to pass.

"Not so fast," he sidesteps, blocking my way. In the darkened hallway, I feel more than see his gaze drag over my body, head to toe. "I haven't seen you here before."

"That's because I'm just visiting." I peer over his shoulder, hoping to catch Nadia, but I see her head disappear back into the crowd.

"Well, let me be the first to welcome you to the Badger Den." He thrusts out his hand. "I'm Adam."

I stare down at the hand, unsure of what to do. It would be polite to shake it, introduce myself and move on. But there's something about him that feels weird. Off. But then again, everything about this night feels off to me. I'm out of my depth socially.

"Nice to meet you Adam," I say, giving him a quick smile. I make a second attempt to get past him, but he adjusts with me.

"How about I get you a drink, so we can get to know one another better?"

"I can't."

"Why not?"

I swallow. "I have a boyfriend."

"Ah." His eyebrow raises. "Is he here?"

I feel like I should lie, but I was raised to be better than that. "No," I admit.

He moves closer, inching into my space. I take a step back and I'm crowded into the wall.

"A girl as cute as you are surely knows you're going to get hit on," he says, lifting his hand to place his palm flat against the wall next to my head. My heartbeat quickens and that feeling of being trapped lunges into my throat. "You've got an innocent vibe going on, but that shirt..." his eyes dip down to my cleavage. "Maybe you're looking to get corrupted a little, huh? I'm happy to volunteer for the job."

Panic rips through me, but I'm not frozen. I duck under his arm. In my hurry to get back to the bar, I nearly slam into Mike holding a bag of trash as he exits the space behind the bar.

"Oh gosh, I'm sorry!" I look behind me, and then to the side, ducking out of sight.

"Slow down." Mike narrows his eyes, the divots of his crows feet becoming more pronounced. He looks down the hallway and back at me. "Is he bothering you?"

"No," I reply out of habit. I don't want to be a bother but... I swallow. "Kind of. He's just a little pushy."

He jerks his head. "Stay here."

"O-okay."

He drops the bag of trash, and strides in the direction toward the bathrooms. A moment later his voice echoes off the hallway walls. "What have I told you about making our female customers uncomfortable? I've given you a warning, Adam, but I can't have you harassing people."

I strain to hear Adam's protests over the loud noise in the bar, but then he shouts, "Whatever. This place has shitty service and shittier beer!"

"Good, then you'll be okay with being banned." Mike returns, picks up the bag of trash and says, "Sorry about that. He's been hounding women in here for a while. He's got a radar for sweet girls. I'd given him a warning before, but tonight's the final straw." He looks at me. "Are you sure you're okay?"

"I'm sure." I nod. "Thank you."

"Hey, your brother is a legend around here and it's better I caught that kid being a dick than him." He snorts. "Can you imagine?"

I laugh. "Axel would peel his skin off."

Trash in hand, he continues toward the back door. I make my way back to the table across the bar with the distinct feeling that if tonight has taught me anything, I'm not prepared for college bars, and as nice as they are, college women like Nadia and Twyler, but most of all I'm definitely not ready for college men.

8

R^{eid}

THERE'S a certain kind of energy needed for an off campus party and I'm not sure that after confronting my ex, three periods of intense hockey, and a surprise visit from my family, that I've got it.

"You want another beer?"

I look down at the girl glued to my side. Mara. She's a sophomore who has spent the last year working her way into the hockey crowd, and the last few weeks working on me. She's been next to me since Jeff and I walked through the door when she pressed a cold beer into my hand, attached herself like a parasite, and hasn't budged since.

"I'm good," I tell her. Reese has this one drink policy during the season, and I try to stick to it, especially when I feel like doing something stupid, and right now, stupidity is really tempting. If I'm going to do something dumb, I may as well remember it.

"Or," she leans into me, tits pressed to my side, "if you want a little more privacy, we can head to my room upstairs."

Jefferson abandoned me fifteen minutes after we walked in the door, a girl on each side. My friend probably has the right idea, there are worse ways to feel better than burying myself into this puck bunny.

Except... I can see it in Mara's dark brown eyes. She doesn't want a conquest. She's looking for a relationship. That's the curse of being an athlete who is known for monogamy. Every girl looks at you like they could very well be the next WAG.

Sorry, girls, I'm done with serious relationships. Those only happen in fairy tales.

Mara shifts, giving me a view straight down the front of her shirt. Christ.

Fuck it. She wants something and I want something. Why am I overthinking it?

"Why go upstairs?" I place a hand on her backside and urge her closer. There's no bigger fuckboy move than a little PDA. She grins, seemingly into it, and slings a leg over my hip.

Eye-to-eye she runs a pointed, manicured nail over my bottom lip. "Did you get this in the game?"

"What's hotter, a busted lip from the game or one from a fight with my roommate?"

She shrugs. "They're both sexy."

I pull her closer, wanting to feel the weight of her on top of me. "Sounds like a win-win to me."

"I've heard things about you, Reid Wilder," she says, kissing her way up my neck.

"Oh yeah? What kind of things?" I wait for the tingle of want. For the urge of desire to take over the dark gloom in my chest.

"That you're sweet." she says. "And this is the first time you've been single in a while."

"No lies detected," I laugh, skimming my fingers along her bare thigh. "Anything else?"

"That you're normally not the typical fuckboy hockey player that comes to parties like this to hook up, but you're nursing a broken heart." Placing her hands on my chest, she grinds down. "Good thing I'm pre-med, I can mend you right up."

Jesus that feels good, or, well, it should. Her hot pussy is rubbing up and down my cock but other than a half-chub in response, my body isn't working.

Maybe she's right. I am broken.

A flicker of an emotion tugs at my gut, but it's when her lips are inches from mine, and a different face flashes in my mind, that a jolt of regret hits me. "Shit, sorry babe." I lift her back up. "I don't think this is going to work."

"But–"

"Hey, it's not you." I stand, adjusting my shorts and grabbing my jacket off the back of the couch. "It is one thousand percent me. You said it. I may be a little bit broken."

She pouts, but I turn away, not sure why I feel bad for having this girl in my lap, and definitely not sure why the person I thought about while some chick was grinding on my dick was Axel's little sister.

Yeah, that's not great.

I pull out my phone and text Jeff, letting him know I'm heading home. He'll get the text when he comes up for air, whenever that will be.

I take the walk back to campus, feeling the need for some cool air and some sleep. Unfortunately, I walk in the front door of the manor and the first thing I see is Shelby lugging her suitcase down the stairs.

There's no missing the look of sheer determination on her face. The second? That tight black v-neck tee. Yeah, I knew she had perfect tits hidden under those innocent girl clothes.

Annnnd that sends more blood flow to my cock than anything else tonight.

"Going somewhere?" I ask, shrugging off my hockey jacket and hanging it on the rack by the door.

She lugs the suitcase down to the first floor. "Just moving into the porch."

"That porch?" I look over my shoulder to the musty room we use to store everything we don't want to deal with. "That porch is cold and gross and I think there may be spiders."

"I cleaned it up," she says proudly. "At least I tried to."

I take the suitcase from her, lifting it by the handle, and I follow her to the porch. It's chilly, but it is a lot cleaner than before. No cobwebs and the couch has been made into a bed with fresh sheets.

"My plan was to move down here and give my brother his room back," she explains. "Even if it's going to be a shorter visit than I planned."

I frown. "What does that mean?"

"Any idea when he's coming home?" she asks, avoiding the question and pushing the suitcase deeper into the porch. The hard wheels clack against the tile floor.

No sooner than the question is out of her mouth, Axel and Nadia stumble through the door. Well, Nadia stumbles.

Behind me I hear a soft "eep," and then a small hand wraps around my wrist and Shelby pulls me into the porch, quietly closing the door.

Looking down at where her hand is wrapped around my wrist I note, "You're surprisingly strong for someone so small."

"He can't see us together," she says, slowly removing her hand.

"We weren't together until you dragged me in here," I point out.

"Shhhhh!" she hisses at me, those big eyes reflecting guilty fear at the two of us being caught together after her brother explicitly forbid it.

I clamp my mouth shut and step behind Shelby, leaning forward to press my ear to the door. My hands are on her shoulders, and her hair smells sweet and clean. Even though I probably shouldn't, I take a deep inhale.

Fuck, she smells good.

Outside, in the main part of the house, Axel and Nadia aren't quiet. The refrigerator door opens and slams shut. They laugh and joke together. The sink runs. There's a long spell of quiet that I'm certain means they're making out. *Finally* I hear the echo of footsteps on the stairs.

"Are they gone?" Shelby whispers so low I almost miss it.

"I think s—"

A rap against the window shakes the glass. "Shel, I see the light on, are you up?"

She cranes her neck and looks up at me. I shrug. She's right. If her brother catches me in here, I'll have worse than a bloody lip. I dip my head and whisper in her ear, "Tell him you're already in bed and you'll talk in the morning."

The column of her neck tenses as she swallows but in a wobbly, clearly not used to lying voice, she says, "I'm up, but I'm already in bed. Can we talk in the morning?"

Can we? Fuck no. This girl needs to learn how to assert herself.

"Nadia told me you moved to give me my room back. You know that wasn't necessary."

"It's fine," she replies. "You know I love to tackle a good project."

He laughs. "Yeah, you do." There's a beat. "You going to be warm enough? I've got extra blankets."

Shelby looks up at me, and there's no missing the flush in her cheeks. "I'll be fine."

"Okay," Axel relents. "Let's talk in the morning then. Good night."

"Night," she says, but doesn't exhale until his footsteps retreat and are on the steps.

Once we're both sure he's upstairs, I take a step back, giving myself a little room from this sweet smelling girl. I should leave, immediately, but I have questions.

I blink. "I only had one beer at the party, so I know I'm not drunk, but you're going to need to explain this to me better."

She peeks out the curtain, like she's making certain he's gone. In a low voice she says, "I just don't think this is where I need to be. There's no need to disrupt anyone this late at night, but I'm going to let him know tomorrow that I'm going back home."

Taking her by the shoulder, I spin her around to face me. "Okay, what happened?"

Her big blue eyes dart away. "Nothing happened."

"You went from cleaning out the porch and moving in to hiding from your brother." I cross my arms over my chest. "Your *notoriously* overprotective older brother." I narrow my eyes. "Nuh-uh. Spill?"

Her hands clasp and she worries that little band on her ring finger. I kind of hate that ring. "Fine. I hung out with Nadia and Twyler tonight at the Badger Den and it was..." she pushes her hair behind her ear, "... a lot."

Nadia took this innocent good girl out to a bar? During hockey season? Say no more. "So they popped your hockey bar cherry."

"Ugh," she drops her face into her hands, "do *all* of you have dirty mouths?"

"Probably. And for the record," I grin, "that wasn't even close to dirty."

"That doesn't make it any better. It just proves how out of place I am. I'm just not used to all this..." She pulls at her shirt. "The tight clothes, which by the way, I think belonged to someone called a puck bunny. And Nadia's language is filthy–"

"Nadia has spent a lot of time around athletes. Same with Twyler. It comes with the territory."

"All I know is that coming here was a mistake."

"Why? Because a few cuss words and that sexy shirt are an affront to your good girl sensibilities?"

She stares at me. "Don't call me that."

My eyebrows raise. "A good girl?"

"I think I lost that title when I ran away and hurt both David and my family. I made a commitment to him and then panicked when I felt like things were moving too fast. But coming here isn't the answer. I don't know what I thought would happen by coming here, but I know for certain that getting cornered by some guy at a bar wasn't–"

"You got what?" I ask, voice tight. "By who at the bar?"

"Oh." Guilt flickers across her face again. "Some jerk at the bar got a little too close. Mike helped me."

"Mike the owner?" We all know Mike. He's a solid guy. Former Wittmore player, class of '91.

"Yeah." She absently tugs at that shirt again, giving me a flash of upper boob. *Jesus.* It's no surprise that some kid tried to make a move on her. "He kicked him out."

"Okay." I take a deep breath, trying to wrap my head around everything Shelby is saying. I gesture to the couch, "Sit."

She does as she's told, and I'm not sure if that's a good thing or not. Where's the fight in this girl?

"Why did you leave home?"

She makes a face, like she'd tasted something bitter. "Things were moving too fast. My mother and David's mother skipped right over the engagement party to the wedding. They'd picked everything out; the date, the colors, even my wedding dress. And if that wasn't bad enough, I found out that my father had plans to build us a house. Plans *he* chose. On property he picked out. Everything just felt really out of control." She rubs a hand over her chest. "Out of my control for sure."

"That makes sense." Darla and I'd started making plans for our future. It was scary but exciting and I thought we both wanted the same thing, until it turned out that we didn't.

"And David? You still love him?"

There's a flicker in her eye, followed by the slightest hesitation, but ultimately she answers, "I do, but he seems perfectly content to have our families manage our lives."

Oh, David. You stupid dumbass. "Okay, tell me why you came here?"

"I didn't really have anywhere else to go. Everyone I know is associated with my family. But I knew Axel would at least listen to me. He and my parents haven't seen eye to eye in a long time."

"That's all?"

She thinks for a minute, then adds, "I guess I kind of wanted to see what his life was like. I'd heard about it all, but I didn't know what it was really like to go to college, play a varsity sport, have a girlfriend that he can spend time with without a chaperone." She stares down at her knees. "I guess I just wanted to know what it was like to have the freedom of no one watching all the time, or judging every little move I make."

"You know what I think?" I ask.

"No, what?"

"I think you're pretty *fu*-freaking brave. And smart. Because it would be easy to just keep barreling down the same path even with all the red flags waving in front of your face." Trust me. Been there, done that. There were a million signs me and Darla weren't going to work and I ignored them all, looking for some kind of ideal. "Giving yourself a little time to experience life is smart."

"Thank you, Reid. I appreciate it, but after tonight I think I'm done."

I take the way she pushes her hair over her shoulder as a sign of resolve, which is oddly why I blurt, "Actually, I don't think you are."

"Excuse me? What does that mean?"

"It means you came here for a reason. You want to experience life a little bit, and I think it's a good idea." I sit next to her, the old couch sagging under my weight. "Look, my girlfriend and I broke up a few months ago. We had long term plans, too."

"You were engaged?" Her eyes widen with surprise. "Seriously?"

"Not quite engaged," I admit, feeling stupid all over again, "but we talked rings and dates. I thought it was happening, but apparently she had other ideas."

"I'm sorry."

"Yeah, it sucked." I exhale, not liking the way the hurt still lingers in my chest. "And honestly, it was a little scary, but it made me realize I'm not ready for something so serious. I'm young, good looking," I raise an eyebrow, "and have a future in the NHL. I need to live my life a little and that may mean that I may not be a saint, but I won't have regrets. I think that's what you need to consider doing with the time you'll be here."

"Live my best life?"

"Yep."

She looks at me with those big blue eyes, doubt creeping in at the edges. "What if I don't know how to do that?"

That's how it happens. How I get locked in. Because you never issue a competitor like me a challenge that I'm going to pass up. Especially when it's a vulnerable, messy, hot girl making the offer. My decision is sealed before I ever say the words, "Then I guess I'll have to show you."

9

———

S helby

REID'S OFFER is the first thing on my mind when I wake up the next morning. I slept well, good even, despite my bed being an old couch.

I want to do it. Live my best life for the next few weeks. Explore freedom and the opportunities I know I won't have when I go back home. But I also know there's one thing I need to do before I take this step.

I call David.

The phone rings as I sit up, getting the full effect of how cold the porch is and pull the blanket to my chest.

"Shelby," he says in greeting. "Finally."

"Hi, David." There's a long pause and it's clear he's waiting for me to speak first. Okay. "How are you?"

"How am I?" He laughs. "I'm... well, I'm the way a guy is when their fiancée takes off without telling anyone, that's how I am."

"I'm sorry," I blurt, then instantly regret it. This is why I haven't called him. I don't want to apologize. I'm not sad about what I'm doing. I take a breath and add, "I'm sorry if I scared or hurt you. This was just something I needed to do."

"That's what I don't understand. Why do you need to do this?" His voice is tight. "Do you not want to get married?"

"No, it's not that." I pick at the seam on the blanket, a smooth line running across the side. "I'm not sure," I admit. "I haven't been sleeping well, and all of the planning just felt like it was getting out of hand. The parties, the wedding date, the wedding clothes…" I take a breath. "The house."

"About the house. I told your father that we wanted to make some changes."

"You did?" I rise up, surprised.

"I did. And he had no problem when I explained to him that I needed a larger office so that I have the ability to work from home a few days a week," he says. "But don't worry, I thought of you too. I asked for a door to be added for a nursery with an adjoining door to our bedroom. So you can be close to the babies all night."

Babies? That familiar hot, itchy feeling spreads across my chest and I struggle to take a breath. "Wait!" I manage to get out. "Did you say you changed the plans to include an adjoining nursery?"

"Yeah," he says, voice full of pride. "To make it easier for you."

I stand, dropping the blanket, letting the cool porch air hit my overheated skin. "This isn't what I want."

He sighs. "What now?"

"You called me your fiancée, David." Anger licks at my spine. "We're not engaged."

"Close enough."

"No. It's just another step forward that I wasn't included in."

"Are you serious with this?" he asks. "You're really going to act like the victim here of some organized plan by me and our families to exclude you?"

I realize that I am serious. I think about how Reid looked when I spoke to him the night before. He didn't judge me. He just listened.

"Yeah," I reply, feeling emboldened. "I'm not saying it's not something I don't want some day, but not like this. Not with you and my parents making all of the decisions while I sit by quietly with no input."

"Do you not want the nursery? Because we–"

I laugh. I actually laugh. The bubble of hysteria rising out of that tight mass in my chest.

"This isn't about a nursery, and until you figure that out, I'm going to need some space. Real space." I swallow. "I want to go on a break."

With a twinge of underlying fear, he asks, "What does that mean?"

"That means that until I come back home, we're not together. I need to think about myself for once and what I want, because to be fair, it's been so long since anyone asked me that I'm not sure I could even describe it if I was asked."

"Fine," he says, the petulance vibrating through the phone. "If that's what you need, take it. I'll be here when you get back."

"Thank you."

"Whatever you need, Shel. I just want the best for both of us."

"Me too."

I hang up without saying anything else. Pacing around the small area I say aloud, "I can't believe I just did that."

There's not much time to dwell on it, because I can hear the guys coming down the stairs and entering the kitchen. Axel. I told him we'd talk. I pull a sweater over my pajamas and run my fingers over my hair, yanking at the tangles.

Stepping into the living room I take in all four guys, each holding a bowl and spoon, look over at me. Well, everyone but Reid, who seems focused on pouring Frosted Oats in his bowl. None of them seem aware that my world just came crashing down.

"Hey," Axel says, through a mouthful of cereal. "I was about to wake you up. Go change. We're about to head to campus. I figured we could go to the coffee shop and talk."

"He's addicted to their bacon and egg biscuits," Jefferson says, tipping back his bowl and drinking the milk in a move that should be juvenile and unattractive but it's not possible with that face. It's a shame those cheekbones are wasted on a boy.

"This isn't breakfast?" I ask, receiving nothing but four confused stares back.

"Nope. This is just a pre-breakfast snack." Axel sets his bowl down and walks over. "I've got a free period this morning, and I figured you may want a little tour of campus." He nudges me and says with an overexaggerated Texan drawl, "And try the best bacon and egg biscuits north of the Mason-Dixon line."

All I feel like doing is crawling back in bed, finding my phone, and calling David to take it all back, but over my brother's shoulder, Reid's gaze meets mine, eyebrow lifted in a challenge.

Right.

I wanted something new, some adventure, and although I'm pretty sure coffee with my brother doesn't count, I can genuinely say it's something I've never done before.

"Holy cow." I cover my mouth while chewing the steaming bite of buttery goodness. "That's amazing"

"Almost as good as Mom's, right?"

"Never," I narrow my eyes, "*ever*, tell her that. She'd cry worse than when you decided to move two thousand miles away." I take another bite. "But yes."

I'd given him a story on the way over about how, for a minute, I got cold feet and was planning on going back home, but that after sleeping on it, I'd calmed down. For some reason, I don't tell him about David. Probably because he'd pull out the champagne to celebrate and that's not exactly how I feel.

"So why'd you do the one-eighty?" He crushes the wrapper of his first biscuit into a ball and reaches for the second.

I'm just thankful my brother is focused on his food and not the heat I feel creeping up my neck. He can't know about Reid's encouragement or he'll pack my bags himself and drive me directly to the airport.

"I admit that I was overwhelmed, and look, I really like Nadia, but–"

"Oh, you don't have to tell me. Taking you to the Badger Den first off was a terrible idea. That was way out of your comfort zone." I want to argue that and tell him I was fine, but we both know it's a lie. I almost ran away, *again*. "Nadia is a piece of work." He stares dreamily at the biscuit, the piercing in his eyebrow glinting in the overhead light. I'm pretty sure the glassy eyed gaze is about his girlfriend. "Fuck, I love her."

Seeing my brother like this is surreal. He's always been so wild, rushing from one high to the next. One *girl* to the next. I never thought I'd see him fall so hard. It makes me question what I have with David even more, because that stupid look on my brother's face? I've never once seen David look at me like that. "You really do, don't you?"

"She's the fucking best." He shoves the rest of the sandwich into his mouth, chewing slowly before he speaks again. "But look, Nadia hasn't had it easy. She acts all tough on the outside, and she is a badass, but she's been through a lot this past year." He licks his thumb. "You can talk to her, is all I'm saying. Twyler, too. She's cool."

Sure, both girls are nice, and with the comment about not being able to talk about things for legal reasons, I definitely get the vibe Nadia has been through something complicated, but have either of them called off an engagement? Have they threatened to throw everything away and disappoint their family? I don't know, but there's someone that has come close, but I don't think Axel is including Reid in approved friends.

After piling up his trash, he checks the time. "I've gotta head to class. Do you need directions back to the house?"

"No, I've got the address in my phone, but I think I'll stay here for a little bit. It's nice."

And warm. It's so freaking cold outside. Just the thought of venturing out again makes me want to cry.

Axel pulls on his extremely warm looking hockey jacket. "You've got my number. And Nadia's and Twy's. You can call Reese too if you need him."

"I'll be fine. Go learn something smart." I shoo him off and he exits, leaving with a cold gust of air coming in through the open door.

First order of business? Warmer clothes.

I'm googling the nearest clothing store when a shadow falls over the table. I look up and my heart jolts. "Oh!" I gasp, looking up at Reid, "you startled me."

"In the zone?" he asks, setting a full cup of coffee on the table. He's so tall, big, his shoulders filling out the team jacket that matches my brothers. There's a number 8 patch on the arm, and the name 'Wilder' is stitched over the badger logo on his chest. I'm jealous for a moment, this camaraderie of belonging. I've never had that before. He pulls the black beanie off his head and runs his hand through his dark hair, leaving it in loose waves.

I don't know why I'm noticing these things about him, or why my skin heats every time I look at him. Probably because the first time I met him, I climbed in his lap like a maniac and kissed him.

"I guess you could call it that." I flash him the screen. "I need to get some clothes. I'm woefully underprepared for this weather and some of us aren't comfortable freezing our arms and legs off."

"I won't apologize for running hot," he says with a quirk of his lip, "or for being hot." Without asking permission he sits across from me. "Where are you looking?"

"I don't know. It looks like there's a shop on campus." I glance up. "Do they have clothes?"

"They do, but it's Wittmore centric, fan stuff mostly. Although they do have sweatshirts and hats."

"I really think I need a heavier coat and a few sweaters." I stick out my foot, revealing the ballet flat. "And shoes. My toes are freezing."

He grabs my foot and pulls it into his lap. The move knocks me off kilter, and I swiftly shove my skirt under my thighs to avoid exposing myself further. Then he runs a warm thumb over the top of my foot and I freeze. "What are you doing?" I whisper, way too aware of the rough skin of his thumb touching me.

"Just helping out."

"We're in a coffee shop." I pull my leg back, but he holds tight. "People can see."

His eyebrow cocks. "You don't know a single person in here but me. Why do you care?"

"Because it's not appropriate." I wiggle my foot away, and this time he releases me. My foot feels like it's on fire. "And I may not know anyone in here, but I get the feeling everyone else knows exactly who you are."

I noticed it the second he sat down. Every eye in the room followed his movements. Especially the table of girls, talking quietly in the corner.

"You really are a good girl, aren't you?" he asks.

"What if I am?"

He leans back in his chair and assesses me. "You know, if I were your brother you'd have a nickname by now."

Axel is notorious for shortening everyone's names, including my own. In a low voice I beg, "Please don't start calling me Shellybean."

Reid laughs. "Noted."

"Thank you."

"There's a shop a few miles off campus that should work." His eyebrow lifts. "You want a ride? I've got time before my next class."

"In your car?"

"Yes, in my car. Well, truck." He frowns. "Were you expecting a bicycle or something?"

"No." What I wasn't expecting was to be so flustered. "But yes, that would be really helpful."

While I put on my coat, he grabs my trash and tosses it in the bin. "I'm in the lot," he says, turning down a pathway that leads away from the campus. "I had to run an errand between classes anyway."

His truck is older and a little beat up, with small patches of rust along the tailgate. He opens the door for me. "I'm from Texas and know my way around a truck, but you need some running boards."

"Sorry about that," he says, offering me his hand. My skirt goes to my knees and I have to hike it up to take the step in. I'm halfway up when I feel his hand on my hip and a crackle of heat zaps up my spine. I'm leveraged onto the bench seat and I quickly shift over. "You good?"

"Great." I say, flashing a quick grin.

He slams the door shut and walks around to the other side of the truck, while I buckle up. The cab is cold, but has a warm spicy scent that reminds me of Reid. I shove my hands into my pockets as the engine rumbles to life. He fusses with the knobs, and a blast of heat spills into the small space.

"So how'd you end up with a truck like this?" I ask.

"I bought her." he says, placing his hands on the big steering wheel. "It was all I could afford with my part time job."

"Her?"

"Lurlene." At my raised eyebrow he adds, "My grandmother's name."

"That's sweet." And a little adorable, I think as he eases the truck out of the lot. "What kind of job?"

"Coaching hockey at the local rink."

"Ah, of course. Hockey." I rub my hands over my knees. "Well, I'm impressed. I can't imagine earning enough money to buy something like a car."

"No?"

"I've never even had a job," I admit, feeling a little embarrassed by it. "At least not a paid one. My father always wanted me available to volunteer at Kingdom."

He nods, and I stare at the hard line of his profile, the sharpness of his jaw. "Axel's mentioned how he wanted you both to follow in his footsteps."

"Well, he wanted Axel to follow. I'm more of a supporting role."

"To David." He glances over and I avert my eyes, suddenly feeling hot and distracted by his overwhelming scent in the boxy cab.

"Yeah." It's on the tip of my tongue to tell him about breaking up with him, but it also still doesn't seem real. Or maybe I don't want it to be real? What if I made a mistake?

I focus on the view outside the window, and not my crumbling life, and the streets turning more commercial until I see a strip of shops up ahead.

He parks on the street, but even after Reid turns off the engine, I can't bring myself to open the door. "You ready?" he prompts.

"Just bracing myself for the arctic blast."

He rolls his eyes, but says, "Here."

I watch as he shrugs out of his jacket. "What? No. It's fine. I have this coat."

"Yeah, well, it's obviously not enough and I've got on layers." He's wearing a sweater with a shirt underneath and the beanie covering his head. "I'll be fine."

He holds it out in the small space between us, the expression on his face unwavering. I take it and say, "Thank you."

He exits the driver's side and I pull on the oversized jacket, engulfed not just in his lingering body heat but more of that intoxicating scent. I've got my nose pressed against the collar when he opens my door.

"You didn't have to do that," I tell him, dropping the collar quickly. "I can get down easier than up."

"Yeah, well, I'm not taking any chances." I slip my hand into his larger one, and he pulls me to the edge of the seat. I don't miss the way his eyes skim over my legs. "You've really got to get some pants," he mumbles as he helps me to the ground.

"I know. It's top of the list." I shift under the heavy weight of the jacket. "After a new coat."

We've just started walking down the sidewalk when someone calls out, "Good game, Wilder," followed by another, "Can't wait to see you in the playoffs." Soon a small crowd has gathered to grab handshakes or even ask for a selfie.

"Is that your girlfriend?" one fan asks, looking over to where I'm standing a few feet away.

"Just a friend," Reid replies, looking back at me and giving me a wink. He takes the phone into his hand to get a better angle for the camera.

"Thanks man," the guy says, grinning at the image on his camera.

"Anytime." They bump fists. "Thanks for the support."

I turn to him. "Does everyone know who you are?"

"I know you're from the land of football, but yeah, most people know who we are. Hockey is big up here, especially when we're winning." He smirks. "And if you're uncomfortable with the attention, I suggest you keep your distance from Reese and Axel in public. Those two are the real celebrities."

He sounds modest but there's a cocky swagger to his stride as he leads us to a small boutique. "You don't have to come in with me," I say, just outside the door. "I'll hurry."

"Nope. Not a chance."

"What do you mean?" A gust of air stings my nose.

"Remember how I told you I'd help you start living a little? Well, this is it. New clothes is step one." He grabs the door handle and pulls it open. "And I just happen to have excellent taste."

He gestures for me to walk in first. I duck under his arm and enter the warm, cozy shop. It's filled with different styles. There are racks of vintage coats, a wall of well-worn jeans, and cubbies filled with T-shirts.

"I just need a few warmer things, Reid, not a whole makeover. This isn't a teen drama."

I point to a coat that looks like the afghan throw on my grandmother's couch. "And there's no way I'm wearing something like that."

"I want you to feel yourself, find what you like. There's a dozen different styles in here rather than the cookie cutter stuff at the mall, or," his eyes sweep over me, "wherever it is you got these boring clothes."

"They're not boring," I snap, but I know it's not true. My mother picked them out, lined up to my father's specifications. I look down at my knee length skirt and sensible shoes. They're modest. Neutral. *Appropriate.* I sigh. "Fine. They're boring."

"For the next three weeks you're living the life of a college student. You should dress like one." He looks up at me and winks. "Only better."

I follow him through the store as he picks through racks and piles items in my arms. Occasionally he'll ask me a question, about color or size, but apparently I'm in his hands.

"Okay," he says, carrying everything back to the dressing room. "Try those on."

I stare at clothes. It's a hodge-podge of everything, including velvet and leather. "All of them?"

"Yep."

Who does this guy think he is? "What are you going to do?"

He nods at a purple chaise lounge, "I'll wait here and you can model them for me."

I blink, but he seems completely confident in this plan, and as he settles on the chair, crossing his boot clad feet at the ankles, I give up and head into the dressing room. I quickly undress, kicking off the skirt and unbuttoning my blouse. My white bra and panties reflect back at me in the mirror and I consider that if Reid saw these he'd be horrified at the plainness. I bet Darla or any other girl he's been with would wear something sexy and provocative.

Quickly, I change into the first outfit. The sweater is robin's-egg blue, ridiculously soft and oversized, with a wide neck that creeps over my shoulder while the pants are low waisted jeans that fit tight over my hips and butt but flare at the bottom. There's a swath of exposed skin between my top and the waistband of the jeans, that feels scandalous.

"How's it going?" he calls from outside.

"Fine."

"Let's see."

I walk out with one arm around my waist and another clutching the neck of the sweater in place. Reid's eyebrow raises. "Hands down, please."

Reluctantly I drop both and feel every inch of my body itch under his scrutiny. He reaches out and yanks the sweater back over my shoulder, shifting it into place, then he asks, "What do you think?"

"David would hate this." He'd think it's flashy and attention getting. Tacky.

"Well, David isn't here," Reid says, "and I don't give a fuck about what he would think. What do *you* think?"

I catch my reflection in a mirror behind him. The outfit is different from anything I've ever worn before. There's no pretense, like I'm trying to present something to the world, but more than that, for once in my life, I'm trying to fit in. "It's warm."

"Of course it's warm. Do you like the color?"

"Yes."

His eyes skim down to my hips. "And the jeans?"

"They're tight," I admit, running my hands down my sides.

"In a good way or a bad way?"

"A different way, I guess." I twist and look at my reflection. "I've just always worn skirts and dresses. It wasn't exactly a rule, but the alternative was frowned upon."

"Do you want my opinion?" he asks, looking like he's unsure if he should speak it.

"Sure."

"They make your ass look spectacular."

"Oh." My body goes through a series of acrobatics. Heart skipping, stomach flipping, skin burning. "Well, thank you?"

"You're welcome." He looks instantly regretful. "*Never* tell your brother I said that."

I flash him a grin. "Not a chance."

"Okay go try on the other stuff I picked out and we can get out of here."

I end up choosing several outfits, all more weather appropriate and a bit more casual than what I brought with me from Texas. I'm sorting out what I'm going to keep and return to the rack, when I spot a dress included. It's floor length and a dark emerald green with ruching up one side. There's a long split down the leg, that even though it's not that revealing, feels scandalous. I shove it out the curtain and say, "What's this?"

From the comfort of the chaise he replies, "A dress."

"This is neither warm or anything I'll have a reason to wear."

"True," he admits, "but it's sexy."

"I don't need se–" I swallow back the word, "anything like that."

"Why not?" he sits up. "You never know. If you don't wear it while you're here you can take it back home for your engagement party or whatever."

I look at the dress in my hand. It's barely two scraps of fabric held together with a little ribbon. "I could never wear that to an engagement party," then add quietly, "not that there's going to be one."

Reid stands, a line slashed through his forehead. "What does that mean?"

I take a deep breath. "I called David this morning and told him I wanted to take a break. A real one."

His eyes flick down to the ring and I drop my hand out of view. Baby steps.

"That's big news," he finally says. "You handling it okay?"

"I'm fine. Better than fine, actually." The words ring hollow. I'm not upset, it's just weird.

"Good," he says, tone unconvinced. "Did I... or our talk last night, did that have something to do–"

"The decision to break things off with David was mine and mine alone." I cut him off and shove the dress at him, then gather the other items I plan on returning to the rack. I pile them all in his arms. "Take those, please, while I get ready. I know you need to get back."

I duck back into the dressing room before he has a chance to reply, and by the time I come back out in the new sweater and jeans, he's got his elbows on the counter, talking to the sales girl. She's cute, with pink streaks in her pale blonde hair. "Friday night," I hear him say, "after the game, at the Manor."

"I'll think about it," she replies, picture perfect cool.

He grins and then straightens when he sees me. I quickly pay and meet him at the door.

"The only thing I didn't find was a coat," I tell him. "Afghan excluded."

"No worries." He hands his jacket back. "You can wear mine until you find something better."

"You sure about that?" I ask, aware that the sales girl is watching us closely. "What if Axel," or anyone else, "sees."

He shrugs, and wraps it around my shoulders. "If your brother has a problem with me making sure his sister doesn't freeze to death, then I'll deal with it at the time."

I'm not sure what it says about me that I feel more comfortable underneath the weight of Reid's jacket than anything else I tried on today, but I'm too worn out to fight it. I took some big steps today and I'll call that a win.

Even if I have to go against everything I believe in to accomplish it.

10

———————

R^{eid}

I'VE ALWAYS SUSPECTED IT, but after the last hour with Shelby I know for a fact, I'm a glutton for punishment.

I blame Axel. He never should have told me his sister is off-limits. It's like waving a red flag in front of a bull and expecting him not to come running. Despite my reputation as a 'good guy' I've always had a streak of defiance. Ask my foster parents–the seven homes I was in before the Wilders took me in. In home number three, Mrs. Williams told me not to touch the cookie jar after baking a fresh batch of peanut butter chocolate chip cookies. In home number five, Mr. Case told me not to mess with his tools, yet left the hammer on top of the chest. And in number seven, The McMurry's made it clear the computer was for "family" only, but stupidly left the security password as 1234, making it impossible to resist.

Shelby Rakestraw is like all three of those, but smells good and has an innocent, don't mess-her-up vibe that is increasingly hard to resist. Especially while wearing my jacket.

"Where are we going next?" she asks, arranging the bags on the floorboards. "Didn't you say you had an errand?"

Damn. I was hoping she'd forgotten that.

"Yeah, I need to make one quick stop before heading back to campus."

The studio isn't far from where we are, but it is in a more industrial area. I pull the truck in front of the little brick building. I'm about to tell Shelby to stay in the car, but she's already got the door open and has hopped to the ground.

"So what is this place?"

"A metalsmith studio."

"Metalsmith?" she repeats, as I press the security buzzer. I look up into the security camera and wave. "You mean like–" The door unlocks and I pull it open. One step inside and she finishes her sentence, "–a jeweler?"

The glass cases on either side of the small space answer that question for her. They're filled with rings, bracelets, necklaces and pendants. The artist is at the back of the room. Dean is a little older, with long gray hair pulled back in a ponytail that sits at the base of his neck, and an oiled handlebar mustache.

"Dean is a jewelry designer, yeah," I say, tension rising up my neck. No one knows about this place; one of my art professors suggested him when I asked for a quality craftsman. Why the hell did I bring her with me? It's like having a witness to my biggest, dumbest, crime.

Dean looks up from the project on his worktable, pushing the safety glasses to the top of his head. "Hey man, how are you?"

"Pretty good," I reply, even though my insides are twisted in a knot.

Dean's blue eyes skip over to Shelby. He grins and says, "You must be the fiancée."

Shit. I mean, she is draped in a jacket with my name on it.

"Me?" Shelby's voice comes out in a surprised squeak. "Oh, no. I'm not–"

"This is Axel's sister, Shelby," I say quickly. In an attempt to save both of us further awkwardness, I fall on the sword. "But, that's why I'm here. My girlfriend and I broke up. I'm not going to need the ring."

Dean's grin falters. "Damn, man, seriously?"

"Yep, and I know you get to keep the deposit and that's fine, but I wanted to get the designs back."

"I've got them back here," Dean says, turning to a file cabinet and pulling open a drawer. He flips through until he finds the right file. "Too bad, I was looking forward to creating it."

I reach for the file, but before I can, Dean flips it open revealing the design.

Shelby leans forward and looks between the design and my face. "You drew this?"

There's no mistaking the incredulous tone in the question.

"It's just a few sketches." I snatch it off the counter, but Dean isn't having it.

"Your friend is a talented artist. Unlike the rest of us who need validation and praise, he likes to hide it."

"I can see that," she says, giving me a look that makes me feel like she's trying to peek under my skin. "I'm impressed."

Dean reaches under the counter and returns with a stack of cash. He counts it out and sets it on the glass top. "What's that for?" I ask.

"I'm not taking your money, Wilder. I hadn't even started to work on it."

"But you booked me in," I argue, "and probably said no to other projects."

"Look," Dean says, tapping his fingers on the countertop, making the silver rings flash in the overhead light. "The next time you need a ring or any other piece of jewelry, come back and I'll fit you in. Maybe it'll be a ring," his eyes flick to Shelby, "or maybe it'll be something to commemorate your Frozen Four win. I'm not here to cause more pain. My karma is worth more than that." A slow grin curves at his lips. "Plus, I'm banking on your making it to the NHL and tagging me in all the photos wearing my shit. I can wait it out."

"Dammit," I mutter, taking the money and shoving it in my pocket. "Fine, but you better hope I'm not involved in some kind of scandal before then."

"There's no such thing as bad press," he looks at Shelby and winks, "right?"

"I don't know," she says with a laugh. "My father is a minister. He'd probably disagree with that one."

I take the designs and finish up with Dean, promising to be back when we win the championship. I'm opening the truck door for Shelby when she stops and looks up at me. "Are you okay? I know that had to suck."

"I'm fine." I swallow back the lingering pain. "I'm just learning there's a lot more to getting out of a serious relationship than breaking up."

"Yeah," she says. "I get that."

I help her up, even though she doesn't need it in the new clothes. There's a part of me that likes helping her. Likes feeling her body in my hands. A distraction from the pain in my chest. And as I shut the door, and walk around the front of the truck, I know that even though I will never admit this out loud, I just want to see her cute little ass in those tight jeans.

It's not until we're both in the truck and I'm sliding the key into the ignition when I notice she's studying me from the passenger seat.

"What?" I ask, unable to sit under her scrutiny any longer.

"There's more to you than I realized."

I laugh, although it's not in amusement. "What's that supposed to mean?"

She shrugs. "Axel's never told us much about his friends or teammates. I figured you guys were all just a bunch of meatheads like the football players back home. But you're a talented artist, and strangely good at picking out women's clothing–"

"And men's," I add.

"Yes, your outfits definitely make a statement." From the way she says it, I can't tell if it's a compliment or not, but I decide to take it as one.

"I'm getting a degree in graphic design," I tell her, "and recently I've been doing a little more with fabrics, like working with textiles or block and screen prints."

"What about hockey?"

"Hockey is in the forefront, but I knew I needed something to fall back on just in case." I take the turn into Shotgun. "The team is doing a charity fundraiser next month and the PR department for the team chose a few of my designs for the T-shirts that will be for sale."

"That's so great." She grins. "I'll be able to get a Reid Wilder original."

The image of her in one of my shirts, with nothing on underneath, pops into my head *and* creates a throb between my legs. God, I like that idea way more than I should.

"What kind of charity event?"

"It's a community outreach day for kids in foster care. They get to come to the rink and take a few lessons from the guys on the team, then load up on junk food and watch a scrimmage."

"That sounds really fun." She tilts her head. "Is this something you did as a kid?"

"Actually, yeah. It's how I started playing hockey. My foster parents took me to one of these when I first moved in with them. I'd never even put on a pair of skates before, but I took to it quickly. My parents were grateful. They'd been looking for a sport or activity to get me involved in and hockey was perfect. By the next weekend they had me signed up."

"And now you're giving back to the same program." She beams. "I love that for you."

"It's not a big deal. I'm happy to help out." I pull up to the Manor. "I've got to get back to campus for class, but I can help you with the bags if you need it."

"I'm fine." She shrugs out of the jacket and rests it on the bench between us and grabs the bags at her feet. "Thanks for taking me today. I really appreciate it."

"No problem," I tell her, watching as she hops out of the cab and walks toward the house.

"No problem," I mutter to myself as I drive off, knowing I have more than a problem.

I'm fucked.

~

3:04.

Every fucking night.

It's usually something different that rouses me. Jefferson stumbling in late at night. Nadia using the hall bathroom. The way the upstairs of the house gets so much warmer than downstairs and I have to peel off a layer of clothes. It doesn't matter what wakes me up, the next thing happens automatically: I think about Darla.

It's not in a romantic way, but more trying to figure out what went wrong. I can't stop going over every fight, every final word. This time it's about the ring, because that's the thing I keep going back to. I didn't make up the seriousness of our relationship. Darla was a full participant, every step of the way. Including the idea of me designing a ring for her.

"This is stupid," I mutter, flinging off the sheet. On the nights I can't get the ruminating to stop, I know the only answer is full distraction. Using my phone light, I look for my laptop next to the bed and *shit*. It's in my backpack downstairs.

After pulling on a pair of sweatpants, I exit my room. Once I get to the first floor, a glow of light spills from the kitchen, or really the refrigerator. I expect to see Jefferson digging around for a late night snack, but it's not his bulky frame leaning into the freezer. It's a pair of bare, smooth legs. It could be either Twyler or Nadia, but, immediately, I know it's not.

Neither of those girls send a jolt to my cock when I see her, or a sweaty annoyance that I can't get away from the one girl I'm not supposed to be engaging. I make the right move–the smart one–and grab my backpack off the couch and head for the stairs.

My foot is on the bottom step when I hear, "Oh cra–" followed by the sound of hard objects hitting the floor.

I drop my bag and rush over, wrapping my hand around the freezer door to open it wider. "Hey," I skim my eyes over her–fuck, no bra–then down to the pile of frozen items all over the floor, "are you okay?"

"Reid?" she blinks, surprised to see me. Fair. It's 3 AM. She sighs. "I was looking for an ice pack." She glances down at the mess. "You guys need to clean your freezer."

"It's a pretty well-known fact around here that you don't go poking around in there." I bend and grab a few foil wrapped leftovers and a half eaten carton of ice cream. "We open it, shove something in and pray for the best." I cram the stuff back in, wedging each one in after the other. "See?"

She holds out one last box of popsicles and I shove it in a small space and quickly shut the door before it all falls out.

She stares at me with a small twist to her lips. "That's ridiculous."

I shrug. "Hey, it's better than the alternative."

"You mean, cleaning up your shit?"

I raise an eyebrow. "Did you just say a curse word?"

She scowls, and to my surprise doesn't trip over herself to apologize. "Ugh, I'm tired. My neck hurts, and all I wanted was an ice pack. You're hockey players–you should have ice packs, right?"

"We do," I tell her, making a valiant effort not to stare at her chest. The cold air from the freezer has done a helluva job perking up her nipples.

This is why I was going back upstairs.

"But," I continue, pushing past her and all the temptation that comes with her, "we keep them in the freezer chest in the laundry room." I open the lid to the freezer to reveal a well organized system of packs. "Why do you need one?"

"That couch looks friendly, but I think it may be the devil." She winces and moves her hand to her neck while taking a peek in the freezer. "This is impressive."

"Yeah, that's all Twyler. Perk of having a trainer as your roommate's girlfriend." I grab a soft, pliable, pack and ask, "Show me where it's bothering you."

"Right about here." She gathers her hair to one side and touches the base of her neck.

Running my fingers over her warm skin, I touch the spot. "Here?" She swallows, keeping her eyes forward, and nods. Laying the pack over the area, I say. "If it's still bothering you in the morning, ask Twy to check it out. She's good."

"Thank you." She rests her hand over the pack, keeping it in place. "What are you doing up, anyway?"

"I couldn't sleep," I admit. "I came down to get my laptop to watch a show." And because my brain and impulse control seem to be on a break, probably because I keep having to drag my eyes away from her tits, I ask, "Want to watch with me? An update just came out about this decades old missing person's case I've been following."

She hesitates. Which she should. I never should have asked. I open my mouth to take it back and she says, "Sure, why not?"

11
____

S helby

"I WAS GOING to go back upstairs but..." Reid's words trail off but it takes me a moment to notice. My brain has been misfiring since he showed up in the kitchen bare chested and in those low slung, black sweatpants.

Is it normal for men to have this many muscles?

Is it normal for my mouth to water looking at them?

I blink, trying to catch up and it clicks. Upstairs is his bedroom. Across the hall from where my brother is hopefully deep asleep. "Yeah that's probably not a great idea. What about here?" I gesture to the couch in the living room. His eyes dart to the stairs and I know he's also thinking about my brother casually walking downstairs and catching us together. "Or how about on the porch?"

There's nothing sexy about the devil couch or the newly spun spider web in the corner.

"Sounds good."

With the space heater Reese gave me whirring on the floor, the room is pretty comfortable. I hear the porch door click shut behind me and I grab the blanket off the couch and sit, keeping the ice pack in place, while pretending like all of this is normal. Completely. Totally. Normal. Like, I'm not closed off in a room alone with my brother's friend and his oversized, very shirtless body.

Apparently Reid is impervious to the unsexiness of the porch.

Clueless, he sits and opens the laptop, propping it on his knees. With a lifted eyebrow, he says, "You're going to need to get a little closer than that."

Shifting, the old cushions sink underneath me, and I slide closer than I planned. Our legs crash together, mine bare, his covered in soft cotton that does nothing to stop the body heat from emitting through the fabric. Whatever I'm feeling is definitely one-sided, because he's focused on queuing up the show and not the whirl of emotions running through me. I mean, Reid probably hangs out with girls all the time. Sometimes shirtless. Often alone.

I'm the one out of my element here. I've only seen David shirtless at a church sponsored pool party, surrounded by other people. I've never been alone with a man, shirtless or not, like this.

"What's this show about?" I ask, trying not to completely spiral.

His expression lights up. "Twenty-six years ago a ten-year-old boy, Andrew, and his brother, Ashton, went to bed on a Sunday night, like normal. The next morning when their mother came to wake them up, Ashton wasn't in his bed. The family immediately searched for him in the house, around the house, in the neighborhood. No one could find him, but later police heard from several eyewitnesses that saw him in the middle of the night, miles away from home on a stretch of deserted road. Although they did find a few signs that Ashton had been in the area, he was never seen again."

"Wow, that sounds really strange."

"Yeah, back then cell phones and having internet in the home wasn't as common. No one has any clue why he left and where he was going, but last week police in the area did a search of a property that's owned by a prominent family." He gestures to the screen. "This is an update of that."

I do my best to create a little space between us once he starts the video, but physics and the breakdown of the foam in the couch cushions work against me. Like in the truck, I'm overwhelmed by being so close to him. His scent. His warmth. The trail of soft-looking hair that travels between his belly button and the waistband of his pants.

So it's no surprise when I have to say, "Wait. Stop the video." He presses pause. "So no one saw him again after the trucker watched him run off the road in the dark, but they found candy wrappers near an old shed, and then a year later found his backpack and a Bulls basketball jersey twenty miles away in a ditch?"

"Wrapped in a garbage bag, yeah," he says, with enthusiasm. "His mother claims the jersey wasn't his, but the backpack is. So the big question for decades has been, who does the jersey belong to?"

"Do you know?" I ask, already invested.

"That's the big news. The police just announced that they found DNA on the shorts that match someone that lives on the property they're searching."

"Wow." I nod slowly, taking it all in. "This is a crazy story."

"Right?"

"And you do this a lot? Follow old cases like this?"

"There are a few in particular I'm interested in. Usually ones with a strange mystery like this that is seemingly unsolvable." He leans against the arm of the couch, assessing me. "Do you think it's weird, because Twyler loves true crime too, although she's way more into the cult stuff. Reese definitely thinks we're weird."

"No, but what is weird is that I'm starting to realize how all of you have so many interests and I'm just kind of floating around, waiting for someone else to tell me who I am and what I like."

"Well," he says slowly, "how do you feel about watching this show with me?"

I consider it. "The show is interesting. It's like a whole other world, with people going through things I never even considered. Not from inside my well-crafted bubble where no one goes missing and if bad things happen we just pray over it and bake a casserole and go about our business."

The ice pack slides off my shoulder. He snags it before it falls and puts it back in place. His hand is heavy, solid, and he doesn't move it right away. "How's the neck?"

"Sore," I admit. "I'm sure it'll be better in the morning."

"Is it here?" he asks, pressing down his thumb. I feel a sharp twinge and grimace. "Yeah, I can feel the knot."

"That's it." I roll my neck. "I'm sure it'll be fine in the morning."

His eyes linger around my collarbone, before returning to the laptop. He starts the show again, but doesn't move his hand. I feel the firm press of his thumb into my neck, although softer this time. He hits the tender spot and my shoulders rise.

"Too hard?" he asks quietly.

The amount of pressure isn't a problem. I try to form coherent words, "No, it's just sensitive."

"Here, take this," he holds out the laptop. "And shift this way a little so I can see if I can work this out."

The video continues to play, with the hosts detailing the events of the house search, but I can't focus on anything other than the way Reid's hands feel as he pushes my hair to the side. My skin is cold from the ice pack, making his fingers blaze a trail of heat. He works against the muscles, and I feel the effect not just in the places he's touching but every other inch of my body.

"Is that good?" he asks, voice gruff in my ear.

I nod, and he pulls me back just an inch, making me sink back into his hard chest.

His hands rub over the caps of my shoulders, and down to my arms, turning my muscles into jelly. My T-shirt is thin and I'm aware of how every pass he makes tightens my nipples. I want to cover myself, but I don't want to draw attention. Maybe he won't notice, or maybe my body feels so relaxed, so good that I'm willing to pretend.

Then, like a string pulling against my spine, I chase his touch and arch my back.

Reid's hands still, and behind me I hear a deep inhale and then a strained, "Fuck, Shelby."

No one has ever whispered my name like that, but there's no doubt of the intention. His knuckles lightly brush over the side of my boob and I feel a zing of heat travel straight between my legs.

"Has a man ever touched you like this before?" he asks, continuing to trail his knuckles gently in the same spot.

"No," I admit, too turned on to be embarrassed at my inexperience.

"Not David?" His fingers are clenched around my biceps.

"Definitely not." I exhale. "He would *never*."

The video comes to an end, but rolls into the next one, some kind of hockey highlight show. I'd stopped paying attention long ago, and even though I can't see Reid's face, I can tell he's singularly focused on me.

"He's either a masochist, a saint, or gay," he remarks, "because I'm not that strong." The pain in my neck has vanished and I only feel the heat of his breath on my ear. "Tell me to leave, Shelby."

I should. I shouldn't have ever invited him in here in the first place. But I did. I *wanted* to.

I also don't want him to stop.

"Stay," I say in a voice I don't recognize.

His fingers find my chin and he turns my face to his, until our eyes meet. "You're sure?"

"I'm sure."

I wait for him to give me some relief, to touch the parts of me that are craving more, but he goes back to what he was doing before, massaging my arms with firm strokes. "Relax," he says quietly, nudging me to lie against his chest. "Good girl."

His fingers drape over my shoulders, making tiny circles, dipping lower and lower with each pass. Desperately, I arch my back, and his hands meet my body, cupping my breasts.

"Still okay?" he asks, thumbs dangerously close to my nipples.

"Mmhmm."

"Tell me what you want, Shelby."

I fight the urge to squirm as heat builds in my lower belly. "I don't know."

"I think you do."

He's right, but it goes against everything in my nature to verbalize it. When I don't speak he asks, "Here?" and circles the hard peaks, while still not touching them.

My body tenses, as if I ease up, I may completely lose control. "You're teasing me."

"It's called consent, Shelby." His chin, prickly and unshaved, brushes against a bare spot on my shoulder. "And I'm sure as fuck going to get it from you. Not just because it's the right thing to do, but because you need to learn how to speak up for the things you want." His fingers continue to make those lazy circles. "So tell me, do you want me to touch, suck, or fuck your tits?"

That one sentence is enough to tip my world on its axis. I know he's being dirty on purpose, trying to shock me into a reaction, but all it does is embolden me. I know I'm not ready for the second two, but I'm confident enough to say, "I want your hands on my tits."

There's no more messing around and Reid finally gives me what I've been craving. His hands are firm as they knead my breasts and squeeze them together. I watch him skim his thumbs over the cotton covered nipples, drawing them into tighter peaks. My belly flip flops, churning with an explosion of butterflies, but most of all, I notice how each touch sends a rush of warmth between my legs. This time I can't hide the squirm, and clamp my knees together.

"It's making you wet," he says, describing what I feel. "Every time I touch you here," he gently tweaks a nipple, "you feel it in your pussy, don't you?"

A shudder wracks through me and I try to curl into him, but he holds me in place.

His hand is big enough that he holds both of my tits in one, while skimming his palm over my belly. "I bet you can come like this, can't you?"

I have no idea, because I've lost all sense of where my muscles end and my bones begin. All sense of decency. My breath comes in short pants as he runs his hand up my shirt. The first touch of his finger tips, skin to skin, against my breast ignites something in me. Something hot and feral. Wild and desperate.

My hips buck and I grab his hand, thrusting it between my legs. The lightest touch of friction is all I need to trigger a shockwave, the first one releasing a deep moan. My tether to my body is disconnected, and I float high on the aftershocks, basking in the heady glow.

Until I fall back into place.

Back to reality.

To what I've done.

To the feel of Reid's very hard erection pressing against my backside. I bolt upright, yanking my shirt down, and look at him, catching the way his tongue darts out and swipes over his bottom lip.

"Fuck, Shel," he says, "I didn't–"

"It's fine," I say quickly, unsure if the heat on my cheeks is from embarrassment for what he just witnessed or the result of my body going crazy. "That was... we shouldn't have."

"I know. Fuck, fuck, *fuck*." He runs his hands through his hair. "I didn't mean to go that far."

"Of course not." A laugh slips out, sounding more hysterical than I mean for it to. "I'm Axel's little sister. The good, innocent, and scared girl that showed up at your house one night and humiliated, well, who *continues* to humiliate herself."

I start to leverage myself out of the sink hole between the cushions, but his hand wraps around my wrist, holding me in place.

"Don't. Nothing you're doing is embarrassing." His eyes skim over my face. "Not the night you arrived or tonight."

"Thank you for saying that, but you're just being nice."

He laughs.

"What?" I ask.

"Everyone thinks I'm a nice guy, but that's giving me too much credit. Would a nice guy be down here in the middle of the night, secretly with his friend's little sister after being explicitly told to stay away? Would a nice guy figure out how to get his hands on you even though you're inexperienced and naive?" He leans forward, face inches from mine, and brushes his thumb over my lips. I swallow, enthralled and terrified of what he'll say next. "Would a nice guy wake up every morning, with my hand on my cock, thinking about what your lips would look like wrapped around me?"

I shake my head, taken aback and flushed with a million feelings. "You're trying to scare me."

He drops his hand down to my neck. "I'm trying to make it very clear who I really am, GG."

Good girl.

That's who he thinks I am, just a good girl who can't handle what he's saying–or maybe more likely, who he really is.

"As I just revealed, I'm not some good guy like your boy, David." His thumb swipes over the sensitive skin on my throat. "I'm red blooded. *Hot* blooded. And being this close to you is a problem for me. I knew it before I walked up to you in the coffee shop, and I definitely knew it before I came in here with you tonight." His eyebrow lifts. "But that's the problem. I did it anyway, consequences be damned."

He rises off the couch, leans over and grabs the laptop, giving me a bold view of the hard bulge underneath his sweats.

I avert my eyes and ask, "Where are you going?"

"I'm doing what I should have done the minute you walked in the front door," he tucks the laptop against his side and peers out the curtain into the living room, "leaving you alone."

12

R eid

I *HATE* LOSING CONTROL.

My social workers would say it's due to the constant moving when I was a kid. The revolving process of being placed in a new home and meeting a new family and getting settled in a new room, new school... new everything. Only for her to show up days, weeks, months later, helping me pack up my sad bag of belongings and start the process over again somewhere new.

That uncertainty made me want to control everything. Having a job and my own spending money in high school. Earning a scholarship for hockey. Even after moving in, and being adopted by the Wilders, I didn't want my life to be left up to someone else.

I think it's why I make a good D-man. Every inch of the ice is my domain. No one is getting past me. I try to stay two steps ahead, protecting what's mine: The puck, my teammates, the goal.

Even though it's hard to admit it, that urge for control is what made me get in so deep with Darla; planning engagements, designing rings, setting up a future. That urge was exactly what tore us apart. I wanted too much, too fast, and too soon.

So yeah, I hate losing control, which is exactly why Shelby Rakestraw is a problem.

Every time I think about or see her, it's like the ground has fallen out from under my feet and I'm doing my best not to stumble. I can't stop thinking about how she looked that night, body warm and pliant in my arms. I knew she was turned on with those breathy little moans and hard nipples. I knew her tits would feel good in my hands and I was ready to draw it out–to show her how good I could make it for her. But then it all happened so fast, the way she grabbed my hand, shoving it between her legs. She came so fucking quick, falling apart in shuddering bliss. I've never been so hard, so fucking horny, as I was watching every inch of her body turning red.

It took every ounce of control not to take it further. So I did what I do best. Draw up the shields. Act like a dick. *Take control.* Scaring her off was the only thing I could do to get out of that room without bigger regrets.

More proof that I have absolutely no control when it comes to Shelby? She's not the only one on a hair trigger. I've just about rubbed myself raw three times a day since.

"Wilder!" My eyes snap up and I see Jefferson waving to me from behind the net. I'm on the bench just outside the rink, fixing a broken lace. "You finished?"

"Yep." I tie it off and glide onto the ice toward the other defenders already in place for the series of 2 v 2 drills we're about to start. Reese, Emerson, and the other offensive players face us from the opposite end.

Coach blows his whistle and slides the puck down the center line as the first two match-ups take off in a burst of speed to see who gets there fastest. Jefferson places his hands on the top of his stick and leans against it. "By the way," he says, "that Mara chick has been asking about you."

"Mara?" I think back through the girls I've hooked up with lately and finally land on the one I didn't. "Oh, from the party."

"She said you were about to hook up and you bailed."

"Next!" Coach Bryant calls.

The puck slings into the empty middle of the rink and I sprint toward it. Reese gets there first, and Jefferson and I fall back into defensive zones. Reese slaps the puck through the gap where Emerson is waiting. Unfortunately for them both, I'm there first and Jefferson's got Reese fully defended. I clear it out of the box and down to the other end.

"Nice effort." I grin at Reese, who swears under his breath. Cap is a competitor all the time, so even losing during practice pisses him off.

"So why'd you do it?" Jefferson asks as we get out of the way of the next challenge. "Bail on a hot chick who's into you?"

"I had a headache."

I hear a snort and glance over at the goal where Axel is seemingly both watching the play down the ice *and* eavesdropping.

"What's that about?" I ask.

"Aren't headaches a chick excuse?"

"I just wasn't into it," I say, while keeping it to myself that the instant she sat in my lap, all I could think about was being in the same position with his sister. "Why do either of you care anyway?"

"Are sure you're not sulking about the break up with Darla?" Jefferson asks.

Ah, there it is.

"I'm not sulking. I just wasn't into it," I say, not adding that the only girl I can't stop thinking about is Shelby. I may not be making the best decisions right now, but I'm not stupid enough to tell Axel that.

Neither of them look like they believe a word I'm saying, because even if they don't know the truth, it's still bullshit and we all know it.

My reprieve comes unexpectedly from down the ice when Coach Bryant's angry voice carries down the ice, "Hey! Knuckleheads! Stop distracting my goalie!"

NO MATTER HOW OLD, how accomplished, or how well you're doing, getting called into the Coach's office is always unnerving. I get flashbacks to all those days of sitting in my social worker's office, meeting the administrators at new schools, being told that things were changing again.

"You wanted to see me?" I ask, standing in Coach Bryant's office doorway. I'd just been coming off the ice when one of his assistants told me to head to his office after I showered.

"Take a seat," he says, not looking up from the papers on the desk.

I wrack my brain trying to figure out where I'd fucked up. I hadn't missed any practices, my grades are solid, I'm carrying my weight during the games... I mean, at least I think I am. Running my hands down my thighs, I shift in my seat.

"Stop squirming." He drops the papers and leans back in his chair. "This isn't an interrogation. I just wanted to check in with you."

"Check in?" I repeat. In three years he's never 'checked in' on me. "Did I do something wrong?"

"Christ." He rolls his eyes. "I'm meeting with all the seniors. Things can get a little tense heading into the final weeks of the season and with the playoffs on the line, I want to make sure everyone is steady."

"Oh." I relax a little. "Well, then, sure, everything is fine."

"The PR department told me you offered to help out on some design work for the fundraiser in a few weeks. How's that going?"

"Good." I nod. "Everything is finished. I submitted the designs last week."

"I've seen your work. You've got talent, Reid, but just being a student-athlete is hard enough. You didn't have to take on this extra work."

"It's not a problem, I enjoy it," I reply truthfully, although I don't add that anything extra to buffer my portfolio is worth the time and energy. That portfolio is tangible. *Real.*

Like he's reading my mind he says, "I heard from New York. They like what they see. Do you still feel comfortable with the deal?"

"New York has a good program, anyone would be lucky to get a position from them or the farm team."

It's a side step, because even though playing for the NHL is the plan, I'm never going to be comfortable when my life is on someone else's terms. But I want to do something big. Not just for my parents, but for Coach, because he gave me a shot when no one else would.

The expression on his face tells me he's aware I avoided the question, but thankfully he doesn't push. "Just make sure you stay balanced. And by balanced I mean that until that trophy is in the case in the lobby, hockey is your priority, got it?"

"Yes, sir."

I don't take another breath until I'm dismissed and out in the hall. Some guys on the team have the benefit of focusing on one thing, one girl, one future. I know all too well how easily it is for plans to get yanked out from under your feet.

So yeah, I'll give the American Dream a shot–give the team what they need, and I'll sign deals to make my family proud, but I'll always have some kind of back up plan in the works.

Because at the end of the day, guys like me, don't ever get what they want.

13

S helby

Out of a massive double dose of humiliation and shame, I spend the next few days avoiding everyone from the Manor. I don't know who I'm hiding from more: my brother who I'm terrified can read exactly what I've done on my face? Or Reid, who is the one that did it to me?

It as in giving me an orgasm.

My *first* orgasm.

That little fact alone is enough to keep me in my makeshift room until the guys leave every morning and sneak back into it before they get home at night. I'm thankful for their long practice schedule at the arena, but after a day or two, I'm bored. Sitting around alone, watching daytime TV, and cleaning up after my brother and his roommates, I had to acknowledge that this isn't why I left Texas and broke up with David.

After my sixth episode of Judge Hatcher doling out ridiculous consequences to ridiculous people, I catch myself shouting at the TV,

"You're both idiots!" at a broken up couple fighting over damage to a car, and realize I need to get some air. For my sanity.

That, *and* to escape Reid's scent that seems to linger in the air.

Since I have no car, I bundle up in layers and start the walk toward the small strip of shops and establishments near campus. There aren't many people around as I pass Twyler and Nadia's cute little teal house, but it gets busier with students heading back and forth to class, the closer I get. I blend in, looking the part of a college girl with my new clothes–even if I'm freezing without an appropriate coat.

I stop for a coffee at a different shop on the strip, and continue on my way. There's a car outside the Badger Den and I see the owner, Mike, struggling with a large box in his hands while trying to open the door.

"Let me get that," I call out.

Mike looks up and grins in recognition. "Axel's sister Shelby, right?"

"That's right," I open the door wide enough for Mike and his box to get through.

"Thanks," he says, carrying the package to the bar and setting it on top. Mike is a little older, with more bald spot than hair, but he's got the same swagger I've noticed my brother and his friends carry. It's a confidence I can't really comprehend. Mike nods back at the door. "Any chance you can hold that while I get the rest of these things in?"

"Sure." I set my coffee on the bar. "I'm just happy to warm up for a minute. I'm still not used to this weather."

With a box of paper napkins in his hands he gives me the once over, "You definitely need a heavier coat."

"I know. I just haven't found one I like."

"That's the difference in harsher weather. We worry less about want than need." He grabs the last box and after he carries it in, I let the door swing shut. I follow him back in and pick up my coffee, taking a warm sip.

"Other than the cold, are you enjoying your time with your brother?" he asks, using a blade to cut the tape on the box of napkins.

"It's different than my life at home." He raises his eyebrows, waiting for me to continue. "I'm not in college there, and I don't really have a job other than supporting my father's ministry." I watch as Mike grabs a napkin dispenser off the side of the counter and stuffs the paper rectangles inside. I pick up one of the dispensers and a stack of napkins and do the same. "I'm not used to this much freedom."

"Are you enjoying it?"

"I think it's more overwhelming than anything else." And confusing.

"Transitioning to adulthood isn't easy, but if you're anything like your brother, I'm sure you'll be fine."

"Where do these go?" I ask, and a moment later I'm placing them on all the table tops across the bar. When I finish up, I head back to the bar. "Anything else you need help with?"

He studies me for a moment. "You looking for a job?"

"Oh, I meant right now." I laugh. "I doubt I'm qualified." I look at the lines of liquor bottles behind the bar. "I've never even tasted alcohol."

"No drinking required," he says with a smile, "but I could use a server."

"I'm only planning on being here for a few weeks."

"I had two employees quit recently and haven't been able to find a good replacement." He lifts an eyebrow. "And the fact you just helped out with little to no direction shows you have the number one thing I look for in an employee: initiative."

A strange swell of pride fills my chest. "If you're okay with this only being temporary, I'm game."

He grins. "You're a lifesaver! Thank you."

"When do I start?"

"How about tonight?" he suggests. "There's no game, so it should be slow enough to get your bearings."

That fluttery panic rises in my throat, but I take a deep breath, and swallow it back. "Sure, why not?"

Seriously, I've got nothing to lose but hours in front of the TV and obsessing over Reid Wilder.

Mike reaches under the bar and tosses me a T-shirt.

"Welcome to the team."

I'VE DONE a lot of uncomfortable things this week, but for some reason this feels big. Raising my hand, I knock on the door. Before I can even regret doing it, the door opens and Nadia peers out of the Teal House.

"Shelby! Hi!"

The first words out of my mouth are a rushed apology. "I'm sorry I showed up without calling, I know you're probably busy."

The divot between her eyes appears. "We're definitely not busy. Twyler's just watching TV and I was pretending to study for an exam while really shopping online."

Behind her I hear Twyler yell, "Nad, ask her to come in and close the door! It's freezing out there!"

She swings the door open and I step inside the tiny house. The off campus neighborhood is called Shotgun and the Teal House is the example why. The houses are from back when the neighborhood was a mill and filled with workers and they lived in these narrow homes where you can see straight through the house from the front door to the back. In the small living room, Twyler sits on a couch, the TV on pause and a bag of chips next to her. "Hey, Shelby." She does a double take. "Girl, you really need a coat."

I really do, but that's not why I'm here. "I think I did something stupid."

Nadia gestures for me to take the armchair, but I don't miss the look they give one another.

"How stupid?" Twyler asks, holding out the bag of chips to me.

I shake my head, stomach too anxious to eat. "Earlier today I was walking down on the strip and–"

"Oh my god," Twyler's back straightens and her blue eyes widen, "did someone try to get you to join a cult?"

"What? No." I pause. "What cult?"

"There used to be this cult nearby, Serendee." Twyler's entire expression grows animated. "They had a recruitment center just off campus and would specifically target weak-minded students." Her eyes shift to Nadia.

"One meeting!" Nadia declares, throwing up her hands. "And they offered free food! It's not like I gave them all my money and started wearing those weird, ugly dresses and agreed to an arranged marriage."

Twyler rolls her eyes. "Anyway, they're disbanded now that the leader is in prison for being an awful, abusive person, but there are a few of his people still around and they're freaking persistent."

"Okay, well, no," I say, "I can assure you that I did not get recruited by a cult, but I was offered a job by Mike at the Badger Den."

"Oh," Twyler says with relief. "Well, that's great."

"I didn't know you were looking for a job," Nadia says, grabbing a handful of chips.

"I wasn't." I explain what happened that morning and how offering a little help turned into an offer. "I took it, which is idiotic, because I've never even had a real job before. He gave me this shirt," I dig into the bag I brought with me, "and I can't even figure out what to wear it with. Jeans, a skirt, leggings? This is all falling into 'normal' people stuff and I have no idea how to do that."

"Normal people stuff?" Twyler asks.

"Like things that are different from how I was raised. What was expected of me. My whole life has been centered around my father and his role at Kingdom. We didn't get after school jobs or wear clothes that it would be okay to get beer splashed on. What if they ask for something and I don't know what it is? What if someone gets the wrong order and gets angry? What if–"

"Okay," Twyler huffs out, resting her hand on my arm, "slow down and take a deep breath." It's harder than I want it to be, but I manage to suck in and exhale. "That's good. I understand this is all new to you, but it's a serving job, not rocket science. At the most, you'll serve food and drinks, clean up, and make sure rabid hockey fans are happy."

"Honestly, that doesn't sound any different than handling the events I help my father with at his church." Although I don't get paid, and I guess they're rabid God fans, not hockey ones. "We have a lot of social events and receptions, and trust me, those church ladies can be demanding. Although, to be fair, no one is drunk," I laugh, "unless it's on the holy spirit."

"See? You're more prepared than you think you are. It'll probably be a little chaotic and customers can be asses," Nadia chimes in, "especially if Wittmore is losing, but Mike and all the other workers are super nice. I think it's a good idea."

"You do?"

"Why not? You don't need to sit around the Manor all day waiting for Axel to come home." She pops a chip in her mouth. "Don't get me wrong, he's happy to have you here, but he's so busy right now with school and the team. Go out there and live your life."

"Do you think he'll freak out when he finds out?"

"Of course." She grins. "Which is even more reason to do it."

I do kind of like the idea of that. "Okay, I'll do it."

"Excellent. So, now that we've settled that," Nadia grabs the shirt from my hands and holds it up, "we have to get you ready."

The shirt is black with the Badger Den logo on the chest. "That's what I really need help with. It doesn't seem like there's really any official dress code. I just want to make sure I'm comfortable and fit in."

"If there's one thing I know how to do, it's how to dress for sports fans."

"Nadia..." Twyler warns.

"Nothing slutty," she argues, "but you do want to make some solid tips."

"While not having her brother and *your* boyfriend lose his mind," Twyler reminds her.

"That too." She stands. "Come on, let's go find a happy medium."

"Okay," Nadia says, twisting her finger around a lock of hair, "I think this should do it."

I'm learning quickly that my brother's girlfriend loves a makeover and apparently I'm the perfect target. After digging through Twyler's closet for a pair of black skinny jeans with ripped holes in the thighs and then attacking the hem of the oversized shirt Mike gave me with a pair of scissors, she started on my hair and makeup. She turns me to the mirror and adds, "What do you think?"

The girl reflected back at me looks older and more mature than the one that came out here the week before. Nadia has coated my eyelashes in thick mascara and a wide swath of eyeliner that curves at the edges. My hair is pulled back to stay out of my way while I'm working, but she left enough loose pieces to curl by the sides of my face.

"Are you sure Mike will be okay with you chopping up the shirt he gave me?"

"All the girls at the Den alter their shirts."

I glance at Twyler who is half paying attention to us and half watching some show about a serial killer. She nods and says, "She's right."

I tug at the hem that curls now that it's been cut, trying to cover my midriff. "Okay but if he's upset, I'm telling him you did it."

"Bring it on. I'm not afraid of Mike."

I take one last look in the mirror and straighten my shoulders, liking what I see. "I guess I should probably head over."

A loud bang rattles the door and a moment later it opens. Axel's spiky blonde hair appears in the doorway. "Hey, T."

"Oh boy," I mutter, realizing I'm going to be dealing with this sooner than I hoped, but before my brother even lays his eyes on me,

I see that he's not alone. My stomach explodes in a flurry of manic butterflies when I see the copper tousled head of hair following him in. As much as I shouldn't track Reid like this when my brother is nearby, I can't help myself.

My brother isn't paying attention to that anyway.

"Where's the rest of your shirt?" he asks, striding across the small room, eyes trained on my T-shirt. "Is that from the Badger Den?"

"It is." I cross my arms over my waist, covering my midriff. "Mike offered me a job."

"Mike," he repeats. "Suddenly you're on a first name basis with a bar owner?"

"He needs help and I need something to do." I drop my arms, placing a hand on my hip. "I don't know why it's any of your business."

"It's my business because you're my responsibility while you're here and I told Mom I'd keep you safe." His hand thrusts in his hair. "Working in a bar with a bunch of horny hockey fans doesn't seem safe, Shel." He looks to Reid who is sitting on the couch next to Twyler, hand shoved in the potato chip bag. "Back me up, man."

Reid freezes, hand full of chips halfway to his mouth, eyes shifting between my brother and then me. His gaze is casual enough, but my body temperature increases by five degrees. He shakes his head. "Nope. I'm not involved."

"Babe," Nadia says, moving between me and my brother, "isn't that what you've always wanted for Shelby? For her to go live a normal life, doing normal things?"

"I was talking about college classes and going to the movies. Not becoming a Badger Babe."

"A what?" Twyler asks.

"You know that's what we call the girls that work at the bar. Badger Babes." Reid chuckles darkly from the couch. Undeterred, my brother looks down at his girlfriend and grimaces before sighing. "It's a compliment."

"Uh, huh." Nadia rolls her eyes. "If it's a compliment then there's no reason Shelby can't join the ranks, right?"

His mouth forms a line so tight I wait for the lip ring to pop off. "Dammit," he mutters. "Fine. But keep your boobs in. *That's* not how you get tips. It's how you get perverts following you around."

"Jesus," Nadia rolls her eyes and looks at Reid. "You think this is fine, right?"

"I already said, I'm not involved in this."

"But come on," Nadia persists, "you're a guy, how does she look? Slutty or cute?"

"She looks like Ax's little sister." His eyes never leave the TV. I know why he says it but, ouch. Not even the smallest urge to take a peek? "I assume Mike knows this, which means he'll let everyone else at the bar know, too. She'll be fine."

Nadia seems satisfied with that. "See?"

"Whatever," Axel says, "but I'll be there to–"

"Sorry, Bud," Nadia says, "but you promised to help me study for this exam."

Twyler hops up from the couch and hands Reid the remote control. "Come on, Shelby, I'll walk with you."

"You sure?" I ask, just happy to be getting out of this room. Between my brother's judgement and Reid's nonchalance, I'm ready for an escape.

"Yep," she stuffs her feet into sneakers. "I have to meet Reese on campus anyway."

I pass Nadia on the way to the door and say, "Thanks, for helping me get ready."

"No problem." She squeezes my arm. "You're going to do a great job."

"Shel–" Axel calls as we step onto the cold, dark porch. "You're going to do great. And if anyone bothers you, knee them in the junk."

"Thanks, bro." I wrap my arms around him and give him a hug, because there could be worse things than having an overprotective brother.

14

———————

R^{eid}

I LEAVE five minutes after Shelby and Twyler, telling Axel I have an assignment to work on. It's not a lie. I do have a project due for my art theory class, but when I get to the sidewalk in front of the Teal House, instead of turning right, toward home, I go to the left.

Toward the strip.

I tell myself it's because I didn't want to hang out with the love-birds, watching them pretend to study while really just eyefucking each other until they just started outright fucking. Then I tell myself it's because I'm hungry and there's nothing good to eat at the Manor, and I need fuel before I can focus on my homework.

But when I open the door to the Badger Den and instantly look for Shelby, I know I'm full of shit.

I came here for her.

Not that I want her to know that, so I pass a table of college girls, and slide into a booth in the back, the one in the dark corner that always seems to be a little sticky and has a shitty view of the big screens. Sure enough, I think, shrugging out of my jacket, I can only see the bottom half of the game, but I've got a direct view of Shelby coming to and from the bar.

I had no fucking clue she'd be at the Teal House when I agreed to go with Axel. I'd done everything I could to avoid her, *particularly* in tight spaces or with her overprotective brother around. But I stepped in the house and it felt like I got rammed into the boards. It took everything in me not to stare at her curvy little ass in those tight jeans, or the small strips of flesh visible at her waist and thighs. It took an act of God to act disinterested when I was asked to give my opinion. I had thoughts, alright, thoughts that went *straight* to my dick.

"Hey, Reid." A familiar waitress appears, blocking my view of the bar. "You here alone?"

"Josie." I lean back, trying to keep an eye on Shelby while she helps a table of frat boys. "Yep, it's just me. Thought I'd grab something to eat."

"What can I get you?"

"Basket of three-alarm wings and fries," I rattle off, not looking at the menu. "And a Coke."

"You've got it."

The bar isn't as packed as it is when Wittmore plays. Not that I'm here during, but the post-game crowd is always thick, standing room only. Tonight everyone has a seat, the frat boys in the center, taking up a long stretch of pushed together tables. A few locals–older people who probably have been coming here since they were students, and then the table of sorority girls, a couple I realize look vaguely familiar and keep not-so-discreetly checking me out.

At the bar, Mike and the other employees are patient with Shelby as she learns the ropes, and although it's obvious she's nervous, there's a spark of confidence in her I haven't seen before.

Well, maybe once, when she was riding my hand between her legs.

Nope, not going there.

"What are you doing here?" Shelby blinks, holding my dinner in her hands.

I nod at the food. "Eating."

Her eyes narrow, but she slides the wings and fries over to me.

"Did he send you here to keep track of me?"

"He?" I ask innocently.

"Axel." Her arms cross over her chest and her shirt rises up, showing off the smooth skin around her waist. "Did he send you?"

"No." I shake my head. "Your brother is too focused on Nadia at the moment. I needed dinner and everyone knows the Den has the best wings."

I pick one up and take a bite, the combination of steam and sauce scalding my tongue. I fake my way through it, swallowing the burning meat down.

"If you say so," she says warily, like she's not sure if she can trust me. Smart.

"Since I'm here," I dip a drumstick into the sauce, "how's it going?"

"Oh, so now you want to talk about my job?" Her hip juts out and her pink lips make a sexy scowl. "Because back at the Teal House when I needed your help, you had no opinion or interest in defending me to my brother. What happened to helping me try new things?"

I take a gulp of soda, not just to wash down the hot sauce but to buy time because I want to point out that the last time I helped her, I gave her what I'm pretty sure was her first orgasm. Instead I say, "I did you a favor, GG. If I said something either way, Axel would get mad or suspicious, or even more overprotective."

She sighs. "You're probably right."

"So," I dip into the sauce again, this time with a wing, "how's it going? Fend off any perverts yet?"

She rolls her eyes, but a small smile tugs at her mouth. "Just the one."

I smirk. "I don't think what happened between us counts as 'fending' off anything."

"Oh my god, stop." Her cheeks burn bright red and it's cute as hell.

"Seriously, tho..."

"Overall it's been pretty good. Just trying to figure everything out, like where everything is stored, or how to use the cash register. Josie's been training me most of the night, but she had to take a call, that's why I brought out the food to you."

"You killed it," I tell her, reaching for the fries. "And so did Dave back in the kitchen."

"I'll let him know, and I'll refill your glass while I'm back there." The quick smile she gives me while picking up the empty glass that I've drained while eating the hot wings, makes my chest feel tight. And my eyes are glued to her cute butt in those skinny jeans as she turns toward the bar. That's what I'm focused on when out of my peripheral I see movement. Two of the frat boys have hopped out of their seats and are roughhousing.

"Take that back, dickhead."

"Not a chance," the other argues, pushing up his sleeves. "Gretzky's days as the GOAT are coming to an end."

"That's insane. He had sixty-one records when he retired. Only *five* have been beaten." It's an argument I've heard a million times in my life, half of them in this very bar, but this isn't like every other time, because just as Shelby passes them, the dickhead decides to shove his friend, slamming him straight into her side.

"Oh shit," I mutter, working my way out of the booth, but it's too late. Shelby's knocked off balance and the glass flies out of her hand. The ice hits the floor and in the next step, she slips, crashing to the hard ground. I try to go for both of them. The girl and the glass and *fuck.*

I get neither.

"GG," I say, bending down next to her, "are you okay?"

"I-I think so," she says, sounding a little dazed. Josie runs over to check on her and once I'm sure she's not hurt, I stand and face the dipshit that did it.

This time, I'm the one pushing my sleeves over my elbows.

"Wilder," the dickhead says, instantly recognizing me. "I didn't mean to–"

"You didn't mean to act like an asshole in a crowded bar and think no one would get hurt?"

"I didn't see her and we were just messing around." He holds his hands up and swallows. "Swear."

"First, this isn't a fucking playground, but even if it were, your mother didn't teach you the first rule of life," I step toward him, "keep your fucking hands to yourself." He nods vigorously, while his friend does his best to fade into the background. "And second, Gretzky is not just the GOAT, he's a fucking God. Keep that bullshit out of your mouth." I jerk my chin toward Shelby. "Apologize. Now."

The dickhead and his friend both start to apologize–or grovel is more like it. Shelby looks both annoyed and horrified, tugging at her shirt that is now sticky with the dregs of my soda and whatever she absorbed from the floor.

"It's fine. Just a mistake," she says to me more than them.

I'm not convinced.

By now Mike has rushed out from behind the bar. "Everything okay out here?" he asks, eyeing the two frat boys, who look at me, like they're not going to speak until I give them permission.

I cross my arms over my chest, a move I'm well aware makes me look terrifying. "I think we're good."

"Shelby?" he asks.

"I said I'm fine. It was just an accident."

"Totally an accident," dickhead promises. "We're really sorry."

"I know." She holds her dirty hands up. "I think I need to go wash off."

Mike nods and then adds, "Why don't you take the rest of the night off."

Her jaw drops. "Am I fired?"

"Hell no," he says quickly. "It's a slow night and you need to go get cleaned up. Josie can cover it." When she agrees, he adds, "You want me to call Axel?"

"I'll get her home," I announce. "She's staying at the Manor anyway."

"Don't bother Axel," she says, giving me a knowing look. Ax would flip if he found out about any of this, including the fact that I'm here. "I can go with Reid."

"Good," Mike starts back to the bar. "Come in tomorrow at four. It's a game night so we'll be busy."

"I'll be here," she says, unable to fight a grin. "Thanks for giving me this opportunity."

"You're doing great," Josie tells her. "And don't worry, I'll split whatever tips those dumbasses leave."

Once we're alone, I say, "Grab your stuff and I'll meet you at the door."

Retrieving my coat at the table, I head to the front door and wait. A few minutes later she meets me, a takeout container in her hands. "What's that?"

"Dave made you a fresh order of wings."

"Wow. Thank you."

"It's the least I could do after you stepped in like that with those guys."

I grunt in response, but notice she's still not wearing a coat. It's late February, night and cold as fuck outside. I hold mine out.

"I can't take that."

"Of course you can. It's cold as a witch's tit out there."

Her cheeks turn pink and I almost say the word again, just to see the flush.

"GG, take the damn coat." I'm not only hot, wanting to go back and punch that dickhead in the face, but my skin is on fire because I want to check her out, head to toe, and make sure she's okay.

She relents, and doesn't fight me when I drape it over her shoulders.

We step outside, into the arctic air, and she nuzzles into the jacket. "We have to walk," I tell her, shoving my hands in my jeans pockets.

"I guess I can add something to my list of new things," she says as we cross the street.

"The job?"

She glances over at me. "Having a guy defend me from frat boys."

"Hey, I told you, I'd help you live your best life." She laughs and the sound is fucking glorious. Something pops in my mind. "You didn't really need defending. They just needed to learn some manners."

"The whole thing was mortifying."

"GG, that's the thing, if you're going to live your life; sometimes embarrassing, uncomfortable things have to happen." I wrap an arm around her shoulder and drag her to me. "You handled it like a champ."

She rolls her eyes. "If you say so."

I don't move my arm around her shoulder, telling myself I'm blocking her from the wind. As we cut through campus, I ask, "Are you saying David wouldn't have defended you?"

"That's the thing. We never would have been in a situation where it would have happened. Being here, getting a job, doing new things, that's the only way it happens. Living life, even if it's a little scary and messy, and unpredictable."

Her words hit me straight in my chest, because I've had messy and unpredictable. It's a terrifying way to live, but I also know that if you don't take risks, search for more, you can miss out on the most amazing things.

I release her and come to a stop.

She turns, looking tiny all bundled up in my jacket. "What are you doing?"

"Being unpredictable."

And probably fucking everything up, but at this moment I don't care. I reach for her and push her into an alcove of one of the Admin buildings. It's less windy in here, and I set the box of takeaway down. Crowding her into the wall, I press my body against hers. She looks up at me and I reach for her face, my cold fingers against her cold cheeks, tilting her chin up. My mouth is inches from hers, and I see her lips part, a tiny cloud of air meeting the chill.

I'm gonna kiss her.

"Wait," she says the instant before our lips meet. I stop, but don't draw away. "I need to confess something."

A million bad thoughts run through my mind. She's not into me. She still loves David. Her brother is standing behind me and I'm about to get a thrashing.

"I've never done this before, well, other than that night we met."

I frown. "Done what?" Fuck. I'd suspected it but there it is. "So that was really your first kiss?"

She nods, eyes darting away. She's embarrassed–again, but now I just feel like an asshole. I knew she was inexperienced but, fuck. Now I need her to say it. "So the night on the porch, that was also your first?"

Orgasm.

She nods, and bites down on that soft bottom lip.

Christ. I gave this girl her first orgasm and just...

I'm more than an asshole. I'm a *fucking* asshole.

But now that I've got her here, tucked away in this little nook, I'm not going to fuck it up again. "GG." I get her attention. "I forget how innocent you are, and that's on me. I need to be more careful with you, which is why I'm going to ask if you're okay with me kissing you."

She nods a quiet, "Yes," in answer. I drop one of my hands and slide it into the warmth inside the coat, my fingertips brushing over the warmth of her exposed flesh. She jumps at the chill from my touch, but I need my hands on her right now.

I go slow, restraining myself from the hard, claiming kiss I want to give her. Instead, I go featherlight, one small brush of my lips over hers, cold meeting cold until we start to warm. I already know Shelby is a good kisser. She proved that to me within minutes of our first meeting. She can act inexperienced, but she's got the instinct, and that's only confirmed when her lips part and she allows me inside.

It's so fucking good. She's so fucking good. Sweet and gentle, but there's a fire in her that I've seen more than once now, and I want to stoke it into an inferno.

She withdraws and takes a deep breath. "Am I doing it right?"

"Fuck yeah, you're doing it right," I tell her, because I feel that kiss all the way into my balls. I look down at her mouth, lips red and a little puffy, and can't help but think that David is a goddamn fool. But then, I realize, I'm grateful for it, because I know that I want to be the one that gives Shelby her first everything. First sexy clothing, first kiss, first orgasm... all of it.

"You're doing it *more* than right," I add, tilting my head and hovering my lips over hers, not ready to stop.

From the way she pulls me close and the feel of her tongue against mine, she has no intention of stopping either.

15

S helby

THE SECOND NIGHT at work goes better than the first.

By the time I clock out and start the walk back to the Manor, I'm still a little sticky from spilled beer, but I did manage to stay on my feet all night. The place was packed with the fans that didn't go to the arena to watch the game taking up every available seat and a good portion of the standing room.

I also quickly learn that there's something surreal about serving drinks and food to hungry patrons while the guy who kissed me senseless is zipping across the ice on the big screen hanging over the bar. I hear his name on the mouths of the fans–both happy and frustrated–and my hackles raise.

Back off–*he's mine.*

Of course he's not. Not really. But tell that to my lips, and the other parts of my body that he set on fire, because they've never been claimed by anyone like that before. I didn't even know it was possible.

Even with that distraction, I think I did a good job–at least that's what the tips in my pocket feel like. I have a job. I earned my own money. I've been kissed.

I didn't even consider these things when I got on that plane from Texas.

Halfway up the main hill in Shotgun, I hear the sound of music and people. The closer I get to the Manor, I start to see people. *Lots* of people. All mingling around the front yard of my brother's house and up on the porch.

It comes back to me that Reid mentioned a party to the girl at the boutique earlier in the week. I search for a familiar face–my brother or any of his roommates. Jefferson is over by the fireplace, beer in hand, talking to two girls. His hand runs gently through his hair, touseling the feathered locks. Damn. No wonder he's got girls lined up. I spot Axel's blond hair, Nadia's arms wrapped around his waist. Reese is sitting at the kitchen table, where they're playing some kind of game. Twyler is on his lap, a wicked grin on her face.

My eyes dart past each face, but I can't pretend I'm not looking for someone specific. My heart skitters when I spot him standing near the staircase, facing away from me. As I work my way toward my bedroom porch, I can't help but admire the way his patterned button down fits perfectly across his shoulders, or the way his pants cling to his backside. There's a swell of pride in my chest knowing what that body feels like up close; muscular, strong in a way I wasn't aware a man's body could be.

"Hey everybody!" Jefferson shouts across the room, "Axel's little sister is here!"

The whole room shifts to look at me, but there's only one person I'm keeping track of. Reid turns, his eyes meeting mine, but that's not what I notice. It's the fact he's talking to a girl–the girl from the boutique. The one Reid invited.

"Shel." Axel disentangles from Nadia and thankfully draws away my attention. He crosses the room and pulls me into a big hug. "How was work?"

"It was good. I made a little cash off all the people super excited you guys won your game." I smile at him. "Congratulations, by the way."

"Thank you and that's awesome about the job." He seems over the fact I've taken the job. Either that, or he's drunk. "Go change and join us if you want."

Definitely buzzed.

"Thanks. I'm a little tired, but I'll see." But I already know I'm not up to seeing Reid flirt with another girl. I know I have no claim to him. All he's doing is showing me how to live a new and different life. Part of that has to be learning how to kiss a guy and not get attached.

"Cool." He steps back and looks me up and down. I brace myself for some kind of overprotective bro moment but he just says, "You know, it's been fun having you around."

I smile. "It's been fun being around."

I don't hesitate, and slip into my room, locking the door behind me, hoping to put some distance between me, Reid and the girl he's here with. As usual, the little porch is a refuge–the sounds of the party muted. The first thing I do is turn on the little heater to take the chill out of the room and pull out the cash I made at work. I really feel proud of myself. It wouldn't buy much in the real world, if I had to think about paying rent or bills, but it still feels good to know I can do it on my own.

I pull off the Badger Den T-shirt and hang it on the doorknob. I work again tomorrow night and I'll need to wash it in the morning. Goosebumps rise on my arms from the cold room, and I rummage through my suitcase for a clean shirt, when I hear a knock on the door. *Not* the door that leads to the living room, but the one that leads out to the porch.

The sound startles me, but I ignore it, assuming it's one of the party-goers looking for a shortcut into the house. There's a second knock, this time followed by, "It's me, GG."

I grab the first shirt I can find and pull it over my head and go to the door. "Reid?"

"Yeah." His voice is quiet, even for being on the other side of the door. "Can I come in?"

Unlocking the door, I slowly open it, seeing his chest first and then look up at his face. There's a small grin toying with his lips. "Hi."

"Hey."

His eyebrow raises and I realize he wants me to let him in. I step back and he enters in a gust of that spicy scent that follows him everywhere. Shutting the door, I secure it and turn to face him.

"I saw you come in," he says. "How was work?"

"Much better than last night." I wrap my arms around my body and look up at him. "I saw some of your game. The fans in the bar thought you did a great job."

He laughs. "I did okay."

"Sounds like we both had a good night."

"I can think of a few ways we can make it better." One of those big hands reaches out for my hip, clamping down and dragging me close. Cupping my face with the other, he tilts my chin and adds, "Don't you?"

He waits until I nod and his mouth is on mine. It's just as unexpected, as thrilling, as the last time. I sink into it, into *him*, the strength in his jaw, the smooth thrust of his tongue. It's so good, so delicious, my mind grows foggy and consumed. Is this what it's always like? How it always feels? I have no experience to know, but it seems unlikely. Otherwise why would you ever stop?

He pulls back and rests his forehead on mine. "I've been thinking about that all day."

He tilts his head to come in again, but I fist my hands in his shirt and pull him to a stop. "My brother is on the other side of that door."

The sharp line of his nose skims from my ear to my jaw and says, "Your brother is busy," before capturing my lips again. My brain short circuits, the neurons and synapses fried at the ends, but the image of the girl on the staircase has held firm.

"The girl," I manage to get out between kisses.

He slows, looking down at me. "What girl?"

"The one you were talking to. The one you invited that works at the clothing boutique."

"Ah. Nikki. I invited her because Emerson has a huge crush on her."

"Emerson?"

"Yep."

I have no idea if it's true or not, but he's in here with me and not her. Plus, his mouth tastes so good. He smells so good. Every single thing about this man feels unbelievably good.

Except he pulls back, a small smile playing at his lips. "Wait, are you jealous?"

"No." I look away, defensively.

"You seem jealous."

"I don't know what I am," I confess. "Or what this is. I've never done this before."

He stills, studying me in a way that makes me even more uncomfortable. "Do you want to stop?"

"No."

He studies me for a long moment, then he pulls me with him as he drops down on the couch, settling me on his lap. I'm still in the black skinny jeans that I wore to work that I borrowed from Twyler. His fingers find the ripped slashes along my upper thigh, and he drags the rough pads of his fingers over the exposed skin.

"Fuck," he says, dragging me over his body. "Your mouth. I can't get enough of it."

"Same," I breathe. I love kissing him too. It's my new favorite pastime, but his hips thrust up and I feel him. Not just him. *It.* His erection. Oh God, and against the crotch of the tight jeans I'm wearing it feels amazing. Chasing the sensation, I rock into him again, and his hands push under my shirt rough and warm.

"Woah," he says, through gritted teeth, "we should..." He inhales and exhales, puffing out his pink cheeks. "We should slow down."

I let out my own breath, trying to calm my heartbeat and lower back down to his lap. He grimaces, then shifts me back, putting some space between us.

"Did I do something wrong?"

"What?" he asks. "Not a chance, GG." He tucks my hair behind my ear. "Why would you ask that?"

I glance between us, my face even redder than before. "You just look like you're in pain."

"Ah, yeah no, not pain." He takes my hand and brushes his lips over my knuckles. "Just sensitive."

"Okay." I suddenly feel insecure. My body is wild with emotions. With feelings. With my own sensitivities that border on pain as much as pleasure.

"GG, look at me," he says, eyes waiting to meet mine when I look up at him. "I know this thing between us feels like a lot, and I should keep my hands and mouth off of you—"

"Please don't—"

He grins, or really, smirks. "I said I should, but there's no fucking way I can stop. I like you, Shelby. You're sweet. Beautiful. Fun." His hand cups the back of my neck. "But you're also innocent, and I don't want to overstep."

"You're not," I assure him. "I like this thing we have. Even if we have to keep it to ourselves." And it's not just Axel I worry about, although I know he'll lose his mind. It's David. My parents. It's the promise I made, that although I've taken a step back, I know I still have to answer for. "You've taught me more about myself and how to live a full life in a few days than I've learned in a lifetime back home."

His eyebrow raises. "You want me to keep teaching you?"

I nod, feeling a ripple of heat rise up my spine. "If you want to."

He leans forward, our mouths nearly touching, and he says, "I want to do so many things with you." His lips brush over mine, but he doesn't deepen it. Instead, he gently lifts me off his lap and rises up. "But right now, I'm going to teach you what every twenty-year-old hottie in Wittmore wishes she was doing right now."

"What's that?" I ask, genuinely curious.

His fingers curl into mine. "How to party with the hockey team."

WE LEAVE THE PORCH SEPARATELY, Reid through the exterior door and a few minutes later, changed into clean, non-beer-soaked clothes, me into the living room. From there, we start a discrete game of never being in the same place or same conversation as the other, rotating around the bottom floor of the Manor in an invisible dance.

Never in my life have I been so aware of another person.

It's ridiculous. Humiliating even, how closely I track his every movement, every laugh. I catch the way the muscle in his jaw flexes, every crinkle near his eyes, and the way he holds a bottle of beer loose between his fingers.

I can't stop thinking about his mouth against mine, the hard way his hands roamed over my body. I try to distract myself with the game Twyler is playing, the sensation of how he felt under me, thick and impressively hard.

"Ahh, my man, Jefferson. So you think you're up to the challenge," Twyler says, her long, dark ponytail bobbing behind her head.

"You may want to rein your girl in, Cap." He cracks his knuckles and scoots his chair up with an exaggerated move. "She's about to get sloppy drunk."

"Twy can handle herself," Reese says, squeezing her shoulder. "And I like her sober or drunk. Doesn't matter to me."

I watch as they prepare to begin and turn to Nadia, "So this game is just about getting your quarter into the cup?"

"Yep."

"And if the other person gets it in your cup you have to drink?"

"Yep?"

"I don't get it," I say, watching Twyler sink her first quarter in Jefferson's red cup. He swears, but takes a massive gulp. Reese plants a sweet kiss on her neck in response.

"There's not much to get," she says. "It's a dumb drinking game. Twyler is just very good at it for some reason, so she loves to torture these idiots who can't handle a girl beating them at anything so they always come back for more."

"Ah, okay."

"Come on." She grabs my hand and pulls me away from the

game. "I think there are some water bottles in the laundry room. Unfortunately, I have to work the opening shift at the gym tomorrow."

She rummages around the other side of the washer and grabs two bottles, then hands me one. The overall crowd at the party has thinned out, but it's nice to be away from the noise for a minute.

"You know," Nadia says, eyeing the washing machine. "This is where your brother came onto me for the first time."

I cough, the water catching in my throat. "Here? Really?"

"Yeah, I mean, it wasn't the first time we'd been together," she continues. "That's what we fondly refer to as the epic fuck up, but yeah." She taps the top of the machine. "Right here."

I squirm at the topic and the fact bare butts have been on the washer that *I* use. She grins. "Fine, we won't talk about Axel. What about you?"

My eyes widen and I squeak. "What about me?"

"I know you're broken up with David. Just wondering if you've met any one you're interested in."

"No," I say, quickly. Too quickly, apparently, because her eyes narrow in suspicion. "I'm not looking for a new boyfriend."

"No one said you were, and look, I'm not going to suggest you go wild or anything–been there, done that–*do not* recommend." She leans against the dryer. "But you came here to experience new things and college guys can be one of them."

Twyler steps in the room. "Oh, there you are." She pulls a keychain out of her hoodie pocket. "I didn't want to disappear without giving you this. I know you forgot yours."

Nadia snags it and crosses her arms. "Where are you going?"

Twyler gives her a look. "Where do you think?"

Nadia smirks at me. "Reese gets horny when he watches Twy win quarters."

"Shut up," her friend says. "It's late and he's worn out from the game."

"Oh please," I take a gulp of water trying to disconnect from this conversation, "we all know why he plants you on his lap like that while you play. He's hiding his boner."

A boner. I *do* know what that is. I may have grown up in a strict environment, but I've heard the boys quietly joking about things like this on the coed youth trips I took with the church. I lower my bottle and ask, "What are you going to do about it?"

Twyler's big blue eyes land on me. "Uh, what?"

"When they get like that, guys, I mean..." I stumble around the words. "Like, when guys' bodies get like that, what do you do to help?"

Twyler's big eyes narrow suspiciously. "Is someone making you feel like you need to fix that? Because that is a classic d-bag move and you can tell them to fuck off."

"No!" I say quickly. "No one is making me do anything. I promise." I clear my throat because they both keep staring at me. "I'm just curious because David and I never went that far and I listen to you guys talk so openly about all this stuff and I feel like there's a lot to learn."

"Shelby," Twyler sighs, "I have no desire to talk about all this stuff either but Nadia is a nosy bitch who has no boundaries."

"It's true." Nadia nods vigorously. "I'm sex positive, so sue me."

Twyler rolls her eyes. "But the truth is that it's not that hard. When and *if* you're with someone that you want to explore that part of your relationship with, just talk to them about it. They know what they want–"

"A blow job," Nadia interjects with a snort. "They always want that."

Twyler shakes her head. "God, they really do, right?"

"Mmhmm."

I gape at the two of them. Like the boner, I know what a blow job is, but I could never.

"They'll take whatever they can get. Blow, hand, feet, tits..." Twyler counts them off like this is the most normal discussion ever.

"Oh, the titty fuck," Nadia nods enthusiastically, "that's always a winner."

I glance down at my boobs, unaware they had a job, other than breastfeeding.

"But," Nadia adds, "that doesn't mean you have to if you don't want to. It's really about communication."

"And consent is important," Twyler inserts. "The most important."

I think back to every moment with Reid that got heated between us. He always asked me if I wanted something, even if he could kiss me. Every step of the way he's made sure I was comfortable with it, and he's always walked away first.

"Twy!" Reese's voice carries into the laundry room from the kitchen. "You ready to go?"

"I better go," she says, grinning just at the sound of her boyfriend's voice. "Just remember, Shelby, you don't ever have to do anything you don't want to. They'll survive or take care of it on their own."

"But," Nadia adds with a mischievous grin, "it's way more fun to help."

16

———

R^{eid}

"She's cute."

"Who's cute?" I grab a bottle of water out of the cooler near the back door. Pete's staring across the room, eyes trained on something–or rather *someone.*

"Axel's sister. Shelly?"

"Shelby," I correct. My good girl.

"Right. Well, it's no wonder he gave the big speech in the locker room."

"I don't think I'd test him on it." I take a swallow of my drink in an attempt to do something with my hands other than throttle my teammate. He's only just gotten out of the cast from snapping his ankle back in the fall. The last thing he needs is another career halting injury.

"I don't want Rakestraw ruining my life–or my pretty face," he grins, "but, someone is going to make a move on her. She's got that innocent vibe a lot of guys are drawn to."

He's not wrong about that. Every single, and a few non-single, guy in the room has checked Shelby out and it's not hard to tell that she's sweet and most likely naive. There's nothing I can do about it, but remind myself and anyone else that brings her up that she's off-limits, and as foolish as it is, I feel a smug sense of satisfaction knowing I'm the one that's felt her lips on mine.

I watch her like a hawk as the party winds down, noticing when she vanishes in the laundry room with Nadia and Twyler, and then later as everyone heads out and we start to clean up.

"Put those down." Axel looks at his sister, who has a collection of empties in her hands. Handing Nadia her coat, he adds, "We'll get it tomorrow."

"Ax, it's gross to leave all of this out overnight." Her nose wrinkles. "It smells and everything is sticky."

The party faded out twenty minutes ago, the last stragglers heading home, including Emerson who offered to walk Nikki back to her dorm. I didn't notice when Reese and Twyler took off, or if Jefferson left with someone or if he's upstairs. Ever since that hot little makeout session on the porch, my focus had been completely consumed by Shelby.

"I'll take them," I say, hoping my face doesn't reflect my thoughts. Thank god for the box of recycling in my hands, it's the only thing covering the half-chub in my pants.

"Thank you." She drops them inside, grabbing two more and tossing them in.

"That's enough," Axel tells her. "Our party, our mess."

"If you say so." She turns in the direction of the porch. "Night, everyone."

"Night, Shel," Nadia says, zipping up her coat.

I follow the two of them out the door, carrying the recycling out to the bin. Axel throws his arm around Nadia's shoulders and he calls out, "Leave the porch light on. I'll be back in a few."

"Got it."

I head back inside and the house is quiet.

I flip off all the lights other than the one by the front door and another by the stairwell, and head upstairs. It was a long day, with a grueling game, a party, and the hasty makeout session with Shelby as the cherry on top. That's the part I can't stop thinking about. My brain *or* my body. I felt like a deviant, drilling into her while she sat on my lap, her hot little mouth on mine. The question about if my erection 'hurt' is a sure signal she's not ready for anything beyond kissing and some light fooling around. Someone just needs to tell that to the monster in my pants, because he can't get with the program.

Although I volunteered to help her explore life a little, I know that doesn't include me taking this to the point of no return. She just wants to learn a few things before she goes back to Texas and the predictable future she has with David the Dud.

Yeah, I doubt that relationship is truly over.

Ignoring the thump of Reese's headboard against the wall, I enter the bathroom, where I'm accosted by the scent of Shelby's shampoo. There's no escaping her.

I start my nightly routine. It's not just washing my face and brushing my teeth and the guys have no fucking clue that I do it, but I've always got a daily mantra. My adoptive mother taught me to do it when I was struggling with some of the transitions in my life. Sometimes it's about hockey. Other times about my goals. But lately it's even more specific. Shoving my toothbrush in my mouth, the words start:

Shelby Rakestraw is your best friend's little sister.

Shelby Rakestraw is off limits.

Shelby Rakestraw is not the girl for you.

Shelby Rakestraw's mouth is unbelievably perfect and would look so good wrapped around–

Dammit.

Taking a breath I start at the top.

Shelby Rakestraw is your best friend's little–

I go through the list over and over, trying to get my head on straight.

Finishing up, I start unbuttoning my shirt before I get to my room, shrugging it off and tossing it in the laundry basket in the corner. I thumb open the button on my jeans and hook my thumbs in the waistband and–

"Stop!"

The voice is a rushed squeak, and I turn. Shelby is standing on the opposite side of my room, the bed between us. Her hair is loose around her shoulders in an oversized hot pink T-shirt and plaid pajama pants, her eyes are glued to my open fly.

Fuck.

I glance out to the hallway, making sure that no one heard her, but Reese is occupied and Axel isn't back home yet. Thank Jesus.

The right thing to do, the *only* thing to do, is for me to send her back downstairs to her room. I should lock myself in here for the night, protecting us both from the inevitable disaster of this situation.

"What are you doing in here?" I whisper.

"Waiting for you."

Nope. Nada. *Hard pass.*

Instead of kicking her out, I shut the door and lock it.

"You shouldn't be in here," I tell her, reaching for a pair of cotton shorts hanging on my desk chair. "Turn around."

"What? Why?"

"GG, I don't think either of us are ready for you to see what's under the denim." Her jaw drops and she spins. I change fast, dropping the jeans and dragging on the shorts. It's probably not a great trade for me, because there's less fabric hiding my increasingly growing erection. "Okay."

She turns and again, her eyes roam over my body. I'm about to ask her again what she's doing here when she blurts, "I just thought maybe, you know, we practice kissing some more, but that's a dumb idea..."

She rushes toward the door, but she has to get past me first. I grab her hand and pull her against my chest. "It's not dumb."

"No?"

"It's fucking stupid and it's going to get us both into a lot of trouble." I tilt her chin, making her look up at me. "Coming to a man's bedroom means something, GG, innocent intentions or not."

"What does it mean?"

"That you want to take things further." I swallow. She needs a warning. Needs it spelled out. "Further than kissing."

"Okay." She nods. "So what if I want that, too?"

"Do you even know what I'm talking about?" Because she's not stupid, but she is innocent, and even in those silly plaid pants she's the sexiest thing I've ever had in my room.

"Yes," she says quickly, but then shakes her head. "Sort of. I mean, what you and I did before, that night on the porch."

"I shouldn't have. I went too far."

"You didn't." Her hand flattens against my stomach and I inhale sharply. "You didn't do anything I didn't want."

I thrust my hand into my hair, this girl is going to be the end of me. The end of my relationship with Axel. The end of my sanity when this all falls apart.

"I understand the mechanics," she's saying, "the biology–but I want to experience it. Is that wrong?"

"With me?" I answer for her. "Yes."

She looks up at me, wide-eyed and determined. "I don't think so."

Outside the door, we hear heavy footsteps as Axel comes up stairs. We both freeze, waiting for him to go into his room. There's a tap on the door, and then, "Yo, Reid."

My balls shrivel up at the same time my heart lodges in my throat. I struggle to clear it enough to speak. "Yeah?"

"I'm going to hit the gym in the morning. You wanna come?"

"S–" the 's' comes out in a squeak. I try again. "Sure."

"Cool. I'll meet you downstairs at nine."

We stare at one another for a long moment, waiting for Axel to enter his room and close the door. I flip off my overhead light, which I should have done as soon as I walked in the room. "He'll kill me, you know that, right?"

"He won't find out," she assures me. "And if he does? I'll handle him."

"It won't be necessary." I cross my arms over my chest, trying my best to act tough. "I think you need to leave."

Apparently, she's not falling for my act and Shelby lowers herself to the edge of the bed before saying, "What if I just sit here, on the edge of the bed. That's safe enough, right?"

"There's a lot of things that can happen on the edge of a bed, GG, and if you don't know that, you should probably head back to your room now."

Her jaw tenses and she lifts her chin defiantly. "The simple fact that I don't know that should be reason enough for you to show me."

I think back to what Pete said. Someone is going to get to this girl. Someone with way less restraint and shadier motives than myself. Maybe she needs someone to push her out of her comfort zone. Make her less trusting. At least in the end, I won't hurt her.

"You really want me to show you?"

"Please."

I sit next to her, the mattress sinking under my weight.

"Don't hold back. Act like a guy who wants to be with me."

I fight a groan. She has no fucking idea how badly I want her, and despite what she's asking for, I can't imagine any situation with Shelby where I'd feel comfortable letting loose. Showing her all the filthy things that run through my mind every time I think of her.

Sliding my hand behind her neck, I draw her face close to mine, and ask one last time, "Are you sure?"

She nods, but states definitively, "Yes."

Our breath mingles before I make contact, giving me a hit of her taste before I even kiss her. But she doesn't wait for me to make the move, surging forward, pressing those hot lips against mine, mouth open. The feel of her tongue teasing against mine sends a jolt straight to my cock. The idea that she's never kissed anyone before seems ridiculous, but tonight she's not content with just kissing and she pulls back, admiring my body.

"Are all men like this?" she asks, pressing her hands to the hard lines of my chest. "Because I don't think David looks like this."

"Does David work out six days a week, four hours a day?" It comes out smug as shit and I'm not even sorry. I'm proud of the work I've put into my body–that I'm no longer the scrawny kid shuttled from home to home, wondering where his next meal was coming from.

Her blue eyes meet mine and she says, "No. Not a chance."

I'm bulkier than a forward like Reese who needs speed on his side, but I'm cut, the hours of working out at the gym and practice giving me a body that I know women love. I let her explore my chest, watching her tongue dart out in hunger. Then her nails graze over my nipples and I exhale a groan. "Fuck, GG, you make me so fucking hard."

"I do?"

I'd pull her on my lap again, but I'm wired to trigger and there's too much of her to explore, so I take her hand and hold it against my length. "You feel that?"

"Yeah."

"You do that to me, and it's driving me fucking crazy."

I refocus, pushing my hands under her shirt, cupping her tits in my hands. Her nipples harden, peaking against my palms and I say, "I think I drive you crazy too." Her inhalation is sharp, but she doesn't draw away as I massage her with both hands. I want to see her tits. Taste and touch them. The night shirt she's wearing is too loose, hiding all the good stuff under the billowy cotton. "Can I see you?"

Her hands drop to her hem, but I'm impatient and help her take it off. Fuck me. Her shoulders curve, letting her hair fall over her chest, like she's attempting to hide herself. "No hiding," I command, brushing the hair back and trailing my fingers down her goose-bumped flesh. I trace the curve, then lift them with both hands. "Fucking gorgeous," I mumble, more to myself than her, then duck my head, swiping my tongue over one stiff peak and then the other.

Her hands thrust into my hair, pulling hard, and her back arches, giving her body to me. My cock throbs, and I squeeze the base, trying to gain back a little control. Her fingers loosen in my hair, and I lay her on her back, not ready to stop sucking on her nipples. There's so much of her to explore and every taste reminds me this could be the one and only time. That this is just an adventure– so I press a kiss to each dusty pink nipple before kissing down her belly. Her skin is soft–sensitive–and she twitches as I move toward her hips.

When I reach the edge of her plaid pants, I hook my fingers into the band, she rises up on her elbows, looking down at me over the flat plane of her belly and the swollen peaks of her tits. "What are you doing?"

"Showing you what can be done on the edge of the bed." I lick my lips. "Eating pussy is one of the best parts."

Her breath hitches, causing her chest to rise and fall. "You want to do that?"

"You have no idea." My mouth waters at the thought of her. Fingers curled into the cotton, I add, "But, if you want me to stop, tell me now."

Her cheeks are red, her lips puffy. She already looks ravished and I haven't even gotten her off. I'm terrified she'll tell me to stop and sure as fuck, I don't want to. I almost shout in victory when she says, "No, don't stop."

Dropping to my knees, I make quick work of the pants, but leave her panties on. I'm patient. Diligent. Perseverance is what makes the difference between playing D1 and everyone else. It's a skill that has served me all of my life. The panties are white cotton, and I think I may come just looking at them. They're an indicator of how sweet and innocent she is. How she really is a *good girl*.

I'm going to dirty her up for the rest of her life and I want to be that man for her. To make it so good for her that she has no regrets.

Starting at her knees, I press a kiss on the inside of each one, spreading her wider as I work my way back up. She's nervous, her fingers fluttering between her belly and fisting in the comforter. She told me not to hold back, and I don't plan on stopping until she either tells me to, or she's coming on my tongue.

The closer I get to her pussy, the easier it is to see the wet spot.

Innocent or not, her body is getting ready for me. Planting a kiss over the cotton, I inhale her scent, feeling my balls tighten on instinct. Her thighs threaten to close, but I push them back apart and hook a finger into the crotch and drag it aside, getting my first look at her pretty, pretty, pussy and then do what I've wanted all night–longer than tonight.

I dart my tongue out and taste her.

Jesus Christ.

Her hips rise up, chasing my tongue and I use the opportunity to peel those panties off and toss them aside. I give her a long slow lick, lathing her clit with my tongue. I know from experience GG isn't going to last long. Her fingers find their way back into my hair, and every time I get near her clit she tugs, sending a sharp pain across my skin. I hear nothing but the sound of my tongue lapping against her body and her quick breaths. She's close, but she's also new at this, and finding her rhythm may be hard. I grab her hips, controlling her movements, getting us into synch.

"Reid," she whispers, voice low. "I'm–I'm–"

Her thighs snap against my head, and the rest of her words are overtaken by a moan. I bury my face into her pussy and let her ride my tongue, licking slowly until she pulls away. "Holy shit," she says, and I think it may be her first time cursing around me–maybe ever. I press a final kiss against the hot bundle of nerves and rise up, crawling over her body. I kiss each one of her tits again, sucking gently on her nipples. All I want to do is drag her to the top of the bed and cuddle with her, but my cock is so fucking hard, I can barely see straight.

"Give me a second, okay?" I tell her, shifting to my knees. "Don't go."

I stand, not so discreetly gripping the base of my cock, trying to will it down. She sits up, watching me. "Where are you going?"

"To the bathroom. I'll be right back."

"Because of that?" she asks, gesturing to my erection.

"Yeah. I'll be quick."

"But–"

"No but's." I lean over to kiss her. "I'm just going to–"

Her hand wraps around mine and it feels like a gut punch. "GG," I say slowly, "I don't think this is what you came up here for."

"I came here to learn. For you to teach me." She eyes the hard line of my cock as it strains against my shorts. "Learning how to make you feel good is part of it."

"I feel fantastic–feeling you come on my tongue was a highlight."

Her cheeks get impossibly redder, but she surprises me by running her hand along my shaft. I inhale sharply, my lower belly caving and I almost come on the spot when she asks, "Can I?"

Touch me? Rub me? Suck me?

Take your pick.

I swallow and reply quietly, "You can do whatever you want."

17

———

S helby

I HAVE no idea how I'm even sitting upright.

My bones feel like mush, and my brain has overdosed on a chemical high, but there's still this flicker of want in my belly that has nothing to do with the orgasm he gave me.

I want him and I want to make him feel as good as he made me.

Standing at the edge of the bed, he watches as I run my hand along his length, the hard line trying to stab its way through the cotton of his shorts. It's bigger than I'd expect. Harder. Again, in theory, I know the basics of sex. But actually seeing it–feeling it–I'm out of my depth. And it doesn't take Reid long to figure that out.

"You won't hurt me," he says quietly. "Trust me, this guy has seen his fair share of abuse."

My jaw drops. "It has?"

"Oh, shit. No, not like abuse abuse, but you can handle him." He places his big hand over mine and together we grip the length. "Like this."

He guides my hand over the fabric, up and down his length. "Does that feel good?" I ask, looking up at him.

His jaw tenses. "Unbelievable."

I'm not sure why, but pride fills my chest. It makes me bold. I press a hand on his lower belly, fingers trailing over the carved lines of muscle. His body is incredible–like a work of art. I trace the dark line of hair, soft and tempting, but force myself not to get distracted. Curling my fingers into the waistband of his shorts, I tug them down. Reid releases my hand and together we lower the shorts over his erection and there it is, bobbing in front of my face, a clear bead of fluid at the tip.

My body grows hot, belly flip-flopping, and that warm heat is back between my legs. Reid grips the base and I reach out, thumb grazing over the head. He groans softly, every muscle in his body locking up.

"It's so soft." I glide my fingers down the shaft, feeling the variations in skin. Soft, but with a long ridge down the back. I dip them down to where he's got a death grip on the base, then come back up.

"You're killing me, GG," he says, knees wobbling despite tensing his powerful thighs. A heavy hand lands on my shoulder as he braces himself. "Your hand feels so fucking good on my cock."

My hand moves on instinct, tugging up and down his shaft. With every pass his breathing grows heavier, strained. His hips rock forward, a hard thrust, and I move against him, remembering how my body wanted friction. When I look up at his face, his eyes are closed, mouth slightly parted. His expression is caught halfway between pain and pleasure–he's beautiful.

"Fuck," he grunts, hand clamping over mine again, "I'm gonna–"

His words are cut off because he grabs my neck and bends over, slamming his mouth into mine. This kiss isn't gentle. It's hard and unrelenting, and our mouths are still fused together when he thrusts one last time and groans. Hot fluid spills down our hands until it lands in a sticky pool on my thigh.

We pull apart and I'm fascinated by the way Reid's chest rises and falls in quick breaths. I did that. I made him gasp for air like he just finished running sprints. I pulled a groan out of him that rattled my chest. Those are the thoughts running through my head as he reaches for his shorts on the floor, wipes off my leg and then himself.

It's then that I realize I'm completely naked sitting on the edge of this man's bed. He must realize it too because he finds my shirt and helps me back into it, pulling it gently over my head as I slip my arms through the sleeves.

"Did I do it right?" I blurt.

His eyebrow lifts. "Are you kidding?"

I shake my head.

"That was fucking incredible, GG." He inhales deeply and tilts my face to look at him. "But what's important to me is that we're good." He brushes the hair off my cheek, tucking it behind my ear. "Are we?"

There's this tiny niggle in the back of my head that says I should feel awkward and weird about what we've just done. That I crossed all of my boundaries and tossed my values to the wind, but then I look at the concerned expression on Reid's face and the satisfied way I feel, and answer him truthfully, "Yeah, we're good."

Bang!

Bang!

Bang!

"Reid? You up? We're headed to the gym in ten."

My brother's voice wakes me up with a jolt. I don't need a reminder that I'm still in Reid's room, warm in his bed. I fell asleep here last night, with the plan to leave before daylight.

From the way the sun glares through the window, it's clear that didn't happen.

Why? Reid's bed, compared to the musty old couch in the cold porch is so toasty and cozy. *Reid* is toasty and cozy, his body spooned into mine all night. Except now my brother is the one waking us up and there's nowhere to hide.

"Yo, Reid!"

The door rattles, and I panic, rolling over and shimmying under the blankets. I pinch him in the side as I vanish and he finally moves.

"Oof." His body spasms from the pinch, hips thrusting toward my face.

Holy Morning Erection.

I barely hear the creak of the door opening over my hammering heart and the distraction of Reid's impressive cock. He put on a clean pair of boxer briefs before bed, but the thin cotton does nothing to hide the tent pole between his legs from threatening to work its way out.

"Sorry, man," I hear Reid say, voice muffled from the blanket. "I stayed up too late last night."

"Working on a new project?" Axel asks, "Or did you scare yourself with one of your murder shows?"

Reid's fingers find my face under the blanket and graze my cheek. "New project."

"I should've known." Axel laughs. "You always get hyper focused when you start something new."

"Yeah, it's in the early stage, but it definitely has my interest." His fingers find my lips and he rubs his thumb across the flesh. Feeling bold, I dart my tongue out and lick the curve of his thumb. "Meet you down there in ten?"

"Yep."

Even after I hear the door click shut, I don't move, frozen in place. Finally, the covers raise and Reid peers down at me. My eyes land on his mouth. His lips. His *tongue*. Oh my god. His tongue. That licked and sucked and—

It's like the fog clears and everything I let him do to me, everything I did to him comes rushing back. Who was that person? And what was she thinking? That orgasms are great, that's what. But with a little daylight and sleep, I see that last night was last night. Today I'm Axel's naive little sister. Whatever Reid and I did last night was an experiment. A lesson for me, and like Axel unwittingly suggested, a project for Reid.

"Good morning," he says, voice low.

"Hi." I ease my way out from under the cover, to the edge of the bed. *Away* from him and whisper, "You go ahead and get dressed, and I'll just hide out until everyone leaves. If he looks for me in my room, you can tell him–"

His hand snaps around my wrist and he drags me back to the bed, and against his hard body.

"You're freaking out."

"I'm not freaking out." It's a lie. I'm *totally* freaking out.

"GG, stop."

I swallow and look at him. Not his face. Straight ahead, which unfortunately is at his abdomen, the ladder of defined muscles, taunting me. Then the hard lines of his chest.

"I know last night was big for you. It was big for me too."

That forces my eyes to meet his. "It was?"

He nods. "I'm not used to people putting their trust in me–at least not off the ice." His fingers slide under my hair, curling behind my neck. "But you trusted me to show you a part of yourself you shouldn't be ashamed of." His thumb strokes a lazy pass along my throat. "A part that is incredibly hot and powerful."

"What do you mean, powerful?"

"You had me on my fucking knees, GG, and my tongue in your pussy." The corner of his mouth curves up in a grin. "There's nothing more powerful than that."

I'M CROSSING campus when my phone vibrates in my pocket. I make a valid attempt to answer it, I really do, but I'm bundled up in a sweater and a too big pair of gloves Axel loaned me and I can't actually get my fingers around it and by the time I manage to wedge my hands around the case, the vibrating stops.

Whoever it is, I can call them back. Or that's the plan, until it starts up again. This time I slip my fingers out of the glove and answer.

"Hello." A visible puff of air exits my mouth.

"Shelby. I was going to leave a message."

"Oh, Mom," I say, looking both ways as I cross the street. "Hi. Sorry, I couldn't get to my phone with these gloves on."

"I thought I would hear from you, but since that hasn't happened I decided to make the call."

"Sorry, Mom." A pack of sorority girls bundled in heavy jackets and boots take up most of the sidewalk. None seem prepared to yield, so I step off the curb to go around them. "I've just been busy."

"Busy?" she repeats, unbelieving. "Busy with what? It certainly hasn't been with your obligations back home."

"What obligations?"

"Oh, you've already forgotten? Maybe that cold weather has impaired your memory. Fine, I'll remind you." Her tone turns sarcastic. "There's all of your volunteer work, including the time you spend with the youth program. There's the Wednesday night bible study, the Saturday Mobile Soup Kitchen."

"All of those run smoothly without my participation."

"David, of course, has been a God-send. Stepping in to fill your shoes while you're off on this little..."

"Little what?" I stop mid-stride, feeling the anger rise in my chest.

"The word that comes to mind is, tantrum."

"I'm not having a tantrum, Mother."

"Oh? Then what would you call running off in the middle of the night, with barely a word to your family or your fiance?"

A dozen words come to mind. Liberating. Adventurous. Fun. I think of Reid... *orgasmic.*

I reach the door of the Badger Den, but don't go in. "What is this about, Mom? Did you just call to make me feel bad for doing something for myself for once?"

"No. I called to discuss the upcoming party. Even if you're two thousand miles away, I'd like your input on a few things..."

"What party?" I blurt.

"Did you start using drugs out there?" she asks. "I'm talking about the engagement party for you and David."

"David and I aren't together anymore."

"Nonsense." In the background I can hear her rustling around. Probably with her fabric swatches and samples. "Like I said, this is nothing more than a tantrum and once you wear yourself out, everything will go back to normal. Now, how do you feel about lilies? Charlotte down at the florist says that–"

"You know what?" I interrupt, feeling like my head is about to explode. "I wasn't throwing a tantrum, but now I am. There is no way I'm coming back for that party. No more than I'm going to marry David. That part of my life is over."

There's a gasp on the other end of the line. "Shelby Marie Rakestraw, how dare you speak to your mother like that. You made a commitment–a promise–to David in front of your family, his family, the congregation, and God. You think you can humiliate us and just walk away?"

Part of me, the big part that grew up subservient, wanting nothing more than my parents approval, shouts 'no!' and to go crawling back to the familiarity of that life. It would be so easy. But staring at the neon lights of the Badger Den, and feeling the warm, cozy sweater I'm wearing, along with the memory of waking up next to Reid's muscular body is too intense to ignore.

Maybe more intense than anything else I've experienced.

"I'm hanging up now," I tell her and disconnect before she can respond, then push open the door and enter the bar. It's dark, dank, and smells like stale beer. The floor is sticky and there's hockey highlights playing on the big screens. Josie waves at me from behind the bar and I grin. This is nothing like the life I left behind, and I'm here for it.

"WE'RE ALMOST OUT OF LIMES," Mike jerks his chin at me. "Can you head to the back and slice some?"

"Yep," I say, zipping out from behind the bar. I grab a box of empty bottles that need to go out to recycle. There's a fast beat to working at a place like the Badger Den. There's always something that needs to be done. Serving drinks, clearing up, taking out trash, placing orders in the kitchen or bar. There's no time to think about anything other than the task at hand. Like, what it felt like to have Reid's face between my thighs last night, or how irritated I am at my mother.

I know, those two things should *not* be in the same train of thought.

The only interruption to the steady pace is when something happens at the game. Loud cheers or deep, frustrated groans, cut through my train of thought, dragging my eyes up to the screens. Instantly, I look at the players' jerseys. Cain. Rakestraw. *Wilder...*

That was earlier, now the place is filled with happy hockey fans celebrating tonight's win that gets Wittmore one step closer to the finals. The game was played about an hour away, over at Hilldale, but unlike the other nights I've worked, the bar seems to be more crowded now than earlier.

Lugging the box, I go out the back door and set the empty bottles in the bin, then head back into the steamy kitchen where I wash up and cut the limes. Even back in the chaos of the kitchen I hear an increase in the rowdiness out front.

"What's that all about?" I ask Dennis, one of the line cooks.

His eyebrows rise into the bandana covering his hair and he says, "I think that means we're about to get really busy."

Armed with a fresh bowl of limes, I dump them into the little container by the bar and sure enough, the place is swarmed. Josie leans over the bar, shouting out an order to Mike, trying to get her voice heard.

"What's going on?" I ask, peering over the crowd.

"The team just got here."

"Oh." Without warning, my heart flutters in my chest. "I thought they celebrated off campus after games."

"Home games," Josie says. "After nearby away games they like to show up here. It's why everyone stuck around. To celebrate with them." She tugs at the new shirt Mike handed out when I got to work. "Why do you think Mike gave you that jersey to wear?"

It's an authentic Wittmore hockey jersey, black and gold, the name of the bar written across the shoulders. Josie showed me how to tie it in a knot at the waist to keep it from snagging on the chair backs when we're working.

"Rakestraw!" My head snaps to the left, but I know instantly that it's not me they're calling for. It's my brother, who has just stepped through the door, bundled up in his heavy hockey jacket, Nadia tucked under his arm.

Reese and Twyler are behind him. Then Jefferson, who makes a beeline to a table of girls that have been slowly sipping seltzer and grazing on a single basket of fries all night. My eyes ping back to the door and I see Murphy and Emerson walk in.

At that point I turn away, realizing that I'm searching for someone I have no right to be looking for. Reid had a great game; he probably has someone else to celebrate with. "I'll grab them some menus," I tell Josie, needing to be busy. "Anything else?"

"I think we could use extra napkins. These guys are going to eat all the wings."

"Gotcha."

The supply closet is down the hall toward the back exit, across from the bathrooms. I push open the door, assessing the huge boxes of paper and dry goods Mike has stored back here. How he manages to get so much crammed into one tiny closet is beyond me. I'm up on my tiptoes, when I hear the bathroom door swing open and I turn, catching a glimpse of auburn hair.

The last thing I see is the number 08 stitched on the arm of the jacket as he vanishes behind the closing door.

My heart flutters wildly in my chest as an idea springs to mind. Something bold and incredibly un-Shelby-like. I glance down the hall making sure no one is watching, and the minute the bathroom door swings open I step out, grabbing Reid by the arm and dragging him into the supply closet.

"I was looking for–" he starts, a sexy grin tugging at his mouth. I don't let him finish, pushing up on my toes to meet his mouth with mine. His lips are warm, and if I thought he'd be startled I was wrong. He reacts immediately, mouth hard against mine, meeting me, kiss for kiss, with such intensity that I feel it deep in my bones.

His hand tightens around my waist, thumb rubbing over the exposed skin. Slowly he eases the kiss and looks down at me.

"Look at you. Making the first move."

"Is that wrong?

He presses his hips into my lower belly. He's already getting hard. "Does it feel wrong?"

I shake my head, knowing that when he's like this, he's into it. Into me. "Excited?"

"Getting jumped by a sexy little thing wearing a Wittmore jersey?" His tongue darts out, and he eyes me like he wants to devour me. "Yeah, you make me a lot of things, GG. Excited is only one of them."

"You like the jersey?"

"Fuck yeah." His fingers toy with the knot by my waist. "The only thing that would make it better is if you were wearing it in my bed, and it had my name on the back."

Heat pools in my lower belly, and I don't know how to respond to that. Turns out, I don't need to, because his lips, his tongue, his hands are devouring me again. Pushing my fingers up his shirt, I feel those delicious, amazing, unnatural abs. How is this man real?

He pushes me backward, pressing me into a stack of boxes. "You taste so fucking good," he mumbles, dipping his fingers between my legs, rubbing me though the denim. "You think you can come like this?"

"We shouldn't," I tell him, but make no move to stop. Anyone could walk in right now. My boss. My brother. My coworkers. The orgasm is a few strokes away and instead of composing myself, I rock my hips into his hand. His lips burn against my throat and in the small room there's nothing but the sound of my shaky breath.

"Come on, baby girl, let go for me. I'll hold you up."

My eyes flutter shut and my body slacks just as the shuddering orgasm takes hold. I barely register the sharp corner of a box jabbing into my shoulder blade or the sound of people out in the hall. It's just me and Reid.

I open my eyes and he's staring at me.

I twist my body away from him, focused on the door. "I-I need to go."

"Wait." He keeps me in place. "You're so fucking gorgeous, you know that?" He pushes my hair off my face. "Especially like this, red cheeked with your pupils blown. Fuck, GG, you're killing me."

Gorgeous? I don't think so. I'm hot and sweaty and more than a little ashamed of myself.

"I really need to go back to work."

He releases me, taking a step back. "I mean it."

The feeling in my chest is way beyond a flutter at this point and I leave the room while I still have control of my mind and body. Every time I touch him, or worse, he touches me–I feel like I'm losing it just a little more.

18

R^{eid}

"It's been fun," I shrug out of my jacket and hang it by the door, "but I'm heading to bed."

"Same," Reese says, nudging Twyler up the stairs. "Don't forget we've got film to review in the morning."

"Fuck, seriously?" Axel groans, definitely forgetting. "Doesn't Coach know we're growing boys who need to sleep in?"

"You know he'll have food." Twyler says. "And it's a good day for the trainers to assess injuries and stuff too."

Axel narrows his eyes at her. "You know, he's not your boss anymore. You don't always have to side with him."

While they bicker, Shelby, who went straight to the laundry room when we got home, comes out with a clean basket of clothes, and heads to the French doors offering a quick, "Night," to the room.

I join in while everyone calls out their 'goodnights' and Shelby slips behind the covered glass panes, unaware that I've been sporting a hard-on since she pulled me into that closet and shoved her tongue down my throat. That and I've been unable to think of anything other than the look on her face as she fell apart.

I'd told her the truth, that she's utterly gorgeous when she comes–all that innocence and desire mingling together into something irresistible. I would've left early, desperate to get home and rub one off real quick, but I didn't want to leave until she did. I can't make sense of it. I just want to be in the same room with her. Watch her ass as she bends over to pick up a discarded napkin on the floor. Catch a glimpse of her smile as she laughs with Josie behind the bar.

I seriously considered luring her back to that closet, just so I could see her fall apart one more time.

Something's wrong with me. It's like an addiction. *She's* an addiction and I haven't even fucked her yet. I almost cried in relief when Axel announced he was waiting for Shelby to get off work before we started home, wanting to make sure she got there safe. I'm glad he said it, because there was no way in hell I was letting her cross campus alone at night, but it feels like all this sneaking around is going to get us in trouble.

Nah, it's going to get *me* in trouble and I can't even seem to care.

As everyone heads to their rooms, I take back all my bitching about my roommates changing now that they have serious girlfriends. For all of Axel's complaints about getting up early, he's eager to go to bed. It's rare for Jefferson to have a girl over anyway, so he doesn't count, but before Reese and Axel found Twyler and Nadia, a night like this would have lasted into the morning. We would have walked home from the Badger Den a little buzzed, stayed up late rehashing every bit of the match up with Hilldale and playing video games. Even when I was dating Darla, or during one of our many break-ups, there was always someone around to hang out with. Now all they care about is getting somewhere private to fuck their girls. A few weeks ago I would have been annoyed. Now, I'm about to crawl out of my skin for the house to go quiet so I can sneak my way to Shelby.

I follow everyone else upstairs but Reese calls out, "Yo, Reid, grab those lights."

"Yeah, I'll get them."

I flip them off, one by one, lingering longer than I should to see if Shelby will come back out, or invite me in, or just throw me a fucking bone.

It's with zero self-control that I hold my breath and tap on the glass pane. "GG," I say quietly, "it's me."

The curtains pull to the side and our eyes meet.

A dozen hammering heartbeats later, the knob turns and she opens the door.

At first I miss it, too focused on trying to not make a fool of myself. Plus her legs are bare, long and sexy, her thighs cut off by the hem of the oversized jersey. It's not until my eyes travel up that I really see her. *It.*

The tear in the sleeve. The number eight stitched just above it. Shelby Rakestraw is standing in the middle of that little porch wearing my jersey and nothing else.

Have. Fucking. Mercy.

I step into the room, not bothering to shut the door, and reach out, fisting the front of the shirt in my hand. "Where did you find this?"

Her head tilts back and I see the line of her throat clench as she swallows. "In the laundry room. I saw it in the basket and just thought... because you said–"

"I know what I said," I growl, pushing her hair off her neck. I plant my lips on her soft skin, sucking hard. "I just didn't know..." I trail off licking a hot trail across her skin because I don't know if I can admit what I didn't know. Like how seeing her flipped a switch inside of me, unleashing something possessive and feral. Like how my cock is so hard that with one touch I'd probably blow. But the one I really can't confess, the biggest one of all, is the urge coursing through my veins that demands that I take her, mark her, and claim her. *Mine.*

I'm not supposed to make girls like Shelby mine. I'm not good for them. Good *enough.*

But I did promise her adventure and experience, and so far she's met me step for step. Wrapping my arm around her waist, I drag her to me with one hand and kick the door shut with my foot. I sit on the couch, pulling her into my lap, afraid that if I get her horizontal it'll go too far, but this, feeling her hot little pussy pressed against me, it'll do.

"We can go upstairs," she says between kisses, "and get in bed like you said."

I laugh running my hand up her shirt and feeling the soft underside of her tit. "Sorry, GG, that's not a good idea."

"Why not?" she asks, breath hitching as I swipe a thumb over her nipple.

I withdraw my hands and use them to cup her face, making her look at me. Her eyes are filled with doubt and insecurity. Not cool. "Remember when I told you that if I were David there were other ways I'd show the world you were mine than a ring full of promises?"

She nods.

"There's nothing sexier than a girl you're into wearing your clothing." Wrapping my arms around her, I trace the letters on her shoulders, starting with the 'W.' "Especially when it has your name on it. It sends a message."

"To who?"

Fuck. She's so innocent and sweet and has no idea how much effort it's taking to control myself right now. "To the guy and to anyone else that sees it."

A shiver runs up her spine and her back arches, drawing my eyes down to where her nipples poke through the fabric. The movement makes her press down on my erection and my mind goes blank. Hell. This girl is going to be the end of me.

"Did Darla wear your clothes?" The question comes as a surprise.

"No. Not really."

"Why not?"

"Darla was more into fashion than I was. It was something we were kind of into together. Dressing like a fan, or worse, a jersey chaser, didn't fit her style." She also made it clear she didn't want to be identified by my accomplishments. I understood it, but it also sucked. There's something motivating for an athlete about having their "person" out in the stands supporting them. "It was fine."

"But you like it." She runs her hand down the side of my face, fingers trailing over my jaw. I've noticed she likes exploring my body. Touching the muscles on my abs and chest, the lines of my face. Something she couldn't do with David. "Shouldn't your girlfriend do nice things for you?"

I shrug it off. "It wasn't a big deal."

Her fingers move south, to the 'V' at the top of my button down shirt. I swallow, growing more aroused with every second. "I don't know," she says, a little of that naivety slipping away. "I think you deserve better than that, Reid Wilder."

I restrain myself as Shelby unbuttons my shirt, giving me a soft kiss between every loosened button. She parts the fabric, revealing my chest, dipping her head to lay her tongue flat over my nipple. There's no rush as she moves her hot, wet lips from one side to the other, toying and teasing me.

Did I say naive? Because none of this feels innocent or inexperienced.

I grab her behind and massage her ass over the cotton covered panties that drive me wild. Another way that she's the opposite of Darla. No pretense, just function, and it's still sexy as hell. I dip my fingers under the edge and feel the warm heat of her pussy. She seems more comfortable this time, leaning into my touch. "Fuck, GG," I groan, stomach caving as she kisses my abdomen, "you're so wet."

She licks the spot under my belly button and I blame that tongue for short circuiting my brain because the next thing I know she's unzipping my pants and has positioned herself between my thighs, down on her knees. Christ, she looks like a goddess.

She reaches for me and my brain comes back on all cylinders. I grab her wrist.

"Hold up," I say, sitting up from where I've slumped down the couch. "What are you doing?"

"Giving you a blow job." She shoots me a look. "Don't pretend like you haven't had one before."

"Well, yeah," I run my hand through my hair and add, "but I'm pretty fucking sure you haven't given one."

"I haven't," she admits. "Do you not want one?"

"Baby girl, every man always wants a blow job."

She snorts.

I narrow my eyes. "What?"

"That's exactly what Nadia and Twyler said."

I roll my eyes because those two. "What's this about?"

"I may not be your girlfriend," she says, "but the things you do to me, like today in the supply closet." Her cheeks flush a deeper shade of pink. "I want to do the same thing for you."

"Sex isn't transactional, Shelby. I did that for you because I like to make you feel good, not because I expect something in return."

I don't add the selfish reason that I like to be the one *making* her feel good.

"I know. This is about new things, right? Exploring all that stuff I never got to do before–all the things I want to do before I go back home."

I raise an eyebrow. "And one of those is sucking my cock?" Her nose wrinkles, horrified by my choice of words. "Look, if you can't handle the talk, then you can't handle having me in your mouth."

"I can handle it," she says, chin lifting defiantly. Fuck, I want those lips around me, but only if she's sure. "And I want to. Just like I want to wear this shirt. I like it. It makes me feel like I belong, like I'm just part of the group."

"That, I understand." It's all I've strived for my entire life–a sense of belonging. "And you are part of the group. You're not just Axel's little sister. You're a cool girl who came into town and blew us all away. You've got a job and although you still need a coat, your style has improved drastically."

She grins. "Thank you."

My eyes dart to her mouth, then back up. "You're also sexy as fuck, Shelby, and thinking about you taking me in your mouth almost made my brain shut off. Don't underestimate yourself and the power you have over men." I swallow. "Especially me."

"I won't." I hold out my hand, giving her the chance to get up off her knees, but she pushes it aside. I watch as she runs her hands down my abdomen, stomach dipping, until she's freed me from the confines of my shorts and has me in her grip. There's no time to even blink before she's let her tongue dart out to taste the tip.

"Shit, Shelby." She's tentative, but that only makes it sexier, feeling her hot breath against my skin. Cupping my hand behind her neck, I stroke her skin in encouragement. "You good?"

"Yes," she says, gripping the base of my cock in her hand. "What should I do?"

"Keep doing that. Whatever. Lick me." Her tongue touches me again, this time swiping under the ridge of the head. My hips rise off the couch, and I tighten my grip on her neck. My touch seems to embolden her, and she opens her mouth, taking me in. Her tongue flattens underneath, lathing me with warm, wet, heat.

"How deep can you take me?" She looks up at me with wide blue eyes and takes me further. Sweat slides down my back. "Fuck, that's my good girl."

A grin tugs at her lips, and Shelby's naivety seems to vanish in the moment, her confidence rising with every bob of her head. She's got me teetering on the edge, my balls tightening, hips thrusting. "G," I nudge her chin, "I'm close."

I'm past close.

My hips jerk and I can tell she's not going to back off, so I do it for her, pulling her up and crashing her mouth to mine. My release spills, hot and slippery, down the side of my shaft. I taste myself on her tongue–taste myself inside of her—and my already hammering heart threatens to break free from my ribs.

Releasing her, I shudder out a deep breath and she rocks back on her heels. I study her, lips puffy and swollen, still wearing that jersey that rises and falls as she catches her breath.

She breaks first, grabbing a towel hanging nearby and offering it to me. Once I clean up, I crook my finger and say, "Come here." She curls into my side, splaying her hand over my stomach. "I meant what I said earlier tonight. You're gorgeous and," I kiss her on the temple, "you're really good at making me feel good. Thank you."

She grins, and my heart stumbles, feeling all kinds of ways that I didn't plan for. All kinds of ways I shouldn't, but I'm too happy to care.

"Remember," Jane, the PR coordinator stands in front of the big screen coach used to show us film, "even though there's no game on the schedule, Wittmore's Badger Family Day on Saturday is mandatory."

For once no one argues about having to participate in a charity event. Why would they? Providing a day for foster kids to learn to skate and play a bunch of games? It's all a good time.

"When you arrive there will be new jerseys for you to wear that day. They'll be in your lockers."

"Come on, Jane," Reese says, that all-American grin flashing. "Give us a peek at our boy's design."

Every eye in the room swings toward me, including Jane, who is blushing at Reese's attention. There's not a woman that crosses his path that doesn't fall for his charm.

"Not until tomorrow." She smiles. "But I can say that Mr. Wilder did an amazing job."

She continues, giving us a firm warning about not being late, and Reese chimes in letting us know there will be no partying the night before. The easy going grin from before is gone. "This weekend is about the kids. If you show up hungover or late, there will be hell to pay."

There's no argument from the team and even Jefferson agrees to follow the rules. I'm headed to the locker room to grab my things when Jane calls out, "Reid, can you talk for a minute?"

"Hey," I say, dodging the guys as they file out the door. "Is everything okay with the designs?"

"They turned out great. Everyone in the office loves them." She pauses while Emerson and Murphy pass by. "When I sent them to the athletic director's office they loved them too and want to use them on new merchandise heading into the playoffs."

"Seriously?"

"Dead serious. You're a really talented artist and have fresh ideas. Merch sales have been lagging for the last few seasons. We've definitely needed a rebrand and everyone thinks you're the perfect style for what we're looking for." She tilts her head. "We can even pay you."

My head spins at the news. "That sounds really cool."

"I've already spoken to Coach Bryant and assured him that if you take on this work it won't interfere with your hockey schedule. Your advisor has also agreed that any additional work you put into this can be used as part of your senior project."

"Wow," I run my hand through my hair, "okay, so you've thought this through."

"Only because the work you've given us so far is so good and that's how much we want to continue working with you." She straightens. "I'll get you the paperwork and any details you'll need. Truthfully, you've already done the hard work. This will just be a little tweaking to expand the design to other products."

Jane walks out, and I continue to the locker room. I'm stunned at the reaction to my design. It started off as a little tweak on the original logo and mascot, something fun for the event, but I had no idea it would build like this.

When I get into the locker room, the guys are still there, talking about who they're inviting to the Family Day.

"Twyler's going to volunteer with Coach Green," Reese says, hitching his bag over his shoulder, "just in case they need another set of hands for first-aid."

Murphy is bringing his parents. Pete's girlfriend from back home is coming up. I'm shrugging on my coat when Axel chimes in, "Nadia will be here and I figure I'll see if Shelby wants to come. It'll be her last weekend before she goes home."

Wait, what?

"Already?" Jefferson asks for me. "She's really going back?"

"I have a feeling if I don't get her on that plane my mother will fly out here and get her herself and no one wants the wrath of Mrs. Reverend Rakestraw to blow through here." He slams his locker shut. "It sucks though. I can already see the change in her. She's more independent and outspoken. Confident."

"Maybe she'll tell your mother to fu–" Jefferson swallows back the curse, "back off."

"Easier said than done." Axel pulls the black skull-cap out of his bag. "As much as I want my little sister to break free of my parents' control, I don't see it happening long-term. She's just not that kind of girl."

What kind of girl is that? I want to ask. Is she not the kind that would go get a job to earn money of her own for the first time? Or to break up with her almost-fiance so she can experience new things without any shackles holding her back? But most of all, is she not the kind of girl that would give his best friend a blow job while everyone else was asleep in the house?

Because that's the Shelby I know and the idea that she could be leaving soon hits me hard.

"What about you, Wilder?" Emerson asks. "Who are you bringing?

"Uh, my dad and probably my sister."

"The cute older one?" Jefferson asks. "Or the cute younger one?"

I shoot him a glare. "The much younger, totally illegal, one."

He winks. "Gotcha."

I know he's just kidding, but the irony isn't lost on me. Who am I to judge or accuse people of hooking up with a friend's sister when I can't keep my hands off of Shelby?

19

Shelby

With no game tonight, the bar is quiet and Mike lets me leave early. When I step into the Manor, I'm hit by the scent of buttery popcorn and surprised to find everyone in the living room.

"Shelby!" Nadia's eyes light up when she sees me. "You're home early."

"Why didn't you call?" Axel asks, shifting over so Nadia can sit next to him on the love seat. "I was going to come pick you up."

"Mike let us go early." I drop my bag on the kitchen table. "And it's only half a mile. I can walk." I walk over to the couch. Reid and Jefferson are sitting on each end. "What are you doing?"

"Cap told us we have to stay home since we have the charity event tomorrow," Jefferson says.

Reese shrugs from the armchair he's sharing with Twyler. Their bodies are intertwined and I'm not sure where hers begins and his ends. "We have to spend the full day with a group of kids. The last thing we need is for someone to be hungover or sick. It's the one day of the year you need to be a good example."

"I still don't know why that means all of your girlfriends get to be here and I can't hit up the Kappa house."

"Because it does," Twyler snaps, grabbing a handful of popcorn from the bowl in her lap. "You can go one night without cuddling up with a puck bunny."

"Just seems unfair, right, Wilder?"

Reid, wearing dark sweatpants and a worn Wittmore Hockey t-shirt, focused on his phone, grunts noncommittally.

"We're about to start," Nadia says. "You can join us."

"Thanks, but I really need to take a shower. I smell like fried food and beer."

"You just described two of the sexiest things ever," Jefferson says, patting the center of the couch. "It's like catnip for hockey players."

"Dude," Axel warns.

"As happy as I am to know you won't be offended," I tell Jefferson, "I'm still going to change and clean up a little. Go ahead and start without me."

When I come back down the lights are off, light coming from the action movie playing on the screen. The only spot left for me is between Reid and Jefferson. Both men are huge and leave me a tiny slice of the middle cushion. Careful not to touch either of them, I sit, and then I'm instantly hit with Reid's scent. If wings and beer are catnip to hockey players then whatever Reid's soap is made up of is mine.

A shiver rolls across my skin.

"You cold?" Reid asks quietly.

"I'm fine."

"Shelly's always freezing." My brother doesn't hide that he's eavesdropping. "Which makes sense because she insists on wearing clothing that is the complete opposite of the weather outside."

I look down at my shorts and bare legs. "I forgot my sweats!"

"Whatever." He rolls his eyes. "She does this in Texas, too, insisting on the AC being way down while she bundles up." He grabs the blanket off the back of the chair he's sitting in and tosses it at me. "Take this. You shouldn't be walking around these hooligans showing your legs anyway."

"Good grief," Nadia says. "She can show her legs without asking for some guy to start humping them."

"Seriously," Jefferson says. "You know I'm all about the tits anyway."

Before my brother can react, Reid leans around me and slams his fist into Jefferson's arm. "Ow!" he whines, rubbing his very muscular bicep. "What the hell, man?"

"You're lucky I didn't do it earlier."

"Seriously, dude, stop being disrespectful to people's sisters," Reese chimes in. "Now, if everyone is finished being an asshole, maybe we can watch the movie?"

"Still thought we should have watched the Ingrid Flockton documentary," Jefferson mumbles, but Reese has already turned the movie back on. With everyone thoroughly distracted, I pull my feet up on the couch and spread the blanket over my lap.

"Christ, your feet are cold," Reid says, loud enough for everyone to hear. I move to shift my feet away, but he grabs one and clamps his wide hand around it, engulfing me in warmth.

"Sorry, all my socks are dirty."

"Shhhh!" Axel hushes, then crams popcorn in his mouth.

We settle in, but Reid discretely adjusts the blanket so we're both underneath.

Oh boy.

I glance over and his eyes are focused on the TV, acting as though he's not rubbing the arch of my foot with his thumb. Acting as though my brother and everyone else aren't sitting a few feet away and all hell wouldn't break loose if they found out.

It's impossible to keep track of what's happening on screen—something about aliens and superheroes saving the world, when the weight of his hand, heavy and warm, starts a slow, tentative, ascent from my foot up my calf, then over my knee. He stills when he reaches my thigh, his fingers dipping between my legs.

I can't do anything but pretend to watch the movie, and tug the blanket higher up my chest to hide my hardened nipples.

We sit like this for the longest time, through a million heartbeats pounding hard against my ribs. Stroke after gentle stroke, never moving past the warm heat of my inner thigh. If he dropped an inch and touched me at my core, he'd feel the wet spot on my panties. He'd know how desperate I am.

Something tells me he already does.

Is that all it takes for Reid to do to get me excited? To touch me discreetly under a blanket? Or getting me to cross boundaries, teetering on the edge of danger? Or is it because I know what comes next? How good he makes me feel?

I know the answer. It's any and all of those things. He knows it too and the only real questions left are: Would I ever let David do something like this to me? Would he ever do it?

The answer is a harsh, undeniable no, and suddenly everything feels very, very out of control.

All of this is running through my mind as his fingers ease down and graze the edge of my panties, dipping underneath. The move is intentional, *erotic*, and when he strokes his fingers over my clit, it elicits a tremor so intense there's no way I can let this continue. Pushing his hand and the blanket to the side, I stand, and announce. "I'm beat." I pray my voice sounds normal. "See you all in the morning."

Even though everyone is so distracted by the movie that I barely get a half-hearted reply, easily slipping from the room, I don't take a breath until I'm closed inside, letting the air of the enclosed porch cool my skin. I keep the overhead light off, the room lit up by the small strand of twinkle lights hanging from the ceiling. I want them to think I'm tired and going to bed, not hot and flustered.

My phone buzzes.

Let me in.

I look toward the living room, where the bluish glow filters through the curtain over my door, and then swivel my head to the exterior door. Quietly, I turn the knob, and he's on the other side, still barefoot. No coat. Jaw set in a hard, tense line.

"Was that too much?" he asks quietly, eyes dark and intent. "Too far?"

Yes. I shake my head.

"Good." He doesn't wait for me to let him in the room. He wraps one arm around me and lifts me off the ground, carrying me into the small room. With his free hand he carefully shuts the door. Or I think he does. His mouth is on my neck, tongue hot. I'm quickly losing my bearings. "Because I wasn't finished."

"This is wrong," I whisper, running my hands up his shirt. "They'll hear."

"Not if you're quiet, GG." He tilts his head, eyebrow lifted. "Can you be quiet?"

I answer by pushing his shirt over his head and he responds silently, peeling off my clothes. A heartbeat later my back is flat against the couch and he's hovering over me, mouth latched to my breasts. It feels so good to have him close to me, on top of me, and there's this tickling urge in my belly crying out: *more.*

My hips rise up and all the sudden it just seems stupid to fight this. To fight him. I never felt this way with David because he was wrong. Reid? God, with Reid, everything feels right.

He responds to my movements, his strong hand pushing my thigh to the side, opening me wide. Before he even touches me, nerves explode in my belly. Dipping his head, his tongue is hot and he groans softly, "Fuck you taste so good."

In seconds I'm a mess, hips desperately thrusting into his face, making him use his hands to hold me down. "I'm close," I whisper, repeating what he said before he came last time, but instead of ushering me over the edge, he pulls his mouth away. I'm about to argue, to ask him what's wrong, but I watch as he pushes two fingers into his mouth and withdraws them, slick and wet.

"Open up for me, GG," he says, nudging my thighs farther apart. "Let me see your pussy."

One leg hits the back of the couch, the other falls flat. Kissing the interior of each thigh, he drags his fingers against my heat. Back and forth he taunts me, staying away from the spot that I know will trigger the fall. It feels both good and infuriating, and just when I think I'm going to lose my mind, he climbs back up my body, tweaking my nipple, while pushing a finger inside.

I still completely overwhelmed by the intrusion.

"Is this okay?" he asks, voice so low I barely hear him. I nod, but my body is stiff, caught in this moment of in between. Reid is inside of me. "You need to breathe, GG, and use your words."

Forcing in a breath, I whisper, "Yes," wanting nothing more than to feel this man inside me.

"Okay, I'm gonna loosen you up."

His moves aren't tentative or hesitant, but he does take care. Working to ease my nerves. He pumps in and out, thumb occasionally grazing over my clit, and all I want is to chase that high.

"One more," he tells me, then slides in the second finger, the sensation is different this time. Less pressure, more of a stretch. "Good?"

"Yeah." I roll my hips, meeting his thrust. "God, yes."

"Quiet," he says, rising up to cover my mouth with his. "I'm going to fuck you like this, and you're going to come, okay?"

It feels like it's too much, like there's no way I can rein in everything I'm feeling. His dirty words, and all the things he's doing to me. But there's a determination coming from him. He wants me to feel good and hell, I want to feel it too. My eyes flutter shut and I let everything wash over me: the feel of him in me, the heat of his mouth, the touch of his fingers drawing me into a chaotic rhythm.

Outside the room, battle sounds filter through the door, missiles and bombs and explosions, but none are as earth-shattering as the orgasm that rockets through me. Reid knows the second it triggers, leaning up to kiss me, swallowing my breath and any noise that comes with it, until I'm limp-bodied, lying under his weight.

Lying there, satisfied, I wait to feel something else: conflict. Regret. Guilt.

It doesn't come.

Instead, Reid rolls to the side, lifting me up and curling me against his body. His lips press against my neck, sticky with sweat, and I'm caught in those strong arms, holding me tight until we both fall asleep.

20

———————

S helby

I WAKE UP ALONE, tucked under a thick blanket that does little to replace the weight and warmth of Reid's body. I spot the note before I sit up. Folded in a tight square, a drawing of a sun on the side facing me.

Had to go before the house woke up.

See you at the arena.

–R

It's too early for me to decipher what it means, if anything, and I gather my clothes and head to the bathroom upstairs. The girls are up and in the kitchen by the time I shower and get dressed. "Is this okay?" I ask, coming out in a sweater and jeans.

"They'll hand out jerseys when we get there," Twyler says. "Different ones for the players, kids, and family."

"Oh, the shirts Reid designed?" I ask, grabbing the Wittmore beanie she let me borrow. Since she worked with the team she has extra gear.

"I think so," Nadia says, slipping on her boots. "I've never been to one of these before. This is the first time I've had WAG status."

"WAG?" I ask.

"Wives and girlfriends," Nadia says, and I catch the pride on her face. "I was firmly in jersey chaser status before I started dating your brother."

"And that means you don't get to come to things like this?"

"It means you stay home with your legs spread, waiting for an athlete to decide you're worth a hook-up."

As usual, Nadia's frankness surprises me, but even more, since she's speaking so bluntly about herself.

Twyler frowns and faces her friend. "Remember: We listen and we don't judge," although I catch the line between her eyes, "and we've all come a long way since then, babe. Especially you."

She says that with conviction, but I can't help but wonder where Reid and I fall between a WAG and jersey chaser. I'm not chasing athletes so that doesn't sound right, but I sure don't have girlfriend status either. Am I just a hook-up? We defined this as a learning experience. Having an adventure. Where does that fall in the realm of relationship status?

I realize that I have no freaking clue. My one and only relationship was orchestrated by our parents.

I'm still thinking about it when we walk into the arena, until Nadia says, "So are you sad to be leaving next week?"

I miss a step, coming to a stop. "Next week?"

"That's when Axel said you're heading back home, right?" Nadia looks at Twyler who just shrugs.

"Right. Yes." I laugh nervously. "I just totally spaced on it."

I didn't just space on it. I completely blocked it out. I'd just gotten used to being here, used to my job and living on my own.

Used to having a man treat me the way Reid does.

"I wish I could stay longer," I confess, "but my mother would lose her mind if I didn't come home as expected." And predictably fall back into the role of Shelby the Preacher's Daughter. The Good Girl.

I shiver at the thought, knowing now that those words can carry a very different weight.

"We'll make the best of it while you're still here," Nadia says as we approach the arena. Twyler peels off and heads back to the locker room with the guys, while Nadia and I check in at the table out front.

"We're here as guests of Axel Rakestraw," Nadia says, giving our name to the volunteer. "Nadia Beckwith and Shelby Rakestraw."

"Your names are on the list," the guy says, checking us off his list. "You'll each get a jersey with the number on the back of the player you're representing along with vouchers for food at the snack bar. You can grab your skates from the equipment manager down by the ice. Have fun."

"Skates?" I ask as we walk away.

"Oh yeah, part of the day is skating with the kids and players." She glances over at me. "You don't want to?"

"I've never ice skated before." We walk down the stairs toward the ice. The rink is already crowded with swarming kids, some more proficient than the others. The ones not hanging onto the wall, or wobbling across the ice, zip around wildly, making me even less inclined to get in the middle of it. I'd probably not only break my neck but one of theirs too. "Ice rinks were few and far between in Texas."

"You never went with Axel?"

I laugh. "Gosh, no. Mother wouldn't have me anywhere near something like that. I was probably at cotillion or choir rehearsal."

"Well, now's your chance." She drops her bag on one of the benches and pulls her shirt out. I do the same, finally getting a good look at the jerseys Reid designed.

"Damn," Nadia says, looking it over and giving an approving nod. "Reid killed it with the design."

I know nothing about hockey designs or logos, but I can tell there's a vintage vibe. The current Wittmore Badger logo is just an illustration of the animal's face, but the design Reid worked up is a full body, mid-strut. A fluid retro 'W' for Wittmore is stitched across the chest. It's simple, but fun. I can see why the PR department approved of it.

I tug mine over my head, lifting my braid out from under the V-neck to rest on my shoulder. "How does it look?"

"Like you're ready for your first skating lesson."

I give the ice another wary look and she sighs, "Come on, Shel, Axel will be so excited for you to be out there."

Just as we get to the equipment manager, Axel skates up, grinning at the both of us. His jersey is similar but different, the primary color black, where ours are purple. "You made it," he says, leaning over the wall and planting a quick kiss on Nadia's mouth. "And representing 01."

I roll my eyes. "I'm representing myself," I tell him, jabbing a thumb at the name on my back.

"Fair." He reaches out and yanks my braid hard.

"Hey!" I spin away. "Don't be a jerk."

"Maybe you should stop acting like a baby!" He lunges, planning on messing with me again, but a body moves between us.

A large, *male* body that smells amazing.

"Do I need to separate you two?"

"No," we both say at the same time, Axel's mouth in a matching frown to mine. Reid's gaze drops down to me and something flickers between us–an acknowledgment of the secret that we have together and my stomach flips in betrayal.

"I picked up our skates." Nadia walks up, a set of skates in each hand. She shoves a bulky pair at me.

"Bro," Axel says, moving past us to help Nadia. "Help Shel get her skates on. We're starting soon."

I start to tell Reid he doesn't have to help me with anything, but he's already grabbed a skate and is loosening the laces.

"Let's get those boots off," he says, dropping down to one knee. He lifts my foot and eases off my shoe.

"The shirts look great," I tell him. "They're fun. Where'd you get the idea?"

"Glad you like them." He keeps his eyes down, but adds, "I was looking through some of the old jerseys for inspiration and found some from early in the program's history. I thought it would be cool to go with a vintage look." His gaze lingers on me a moment longer than I'm comfortable. He jerks his chin. "Other foot."

I stick it out and he catches it in his hand. Once my boot is off, those long fingers graze the underside, trailing over the arch. I am sent back to the way he touched me secretly under the blanket during the movie. The same two fingers he used to–

My eyes dart over to my brother who is fully invested in his girl-friend, clueless to my runaway body and brain.

Carefully, Reid tugs up my sock, smoothing it out, then works my foot into the heavy skate boot. I watch as he methodically tightens the laces, he dips his fingers under the tongue and asks, "That feel okay? Too tight?"

I shake my head. "No."

"You need a little give at the ankles, but not too much."

"I'm pretty sure I'll be like those kids out there," I nod at the rink, "hanging onto the edge, trying not to make a fool of myself."

"You really think I'd let you fall?" He stands and stretches out his hand. I take another quick look at my brother. He and Nadia are moving toward the rink. I take his hand and let him help me up, then lead us toward the ice. Just before we get to the opening that leads to the ice he leans in and whispers in my ear, "As much as I like seeing you in the jersey I designed, it would be a lot better if it had my name on it."

My cheeks burn, recalling how he looked at me when I wore his jersey. How aroused it made him. "You're playing a dangerous game, Wilder," I say, keeping one eye on my brother. He's back in the goal, showing off some of his moves to the kids.

With one hand on the wall and another holding onto his forearm, I take an awkward step onto the frozen floor. My movements are tentative, shaky, like a newborn deer.

"No." He grabs me, spinning me around and pressing my back against the wall. His muscular arms cage me in. "A dangerous game would be me kissing you right now, out in the open, for everyone to see. Which holy fuck, GG, I want to do that so bad."

My knees turn to jelly, and my ankles wobble. It's a good thing he's nearby to keep me from falling over, but it's a bad thing that he's so close, taunting me like this. "I'm starting to think you're trying to get caught."

He shrugs, a smirky grin tugging at his mouth. "Maybe I'm thinking it would be worth the risk."

"You'd risk my brother finding out about what we've been doing?"

His cheeks are ruddy from the cold, and his eyes dart to my mouth. He could kiss me right now and tear the bandage off this secret, blowing up both of our lives. But to what end? What would be the point? Causing an irreparable rift with my brother over an experiment?

"Reid!"

A small body zips across the ice, coming at him full force. He reacts quickly, catching her in his arms. "Hey, Ron," he says, wrapping his arms around the younger girl. She's in the jersey designated for family, the name Wilder across the back. Another person follows, skating slower but still with noticeable skill. "Dad. Mom here?"

Mr. Wilder points to the stands. There's a cluster of women, all in family jerseys. Reid lifts his hand in a wave and a woman with short, stylishly cut, gray hair grins and waves back.

"She's not skating?" he asks.

"Not this year. Her back has been bothering her a little, but she didn't want to miss the chance to connect with other parents." Mr. Wilder's attention shifts to me. "Hi, I'm Roger. Reid's father, and this is Veronica, his younger sister."

"Shelby." I straighten up. "Rakestraw. Axel is my brother. Nice to meet you both."

"Ah, the little sister that's been crashing at the house." He grins. "Hope you haven't been traumatized by living with a group of college boys."

Before I can answer, Ronnie jumps in. "You've been living at the

Manor." Her eyes dart across the ice, landing squarely on her target. "With Jefferson?"

Ah, the infamous crush. "Just for the past few weeks. And everyone is very busy, I don't see him very much." I catch Reid's disgruntled expression and add, "Just so you know, they're all pretty smelly and none of them do the dishes."

"That's not true," Reid crosses his arms over his chest. "I totally do the dishes."

"*Once,*" I remind him. "*One* time you did the dishes after I cooked dinner."

We stare at one another, both of us on the verge of cracking a smile, until the sound of the buzzer cuts across the ice, breaking our eye contact. Coach Bryant is encouraging everyone to move to the middle.

"You coming?" Reid asks.

I look down at my feet, the skates pointed inward as I barely hold myself upright, and shake my head. "Not a chance. But you guys have fun. I'll happily watch from the stands and get some hot chocolate."

They skate off as I wobble my way back off the ice, but Ronnie darts out on her own, making a swooping loop past me. It's on her way back to her family that I hear her say, just a bit loud, "I like her. Better than Darla."

I glance up just in time to catch Reid reply back, "Yeah, I do too."

THE EVENT IS INCREDIBLE. Seeing the excitement on the kids' faces as they both learn a new skill and just have fun is worth sitting on the hard bench all afternoon. I'm not really familiar with kids that come from troubled backgrounds. In that respect, I've lived a pretty charmed life. My parents may be overprotective and demanding, but there was always a sense of security. These kids don't have that, and there's a shadow of guardedness lurking in their eyes. The guys do everything they can to make them feel at ease. That, I understand.

Just like Axel and his roommates have done their best to make me feel comfortable.

It's not long before some of the younger kids tire out and make their way off the ice. Twyler and the other trainers tend to a few scrapes and bumps down by the players bench. A couple of older teens remain on the ice, their skill level higher, and I realize that they've started a game of shootout with my brother.

Axel is positioned in the middle of the goal, body covered in pads, egging on the kids as they each attempt to make a shot. He's not easy on them. Easily knocking most of the shots out of the way, and slowly there's a crowd of players and kids circling the area, cheering on Axel's competitor. After each attempt, Axel calls the kid over and talks to them.

"What is he saying?" I ask Nadia, who tired out quickly and joined me on the bleachers.

"No idea."

"He's giving them pointers." We both turn and come face to face with Reid's mother.

"You're Reid's mom, right?" Nadia asks.

"I am." She not only has on the purple jersey, she has a button on the front with a picture of Reid in uniform.

"I'm Nadia, Axel's girlfriend and this is Shelby, his sister."

"Oh Axel," Mrs. Wilder beams. "That boy may look rough on the outside, with all the tattoos and piercings, but he's really a teddy bear underneath."

Nadia laughs happily. "Right? He tries to act so tough, but he's the most kind and generous guy I know."

I know these things about my brother, but it's hard to reconcile it over the past few years while we've been separated. I've felt so isolated at home. Lonely. And when I saw him, there was no mistaking his disappointment in the direction my life was headed. He always wanted me to do more, but when it comes down to it, I'm not sure that's true.

"The time they give to this, even though it seems minimal, has the potential to be life altering." She gestures to the ice and it's obvious now that the guys aren't just standing around watching, they're all engaged with the younger boys and girls. "Coming to this event was how Reid got his introduction to hockey. He picked it up quickly."

"Was he also always a gifted artist?" I ask, unable to help myself from finding out more about her son.

"He was. That skill was innate, but holing up in his room with a sketchpad wasn't enough for him. He needed to move around and work out some of that energy. He also needed to be part of a team."

"It sounds like you gave him a lot of opportunities."

She shrugs, eyes focused on her son down on the ice. "Other than providing a safe home, it's one of the most important things a parent can give a child." She looks back at me. "I'm sure your parents sacrificed for Axel to get to this level."

"Uh, not really," I admit. "We're from Texas and my father is a minister. He primarily wanted us involved in church activities. Football or baseball would have been acceptable, I guess, but hockey? Ax figured that out on his own."

She studies me for a long moment. "I guess that explains his determination."

My parents provided the home part, but not the opportunity. If it wasn't in alignment with their priorities, then they weren't interested.

The buzzer blares from the speakers and there's an announcement that the concession stand is open. That gets the rest of the kids and the team off the ice to remove their gear.

The next hour is a blur of pizza, hotdogs, and nachos. The kids' laughter is infectious and I can't keep my eyes off of Reid, following his movements as he immerses himself in these children. Antsy, I do what I do best, moving between the tables, grabbing discarded plates and cups. I always feel most steady when I'm doing something with my hands. I'm juggling a pile when a sharp, earsplitting whistle cuts through the chatter and all eyes move to where Reese stands at the front of the group.

"Now that we're fed and warmed up, Coach Bryant said we could go on a tour of the locker and screening room," he says, "but you need to finish cleaning up whatever trash you have left, and then go thank Shelby for doing the majority of it already."

He grins at me, and my cheeks burn red at the attention, but one by one the kids drop their trash into the bin, and stop to tell me thank you.

"You're welcome," I tell each and every one, until the kids are gone and suddenly a line of hulking hockey players is standing in front of me.

"Thanks, Shel," Emerson says, giving me a cheeky grin.

One by one they file through, until Axel appears in front of me. "I keep telling you, cleaning up after everyone isn't your job."

I cross my arms and glare at him. "I could say the same to you."

He smirks and lunges for me, grabbing me in a ridiculous bear hug. I fight against him, but he's obnoxious and refuses to let go until Nadia drags him away.

"Thanks," I tell her, straightening my shirt.

After the last player comes through, I'm disappointed that Reid never came up. I look around for him, but don't see him anywhere. It's probably for the best. The less we interact in public the better.

The parents sit down for a meeting about local teams the kids can join. Nadia excuses herself to go to the restroom and I spot Twyler waving across the room.

"I'm finished," Twyler says, lingering by a door that leads to the locker rooms, "and the rest of the time is pretty much for the foster families and kids. If you're ready to head out, I just need to grab my stuff and then we can go out the back door. Nadia said she'd meet us out there."

"Sounds good to me."

"You going into work today?"

"No." I follow her down the stairs. "Since it's a bye week Mike doesn't think they'll have too big of a crowd."

At the bottom of the stairs is a set of double doors with an image of the badger mascot and the word Wittmore painted across the top. Using a keycard, Twyler unlocks the door and we enter the player's area. Noisy voices come from down the hall and she says, "That's the screening room where they're meeting with the kids. You can wait out here for me. I need to put away a few things and grab my stuff."

She dips into the doorway of a room that has the word "Training Room" overhead. Down the hall I hear Reese encourage everyone to quiet down. Curious, I walk down the hall and peek into the room. I'd heard my brother and the guys talk about watching film, but I didn't really process that they basically have a movie theater of their own. Today the kids have claimed all of the comfy looking seats, and the players stand against the edge of the room. To my surprise, it's not Reese at the front of the room, or even Coach Bryant.

It's Reid.

"I know it may be hard to believe, but I was once a scrawny kid sitting in the same seat as you are right now. Well," he grins, looking out at the group, "not the same *exact* seat, they upgraded those a few years ago, but I came to the Wittmore Family Day with my foster parents."

There's a small murmur of surprise and not just from the kids. From some of Reid's teammates, too.

"I'd been through a lot of homes. Eight, actually. And I'd finally landed in one where the parents decided that instead of finding me too energetic or tough to deal with, they'd find an outlet for me. It was tough. I was way behind everyone else who had been playing since they were four-years-old and attending training camps every year. But something about it just clicked, and my teammates and coaches, they all became a second and third family."

Reid turns around showing the back of his jersey. His name, Wilder, stitched above the number 08. "It took eight homes." Turning back he adds, "When I got to Wittmore I was able to request a number. I asked for eight. I didn't want to forget those days, but I also wanted it as a reminder of how much I went through to get somewhere safe and stable. To find the right team." His eyes flit up, meeting mine, and I realize that he knows that I'm here and watching. "Hockey may not be the right sport for you, but somewhere out there is the right family, the right team, and you'll make it your own."

Again he looks past everyone else, gaze holding mine. I feel a warmth, something unfamiliar but also right. So, incredibly right.

It's in that moment, when Reid is revealing himself for the kids, his teammates and me that I realize what that feeling is.

Love.

I'm in love with Reid Wilder.

"You ready?" I didn't hear Twyler walk up. Not with the pounding of my heart in my ears. "Shelby?" I blink, dragging my eyes away from Reid as he continues to speak to the kids, over to Twyler. There's a line across her forehead. "Are you okay?"

I nod, but I'm unable to say the words, because I'm not sure that I am.

21

———————

R^{eid}

"THANKS FOR DINNER." We're standing outside of Deion's, a nice restaurant just off the strip. Mom and Dad wanted to get in a good meal before they got back on the road. "And for coming, it was good to see you."

"You know we wouldn't miss it." Mom glances over at Ronnie. "Your sister would've been crushed. She loves coming up to see you, too."

"Me or my teammates?" I ask, tugging at her ponytail. The teasing makes me think of Axel and Shelby earlier. Then just about Shelby. Damn. I can't stop thinking about her.

"Are you sure I can't stay the night?" she asks. She's been bugging all of us about it all week, but I hate to tell her that after being on house arrest last night, Jefferson is probably already down on sorority row.

"Ron, we already talked about it," Dad tells her. "They've already got one sister staying at the house, I doubt there's room for another."

Mom reminds her, "And you've got your own game tomorrow."

"You do?" I haven't kept up with Ronnie's schedule this season. She plays on an all-girls team and from the videos I've seen, she's pretty kick ass. She showed her moves today on the ice, even giving Axel a run during the shootout. "Then you better get home and get to bed." I reach for my phone. "Do I need to get Reese to call you and give you a lecture on preparation, diet, and rest?"

Her jaw drops in horror. "God, no."

Dad laughs and says, "Don't worry, we'll see everyone again for the playoffs."

"We have to win the division first."

"I know you guys are superstitious, but you've pretty much got that on lock."

"I just want to make it clear I don't expect you there." Playoff tickets are crazy expensive. "You know it's fine if you don't come in person. Plus you don't even know how far we'll make it."

"All the way," Mom says. "You guys are going to win the whole thing this year, I can feel it."

Dad chuckles. "There's no way Reese is letting a second opportunity slip through his fingers."

He's right about that. Reese has been focused on redeeming our tragic loss from last year every moment of every day since then. I don't blame him. I can almost feel the trophy in my hands.

"Then, I guess I'll see you in a few weeks." I give everyone a hug, even Ronnie who pretends to hate every second of it. I squeeze her tight and add, "Good luck tomorrow."

"Thanks, bro."

It's still weird having this feeling of "family." Veronica was young when she was adopted, so most of her memories are of just being with the Wilder's. To her, I've always been one of her big brothers.

It's a short trip back to the Manor and when I get to the porch I catch sight of Shelby through the window, opening the oven. Her back is to me and the name Rakestraw is visible on the back of the jersey she still has on. I'd still rather it be my name on the back, but I did design it and a flicker of pride spreads across my chest, similar to the one I felt earlier when I saw her watching me speak to the kids. I've always tried to be honest with my past, but having her hear me talk about it felt more personal.

It also felt like a knife to the chest, knowing she's leaving in a week.

I know it's not her fault. She came here with a goal and that was to get her head on straight–to get some space from her parents and David. She did that, and fuck, she's grown so much. But I know she has obligations to the people back there–and I know they're not going to let her go easily.

Anyway, she's not mine to fight for.

I open the door and step inside, hearing the soft strains of music coming from the speaker: Ingrid Flockton. There's no escaping her.

"Sweet mercy," I groan, inhaling the scent filling the room. "What is that?"

"Kolaches." With her hand covered in an oven mitt, she pulls a pan out. My mouth waters.

"You mean the pastries Nadia learned to make for your brother?"

She laughs. "Definitely the way to his heart. I thought I'd make some for everyone."

My god, she's an angel.

She sets the pan on the top of the oven. "How was dinner?"

"It was good." I should have invited her. Spend every second with her that I can.

"Your parents seem nice."

"They are. They were a little shocked at the fact Axel's sister wasn't covered in tattoos and piercings."

"Not everyone is a rebel."

Except I'm not sure that's true. Shelby definitely has a rebellious streak. If not, she wouldn't be here. "Where is everybody?" I ask, noting that other than the two of us and Ingrid Flockton, the house is quiet. "Upstairs?"

She turns and rests against the counter. "At the Teal House. I was invited but it was the four of them and," her nose wrinkles, "I wasn't in the mood to be a fifth wheel."

I shrug off my coat and walk toward her. "So you came home and baked instead."

"Maybe I took the opportunity of having an empty house to do something I enjoy."

"Baking or taking care of people?"

She tosses the oven mitt on the counter. "Why can't it be both?"

"You know," I close the distance between us, "there are better ways to enjoy an empty house."

"Yeah?" Her head tilts, exposing the long column of her neck. I don't think the move is intentional, but I rarely think any of the sexy things Shelby does is. She's got an instinctive way about her–one that makes my cock hard and drives my body wild.

Leaning into her, I lick a hot path along her throat, up to her ear. Her fingers curl into my side, tight in the T-shirt I'm wearing. Kissing her, I push my hands up her shirt, feeling the warmth of her belly, then the soft swell of her tits underneath one of those pretty little cotton bras. I trace her nipple through the cloth, her breath hitching when it pebbles into a tight peak.

"Fuck, I love your tits." I pull down the front of the jersey and kiss the hard plane of her chest. "I'd take this shirt off, but I like you in it too much."

Apparently she doesn't feel the same about mine, because she pushes it over my head and drops it to the floor. She wastes no time getting her hands on me, feeling my chest and abdomen. She reaches for my button, but I gather them in mine, moving them away. "You touch me now, GG, I'll come in my pants and ruin the night for both of us." I kiss her again and tell her, "I'm going to give you your first kitchen orgasm." I tug at the waistband of her leggings. "Right here on the counter."

A car drives by outside, lights flashing up on the porch. She freezes. "Someone could come home."

"They won't."

"Jefferson..."

"Is busy." She knows he's not coming home and neither are the others. But the fact we're alone, with time *and* space, makes things different. I kiss her gently, then pull away, "Do you want to stop?"

My cock wants to punch me for asking.

"No," she says quickly. "It just feels... weird. Like I'm doing something wrong."

I lift an eyebrow. "Why?"

She swallows, hesitating, but I don't let her off the hook. "It's so open," she finally admits. "Exposed. Like anyone could come in and they'd see us–me–and they'd think that–."

She clams up.

I run my finger up and down her side. "What would they think?" She looks down, eyes averted. Lifting her chin with my fingers, I force her to face me. "What would they think, Shelby?" When she still doesn't speak, I fill in the gaps for her. "That you've got desires and wants? That you like to feel good? That you like to make me feel good?" Her blue eyes widen with every truth bomb I toss. "That they may see you with your skin on fire, pussy drenched, crying out as you come. That they may see a different side of you, one that lets loose of that good girl attitude you hold onto so tight?"

"That's very specific."

"Well, I have very specific things I want to do to you." I cup her cheek and run my thumb over her bottom lip. "But only if you want me to."

I'm always going to give Shelby a choice. Always give her a part in any decision between us. That's the one thing I can give her that no one else in her life ever has. But right now it's taking everything in me not to rip off her leggings, spread her legs, and shove my face between her thighs.

"I want you," she says, voice soft–shy. "But–"

Fuck, here comes the but. I'm moving too fast. I'm scaring her off. I'm not good enough. Or right for her, or a million other buts.

"*But*," she says slowly, "I want something else too."

"Anything you want, GG, and I'll give it to you."

I do not expect what she says next.

"I don't want to go back to Texas a virgin." My heart and cock both lurch at the same time. "And I want you to be the one that takes it."

I'M silent for so long, processing what she just said, that it gets awkward. And when it gets awkward, Shelby gets embarrassed.

"Nevermind." She attempts to jump off the counter, but I come back to my senses, and hold her in place. "Just forget it."

"You think I can forget that?" I thrust a hand into my hair. "Jesus, Shelby."

"I know that's not what our little arrangement was about. And you think I'm not ready. I'm too sweet or innocent or will have regrets," she rambles, clearly uncomfortable. "I'm a grown woman, Reid. I know what I want."

"Hey," I tell her, trying to figure out what to say and how to say it, "I don't think any of those things." I clear my throat, because that may be a lie. "Other than the last one."

"I just thought with the way you reacted to me, you'd be into it." Her eyes dart down to my crotch where my erection is ten steps behind, focused on the makeout session we were having before she dropped this bomb. "But I know I'll always be Axel's little sister to you, and I appreciate you doing everything you have to help me live a little."

"Okay stop." I'm standing in front of her, using both my body and my hands to keep her from running off. "You just surprised me, but let me get one thing clear, I don't see you as Axel's little sister. I see you as this cool girl I like to hang out with. That I love to hang out with. You're fun and sweet, and sexy as hell." She needs me a little. Not completely. She came here on her own, got a job by herself, started to build a life, but she still needed me to protect her, teach her things, build her up. And that hasn't happened to me before. "And if you want me to be the one for you, I'm not going to fight it. I just want to be sure that you're sure, because it means something big for you, and I don't want you to do something you'll regret."

"You think I'd regret having sex with you?" she asks.

"Babe, you're kind of the 'marry the first guy you sleep with' type."

"Maybe I used to be." She reaches for me, cool hands on my overheated skin. "But I'm not that girl that showed up on your doorstep anymore."

I nod. "I know."

"And if I can have a choice in who I do this with, I want it to be with you."

Choice. There it is.

I take a deep breath. "How do you want to do this? Flowers? Hotel? Candles and wine?"

She rolls her eyes. "None of those things." Thank god, because finding all of that shit would take too long and I want inside of this girl now. Her hands glide over my chest and move to my shoulders. "Why don't we go back where we started and see where it goes."

She kisses the underside of my jaw, but I've already got my fingers hooked in the elastic of her leggings. We work together to drag them down, taking her panties at the same time. "Lean back," I tell her, "let me get a look at you."

There's no hesitancy from either of us this time, and when I bend, pressing my tongue against her slick heat, her fingers curl into my hair encouragingly. All I want is to get her loose, to make her feel good, and I think she's as worked up as I am because it doesn't take long before her breath comes in short gasps and her hips rise, chasing my tongue. I draw her to the edge, teasing her a little, pulling back just long enough that she cries out in frustration. "Reid! *Please.*"

"You think I'm not going to make you work for it?" I ask, enjoying the moment, because soon I'm going to take her upstairs, lay her out on the bed and everything is going to change.

It'll be worth it, I think, sucking the hot little bundle of nerves that I know will shatter her. Gripping her by the ass, I bury my face into her and she falls apart on my tongue, bucking into me. She moves with abandon, like we're not standing in the middle of the kitchen, windows wide open where everyone can see.

It's all worth it, even if tonight is the only chance I get.

22

―――――

S helby

I'VE BARELY FLOATED BACK DOWN from the orgasm and processed the fact that my bare ass is on the kitchen counter, when Reid lifts me into his arms.

"Er," I ask, my bare crotch flat against his hard, lower abdomen, "where are we going?"

"Upstairs." His mouth buries into the crook of my neck, sucking and giving me little kisses as he navigates his way to the staircase. He stops at the bottom and draws back, leaving my neck wet and raw. "Unless you–"

"Go," I tell him. I'd meant what I said. It came to me tonight when I realized I love him. I want Reid to be my first. "I can walk, you know."

"I know." He wraps those powerful arms around me. "I want to be close to you."

My heart melts and I know none of this is good for me. Reid isn't good for me, and not because *he's* not good. Reid Wilder is perfect.

He moves with impressive agility, taking the stairs quickly while keeping his mouth and hands on me at all times. He's gentle when he sets me on the bed, less so when he strips off my shirt and shucks his jeans and boxers. His erection, which has been hard since he first pinned me against the counter top, bobs eagerly at the freedom. It's not our first time naked with one another, but the crackle of energy in the air indicates that this time it's different.

"Fuck you're beautiful." He drops to his knees, placing one on either side of me as he works his way up my body. I reach for him, for the soft, wet tip of his cock, spreading the fluid with my thumb. A shudder wracks up his spine and I laugh. This man is strong. A wild man on the ice, imposing in real life, but all it takes is the smallest touch and he's putty in my hands.

I feel the same, my body opening easily for him, the orgasm keeping my muscles loose and pliant. I like the way he handles me, mouth closing around my breast while his hand pushes my thighs apart. He teases my entrance with the rough pads of his fingertips, pushing one finger in. He tongues my nipple, keeping my body over-heated and overstimulated. I barely notice the second finger going in until he shifts, using them to stretch me apart.

"Oh," I gasp, liking how it feels. I dig my heels into the mattress.

"Good?" he asks me, hand splaying across my rib cage. He touches me like he owns me. Like I belong to him. "You're so tight. Tell me if it hurts."

"It doesn't." Proving my point, my hips rock, pulling him in deeper. His fingers are big, but his cock is bigger. I shiver at the thought, both excited and nervous.

"Hell, GG," he swears when he feels it, "you close? Already?"

"Is that fast?" I ask, my nerves are on edge. Raw and exposed. If he touched me there again, I don't think I could hold off.

"I just..." he looks down at me, eyes filled with warmth. "I thought you came so fast because you were new to all of this, but I think your body is just sensitive."

He may be right because ever since that first orgasm it's all I can think about. It's all I want and the minute he touches me my body threatens to crack in two.

Heat burns my face, and he must notice because he says, "It's nothing to be embarrassed or ashamed of. It's hot. Making you come has become my favorite thing to do. I'll gladly work harder if I need to, but damn, feeling how ready you are? It's good for a man's ego."

I snort. "Like you need more of that."

Removing his fingers, he leans over me and fumbles with the drawer of the bedside table. I kiss the hot skin of his abdomen, missing the feel of him inside of me. The muscles that seem so hard, so powerful, but quiver at the lightest touch.

Slamming the door shut, he rolls back to me, foil packet in his hands. A condom. I'd be lying to say I ever saw one up close before. Abstinence is what Father's church teaches. We're *way* beyond that, been past it for weeks. I appreciate that Reid's being safe.

Everything from here on is new to me, the slight ache in my lower belly from where he had been inside of me, the quick way he tears the condom wrapper, pulling out the coiled up ring. I watch as he holds the base of his erection, then slides it over the tip.

Reaching out to touch him, I say, "I like the way it feels better without it."

"You and me both, GG," he grins down at me, amusement in his eyes, "but it's not so bad."

He hovers over me, lining our bodies up. I like this view of him, his strong body over mine. Again he pushes my thighs wide, and settles between my legs, slotting himself against me.

He kisses the swell of each breast, "You ready?"

I nod, but his eyebrow raises. "Yes."

Right from the start the pressure feels different, but he has his mouth close to my ear, his voice warm and steady. "It may hurt a little," he says, "but you should be warmed up. You tell me if you want to stop."

"Hey," I say, getting him to look at me, "I want this."

His tongue darts out and he licks his bottom lip, then claims my mouth with his. The kiss is startling, but not as much as the feel of him pushing inside. The stretch is intense, painful but also good. I'm distracted by his hands holding onto me and he buries himself deep.

"You feel so good," he tells me, "so tight. So perfect." He rambles on a little, saying sweet, sexy things to me, before pulling out and pumping back in again. The rocking motion feels good, and I lift my hips to meet him. The move makes him go faster, deeper and he looks down at me, sweat peppering his forehead and says, "I've thought about this so many times. What it'd be like to be inside of you. To feel your walls tighten around me." He pumps in and out, never taking his eyes off of mine. "I knew it would be fucking amazing, but I didn't know it'd be like this."

I don't get a chance to ask what 'like this' means because his cock twitches and it's followed by a low, deep, groan. With a hard thrust, Reid pumps into me twice more, body tensing as he comes.

We stay like this for a long beat, our bodies slick with sweat, limbs joined, letting our heart and breathing return to normal. It's after we're cleaned up and I'm wearing a clean, soft, Wittmore T-shirt that he climbs back in the bed, dragging me against his chest.

I think he's asleep when his fingers thread in mine and he says, "You know what I can't stop thinking about?"

"I have no clue," I tell him.

"Those kolaches in the kitchen." He pops up on his elbow and looks down at me. "Hungry?"

"AXEL IS GOING TO KILL US."

"For the sex or for eating all the kolaches?" he asks, licking butter off his thumb. My cheeks burn at the way he so casually talks about what we did upstairs. I know it wasn't as big of a deal for Reid as it was for me, but I like the way he's so at ease with everything. That we're down here stuffing our faces on the still warm meat and cheese filled pastries like it's any other day.

I love college.

And I'm pretty sure I love this man, too.

When I don't answer his question, Reid adds with a shrug of his shoulders, "What Axel doesn't know, won't hurt him."

"What would he really do if he found out?" I reach for another off the coffee table. We're on the couch, a true crime quietly playing on the TV. Reid has already seen this one and, by request, spoiled the ending. "Beat you up?"

He considers it, ultimately saying, "Reese wouldn't let him fully beat me up. Maybe one shot, but with the playoffs coming up, he couldn't go too hard. He'd probably just be really pissy about it and make everyone miserable around here."

"I don't have to guess what he'd do to me." With our feet tangled under the blanket, I pull at the layers of pastry, eating them slowly. "After an unbearable lecture, he'd send me back to Texas on the first available plane."

He grows silent at that topic, and I don't blame him. I don't want to talk about me leaving either. What Reid and I have is undefined. I *asked* him to take my virginity, as part of our arrangement. I don't think he minded, but it definitely wasn't an organic moment.

"So tell me about the rest of your family." I nudge him with my foot. "The ones who weren't here today."

That lightens him up, and he starts naming more names than I can keep up with. There's the three older sisters, plus Ronnie who's the youngest and two older brothers. They're scattered all over, but they're still close. "The Wilder's insisted on it. If you wanted to be a member of the family, you had to fully commit."

Leaning over, I push up the sleeve of his T-shirt, exposing the tattoo. "Eight homes, huh?" He looks down at the tattoo, at my fingers tracing the number. "That was a pretty impressive speech today."

"I just want those kids to know they shouldn't give up. They get knocked down so many times, it can be hard to get back up. But life gets easier when you have a plan. Back ups to the back up."

"What do you mean?"

"Like with hockey. I've been drafted already and if everything goes well in the play-offs, I'll be in New York next season, but if it doesn't, I'll have my degree and my portfolio."

"That's smart." I sink into the couch. "Take it from someone who has no back-ups. No degree. No career. No skills."

"Bullshit." He scoffs.

"What do you mean, 'bullshit?'"

He smirks, and I have no doubt it's because of my swearing. I think he likes corrupting me. "You have plenty of skills."

"Cleaning up after hockey players doesn't count."

"That's not what I was going to say," he argues. "You're an amazing cook, and you're good at taking care of people. You have an instinct for it. That's why Mike hired you on at the Badger Den. It's not as easy as it seems."

"I already know I'm looking down the long barrel of being a housewife, Reid, no need to rub it in."

"Hey." He grabs me by the waist and drags me onto his lap. "Those are important things. Critical, if you ask me and not everyone has it." He brushes my hair off my shoulder and lifts my chin until I'm looking into his eyes. "All I wanted growing up was for someone to offer a little comfort and stability. Don't underestimate those qualities."

I shake my head. "Wow."

"What?"

"Only you could make taking care of others sound sexy."

His lips curve up and his hands grab my ass. "Everything you do is sexy, GG. It doesn't matter if you're baking delicious food, serving beer down at the bar, or have your lips wrapped around my cock." He presses a kiss against my neck and I shiver. "I knew the second you walked in that door and sat on my lap, you were more woman than I'd know what to do with."

"Same," I confess. "About the moment I saw you."

"Not a minute has passed in every single day since you crawled in my lap and kissed me that I haven't been thinking about you."

I swallow, processing that information, finally exhaling, "Wow."

"Too much?" he asks, looking slightly concerned.

"Not for me."

The big issue hovers around us–the fact I'm leaving in a week and even if I wasn't, he has a career in his future and back-ups and I'm not part of either of those. So I do the thing that started this all: I kiss him.

REID'S ALARM goes off a lot sooner than either of us would like. After a weekend off, Coach Bryant calls for an early practice, in preparation for the playoffs. Reid is gone by daybreak, but not before his hands, and his cock, find me again. I love how he handles me. Firm, like he knows I can take it. I've spent a lifetime being treated like I'm fragile and the way he pulls me to him, the way he *enters* me. I'm still feeling it long after he's left the bed.

I'm also left with the weird knowledge that I'm no longer a virgin and despite all those years of hearing about it being so special and sacred, something for only me and the man that chose me, nothing seems very different, other than the urge to do it again.

Is that what happens? You become consumed? Because yeah, I feel consumed.

The door clicks shut downstairs and I take a minute in the bathroom before heading downstairs. Twyler has just walked in, key in hand.

"Hey." I'm surprised to see her.

"Sorry to just barge in, but I saw Reid on the way out and he said it was cool."

"Oh?" I nod. "I just got up."

"I realized halfway to campus I left my backpack here on Friday night." She walks around the living room, past the empty tray of kolaches, searching for the backpack. "I know it's here somewhere."

We both enter the kitchen at the same time. We both see my leggings and underpants twisted up on the floor. I'm not experienced with the ins and outs of having a secret boyfriend, but even I know that the discarded clothing looks like one thing: sex.

My eyes draw up and the problem with Twyler is she has these big, blue, beautiful eyes that hide nothing. So it's obvious right away that she knows. And while my heart lodges in my throat, making me unable to speak, it's clear. *She* knows that *I* know that *she* knows.

I snatch them quickly off the ground and sputter, "These must have fallen out of the basket when I was doing laundry."

"Sure," she says, shifting awkwardly on her feet. "Laundry."

I don't speak. Because what would I say? Nadia is her best friend. And Axel is Nadia's boyfriend. And Axel can never. Ever. Know.

But I also need to talk to someone about it, because all of this is big. Really big.

"Reid and I are..." I don't have the word. What are we doing? Nadia would have the word. Hooking up? On the down-low? Friends with Benefits? "Close."

"Okay," she says, seemingly okay with just that information. "How long has this been going on?"

"For a few weeks, I guess." I ball the leggings up and clutch them against my stomach. "Axel doesn't know. He *can't* know."

"God no." She barks out a laugh. "Absolutely not."

That reaction makes me feel both better and worse.

"So you two?" she asks, eyes darting to the leggings.

"Yes," I admit.

"Okay, wow." I can see the wheels turning as she processes it. "He's your first?"

"Yes." I swallow. "Last night."

Her jaw drops. "Tell me he didn't do it here. In the kitchen! I swear to god, I will castrate him–"

"No! No, not here. In the bedroom. His bedroom, on a real bed, not the couch in the porch." I glance over to the counter. "Down here was just..."

"Ah. Foreplay."

"I guess."

She nods, still clearly absorbing everything while occasionally saying, "Okay, wow. Wow. Okay." Finally, she leans her hip against the kitchen table. "And it was good? You're good?"

"It was great." I don't even fight the grin. "Both times."

She laughs and her shoulders relax. "That's the most important thing. Well, to me. Nadia would harass you for all the specifics but I believe in privacy, even though I've learned that is nearly impossible in this house." She makes a face. "But I know this is all new to you and I feel like it's my girlfriend duty to make sure you're okay."

"I'm fine," I tell her with conviction. "Reid's a good guy. He's always sweet and respectful."

"Thank fuck." Her expression grows serious. "I've had a shitty boyfriend before and Nadia has her own documented history of toxic partners. I love Reid and the more I think about it, I don't think this is even that much of a surprise."

"No?"

"You both just went through breakups and needed to get some confidence back. Why not do it with someone who is safe, fun, but also not really available for a long term thing?"

"Right." I agree, although I don't like the way that feels in my chest. I can't argue otherwise because I have no idea what we are to one another. Maybe that's all it is–two broken people looking for something safe to have fun with?

"There it is!" She shouts suddenly, leaning over and plucking her backpack from the seat of one of the kitchen chairs tucked under the table. "I've gotta run, but listen, I won't tell anyone about this. Not Reese or Nadia. Not until you're ready."

"Thank you. I really appreciate it."

She hitches the strap of her bag over her shoulder and opens the front door, pausing to add, "But let me tell you something from experience. Secret relationships have a way of getting complicated. And complicated things have a way of getting out."

23

———————

R^{eid}

I'M NEVER a fan of morning workouts. Or morning anything, well, other than sex. I'm a night owl, either staying up late to draw or watch TV.

"Dude, what the hell?"

My arms shake as I struggle to pull myself up. I get there, but I drop to the ground and reach for my water, taking a long gulp.

"What's up with you?" Jefferson asks, eyeing me suspiciously. We're taking turns on the pull up bar, challenging each other to do one more each rep. I'm keeping up–barely. "You go out last night? You look hungover."

Hungover from eating too many kolaches and having the best sex of my life.

Yeah, I said *best*. Sure, she was a virgin and was nervous. But being inside of her felt fucking incredible.

"I'm not hungover. I just didn't sleep great."

Even after Shelby and I went back upstairs, I couldn't settle down. Her body was too close–too warm. She felt so good there. Perfect. *Mine.*

"You know how he is when he's home alone," Axel chimes in. A reminder that he's always around and always listening. "Staying up late to watch those horror shows."

"I caught Twyler watching Murder ID last night," Reese rolls his eyes. "You know she gets wound up by genetic DNA."

We all pause to look at him, trying to figure out what 'wound up' means in this situation but as a group let it drop. It does give me an out though. "Yeah that's the one. I was hoping there was an update."

"I hope you watched it up in your room. You don't need to keep Shelby up by playing the TV outside her door."

"I didn't bother your sister," I tell him, hopping up to start my next rep. Anything to get out of this conversation. "I didn't even see her."

Axel grunts and I feel like shit. Guilty. Like what I'm doing is wrong. Maybe it's not honest, but it's not wrong. It's not like I can tell the truth and say that I'd spent the night taking your little sister's virginity. Because she asked me to. And again this morning. And, fuck, she's all I can think about.

Jesus, now isn't the time to get hard.

I focus on the pull ups, willing my boner under control, and listen to Reese. "I know I'm always going on about the playoffs, but I don't want to get ahead of ourselves. We're two games from clenching this and getting a top seed. One of those games should be a lock, but we've got to get through Milton first."

Milton U has always been a thorn in Wittmore's side. They're notoriously tough on defense and have an All-American power forward, Finn Austin, that has already been drafted to Toronto. There are few players out there that can compete with Reese's skill and leadership. Austin is one of them.

"Finish up your workout," Reese says, "go to class, hydrate, hook up with your girl–" he winks at Tolbert, "or guy if you need to, and everyone be on the ice at four PM."

"What if I can only fit in one of those things," Axel asks, toying with the ring in his lip.

"Then you better see if Nadia has time in her schedule," Jefferson jokes, throwing a towel at Ax's face.

"My girl always has time for me."

But it gets me thinking. I'm busy all day. Shelby's working tonight. There's no way I'm going to get time with her. With the clock ticking, I'm not sure I'm okay with that.

The guys rack their weights and wipe everything down before heading out for the day. Some change in the locker room, others head back home, pulling on sweats and jackets to make the cold walk across campus. Axel is pulling a beanie over his head when my phone buzzes with a text.

He picks it up off the bench and says, "Who's GG?"

"Dude!" I grab it from him and shove it under some clothes in my locker. "None of your damn business."

"Okay then," he holds up his hands. My heart shot straight up my chest and is making an attempt to escape through my throat. "Don't tell us."

"It's no big deal," I tell them, hating myself for lying. "Just a girl I met."

"Sure, okay," Jeff says, like he's not convinced.

Whatever. The less questions, the better it is for me. Neither say anything else and head out. Reese is always the last one to leave, so I linger a bit, fussing with my hair, waiting until it's just the two of us.

"So," I start, tossing a few things in my locker, "yeah, I'm kind of seeing someone."

He waits for a beat and then says, "Is it Dar–"

"No. Definitely not." I can't blame him for thinking it. I also realize, that's exactly what Axel and Jeff were thinking too. Let them. "It's new and I don't know where it's going to go so I'm not looking to make a big deal about it."

"I can respect that." He glances over at me. "So why are you telling me this? I'm your captain, not a priest."

God, this is awkward. "I was just wondering what do you do when things are rushed like this and you need a little time with Twyler?"

"Are you telling me you never were in this situation with Darla?"

"With Darla things were never..." I search for the word, "...intense?"

He snorts. "Desperate."

"Yeah, maybe. You know she was never into showing outward affection." As I talk, I feel like I'm just listing a series of red flags that I should have noticed. "But we also weren't being discrete. Not like you and Twyler in the beginning."

His jaw tightens and he looks around, as if he's making sure no one can over hear. After an exhale he says, "Room number one-ten."

"Room what?"

"One-ten. The athletic tutoring office in the student center." He slams his locker shut. "It's a good mid-day hookup spot."

I've been there before and I think about the couch. The work desk. Yeah, I can see it. "That's pretty smart."

"Well, don't you tell a fucking soul about it." There's not a trace of humor in his tone. "The last thing we need is every jock on campus hooking up in there."

"Gotcha." I pause. "If it's such a secret, then why are you telling me?"

"If you were going to see Darla, I probably wouldn't have. That girl..." he grimaces, and keeps whatever thoughts he has about her to himself. "I'm proud of you for moving on and finding someone new, even if it's just a rebound." It takes everything in me not to tell him this isn't a rebound, but the truth is that maybe it is? Hell if I know. He slings his bag over his shoulder and adds, "There's another reason I'm telling you about the room..."

"What's that?"

"You play better when you're getting laid."

~

REID: Morning. What are you up to?

GG: Making a new batch of kolaches. Someone ate the other ones.

I smile down at my phone as I cross campus and type: **I want to say I have no regrets but my body definitely felt our late night gorge fest during my workout**

GG: Sorry about that

Reid: Don't be sorry. It was perfect. Any chance we can meet up on campus before you head to work and practice?

Do I feel a little bit like a dirtbag asking Shelby to come to campus to hook up with me? Maybe. But there's just enough apprehension that she'll say no. That maybe she has her own regrets from last night. That fear fades when she replies.

GG: Where and when?

I'm fully aware of the smug grin on my face as I walk into class and it's still there an hour later when I walk into the student union. I'm early. Shelby shouldn't be here for another twenty minutes, so I use the time to grab some food from one of the vendors.

I've just taken a bite of my chicken wrap when I sense a disturbance in the force. That's right. Darla.

Without asking she pulls out the chair across from mine and sits.

"I'm meeting someone in a few minutes."

"This won't take long."

I raise an eyebrow. "What won't take long?"

"I still need to get that stuff back to you. Is there a good time for me to stop by the Manor?"

"Eh," I shrug, focusing on my lunch, "it's obviously nothing I've missed so, keep it, toss it, donate it to charity. Whatever is easiest."

She looks a little taken aback by my aloofness, but I'm pretty surprised myself. Just a few weeks ago seeing or talking about her came with complicated feelings. Now? I just want to finish my lunch and go meet Shelby. But Darla has always liked everything tidy and neat. Organized. And having something un-finished has to be bothering her.

Good.

"I've heard that after a month of chasing puck bunnies, you've been pretty MIA." She leans back in the chair. "Is something going on?"

I laugh. "If there was, would you have the right to know?"

"I just worry about you."

I set down my wrap, my appetite gone. "Really?"

"Just because I didn't see a future with us together, doesn't mean I don't care about you. I know the breakup was hard, and the last thing I want is for you to spiral."

I'm surprised. No, I'm fucking stunned. Does she really think the reason I haven't been around is that I'm not over her? It takes everything in me not to tell her I've got someone in my life, even if what we have is temporary, that makes the pain of our break up nonexistent. It proves to me that it's worth fighting for more than a girl that never wanted what I did.

I should keep my mouth shut and just walk away, go find Shelby and move on. But Darla sits in front of me with that expression of fake concern and I snap. "Why did you do it? Why did you pretend you wanted the same thing I did? The long term commitment? The engagement? Why did you not only go along with it, but encourage it? Was everything just a game?"

I hate myself for asking all of those questions, but I'd been holding onto them for too long. I shouldn't be surprised that she has an answer ready. "College is for experimenting. For trying on new things. You were different from the guys I dated before."

"So you thought you'd try on a jock for a few years, lock him down, and then bail?"

"That's the thing, Reid, I always thought you were more than just a jock. You're an incredibly talented artist who could do so much more if you put in the effort."

For most women, making it to the top level in professional sports would be a turn on. For Darla, it's a detraction. I've always been creative, all those hours of sketching and drawing as a kid, helped me develop a real talent. Darla helped me explore that further with fashion. It's not that I don't love those things, but I love hockey too. I love my team. I love the thrill of it. She's the one that can't handle that there is more to me than just one thing.

It takes everything in me not to gloat about the opportunity I have with designing the Wittmore logo, but I keep it to myself. It's not for her to ruin or to claim some kind of ownership.

"Don't pretend like things would be different if I chose a different career path. It's not about what I do that matters to you. It's who I am. I was never good enough for you long term, and you won't admit it."

It's the biggest challenge I've probably ever presented her and in the end she doesn't bite.

"Reid, in three months you'll be in New York somewhere busy with hockey. Sitting in the stands and waiting while you travel around the country, that's not who I want to be. You know that I've never had any interest in being a WAG." She shoots me a sad grin. "But that didn't mean we couldn't have fun for a while."

And there it is. She never supported my goals and dreams. She was just wasting everyone's time. I stand, pushing my chair back and grabbing my trash. I look down at her. "Here's the thing. It hurt when you dumped me, not because we were over but because I realized I let myself get fooled into believing you wanted the same thing that I did. I was honest with you. I told you what I wanted for my future, and you played along, all the way down to designing a goddamn ring. And it turns out you never wanted it. You never even wanted me. That all of it was just some kind of game. That's next level crazy."

Instead of acknowledging this she just shoots back in a patronizing tone, "Reid, there's a girl out there for you. Someone who wants the same thing you do, it may just take a while."

From the corner of my eye, I notice someone coming our direction, then double-take when I see that it's Shelby. Her gaze darts to Darla, and there's a beat where I'm unsure of what is about to happen. That is, until Shelby shifts her focus back on me and gives me a slow, sweet grin.

"Hey, babe." She walks right up to me and presses a warm kiss against my throat before curling into my side.

"Hey," I blink, then instinctively wrap my arm around her, pulling her tight, "beautiful."

"Sorry I got held up. The Manor was a mess after last night." Her hand flattens on my stomach, fingers curling into my sweater. A ripple of warmth spreads from the touchpoint. "You been waiting long?"

"Nope, just finishing up."

"Hi," Darla says, standing. "I'm Darla."

"Nice to meet you." Shelby grins politely. "I'm GG."

If my mind is blown right now, then Darla's is in full nuclear meltdown. My ex stares at us in disbelief, her eyes narrowing slightly as she tries to place her. She may sense the familiarity, but her irritation of... what? Me being happy? Me having someone in my life? Me moving on? Seems to have disrupted her narrative of what is going on in my life.

"GG," she repeats. "Well, that's cute."

"A nickname," Shelby says, grinning up at me, like we share a secret.

"I'm glad you're doing better," Darla says, not sounding glad in the least. For someone very over me she sounds a little annoyed. "Good luck."

I don't wish it back, instead letting her walk away while I focus on the girl glued to my side.

"That," I say, once Darla is out of earshot, "was very impressive."

"What was?" she asks innocently, still glued to my side. There are people milling around us, most paying no attention, but I know my status on campus. Someone will notice, and I hate to say it, but I don't give a fuck.

"Rolling up on me like a badass, being possessive and slightly petty. That's next level. I'm not even sure Nadia could execute a scene like that with such skill." I run my hand up and down her back. "Where did you learn that?"

"You forget where I grew up," she says, accent sweet as honey. "And there's no one better at being passive aggressive while staking our claim than a southern church lady."

24

———————

S helby

IF I THOUGHT I could just pretend like the deadline for returning home wasn't fast approaching, I woefully underestimated my mother's persistence. Out of patience with my need for space and time, she's been calling every day, usually more than once. There's no discussion, just a reminder of my flight the next Saturday, the engagement party the following week, and the many details that need to be addressed the instant I get off the plane. Never mind the unpleasant fact I'd broken up with David. This was just a minor inconvenience that would resolve itself. After all, a promise is a promise.

I don't know if it was her doing or if David sensed some disturbance in the universe when Reid and I had sex, because after weeks of not hearing from him, he called as well. His message was long and rambling, with a quasi non-apology.

Too bad I've been too busy floating on an orgasm induced high to respond.

In fact, I blame the most recent one, provided by Reid's tongue in room one-ten, for fogging my brain so much that I answer the phone on my way to the Badger Den without checking the name on the screen.

"Shelly-bean!"

"Daddy?" My father's voice is a shock. He usually leaves the phone harassment to my mother due to his busy schedule.

"You're a hard girl to catch," he says, going straight for the guilt.

"I've been busy." I take a deep breath and steady myself. "I have a job."

"I've heard." The disapproval is noted. "A waitress in a sports bar?"

"Hockey primarily. They're very supportive of the team." I step around a pothole filled with dirty rainwater. "Axel knows the owner," I add, which I know in my father's eyes doesn't mean much. "But they serve good food. It's a nice place."

'Nice' may be a bit overkill for a place with sticky floors and smells like decades of sealed-in fried food, but it's not like he'd ever step foot in a place like the Badger's Den so a little embellishment won't hurt.

"Shel, I've tried to be understanding about your need for reflection. You're not the first young person who felt the pressures of adulthood too soon. The need to take a journey, spread your wings, and consider your future is ingrained and there are many passages in the bible to support that. I have prayed for your mother to have patience, and I have prayed that you would see reason."

"Daddy–"

"I need you to listen and not speak." His tone is sharp. Stern. I've rarely been on the other side of it, but I've heard him speak this way to my brother more times than I can count. "I can appreciate that this moved faster than you were ready, but as your father, it is my role to protect you and make sure that you are positioned for a good life. That doesn't just include the man you bind yourself to for eternity, but it includes the smaller things. Where you live. How you live–"

"Are you going to pick out the wallpaper the way you picked out my ring?" I can't take it anymore. "I've given you everything since I was a child, Daddy, but not everything–every decision–belongs to you."

He sighs. "The home was a gift. A surprise. I'm sorry you can't see that. The ring? I thought you would like it. David is a good man, but admittedly, not the most creative. He comes from a good family, will be a responsible, safe, respectable, god-fearing husband to you and a worthy addition to Kingdom. Rejecting him is like rejecting me."

His words cut. Years of belief and loyalty war against the new found freedom of the past few weeks. "Is that how you really see it?"

"Of course." His tone softens. "And it's how I raised you to see it too. I'm not trying to control you, Shelby. I'm trying to protect and guide you, like I always have. Your mother? She just wants to make all of this as special as she can. It's important to her. Come home and work things out with both her and David. He loves you and has been patient, but a man can only take so much defiance."

His tone may be soft but his words land hard, like a punch. Tears build in my eyes and I brush them back, hating that it's so easy to get this reaction out of me. Why do I care what he and my mother and David think about me? Why is the temptation to go back to the familiar so strong?

"We'll see you this weekend," he says, then ends the call.

As uneasy as I feel from the call, one thing is certain. That wasn't a request. It was an order.

It's a long shift after the phone call with my dad, but at least the bar is busy. Wittmore isn't playing but they are showing another game, and that brings in the locals wanting a place to hang out and watch. The constant stream of orders, delivering food and drinks, and the sound of the game give me plenty of time to consider all the things my father said.

And just how pissed it makes me.

"Two bottles of Honey Dew," I tell Mike as I pass the bar, and then to the kitchen I toss out, "and a basket of cheesy fries. Extra cheese."

"You're a ray of sunshine tonight," Mike says, filling up one glass and then the other.

"I haven't seen a piece of the sun in two weeks," I reply, leaning against the counter. I've grown to love Wittmore, but this weather sucks.

"She's just sad that she's leaving us in a few days." Josie swoops around the bar, tossing empty bottles into the recycling. "No wait. That's me."

I give my friend a sad smile. That's how I feel about everything. Sad and a little angry.

Leaving Texas was big. Refusing to come home when my mother told me to, was bigger. But speaking to my father and defying him directly? That's huge.

And it doesn't sit right with me.

None of this does.

"I'm going to miss you, girl," she says, wrapping her arms around me. "And if you ever want to come back, just tell me, and I'll make Mike give you a job."

Mike rolls his eyes at Josie's confidence but he doesn't disagree. He just pushes the beer toward me and I carry them out to the customers.

When the game is over, Mike cuts me loose, and I grab my stuff from the back. Slinging my bag over my shoulder, I call out, "Night everyone," and head to the door where I'm surprised to see Axel waiting.

"What's wrong?" I ask, taking him in.

"Why do you think something's wrong?"

"Because your jaw is so tight that there's a big knot at the back and that tells me you're freaking out but trying to stay calm," I push past him, out into the cold night. So. Freaking. Cold. "So what is it?"

"Can't a guy come walk his sister home from work?"

"Yes, but I know that's not why you're here." After the call with my Dad, I'm expecting the worst. "Spill."

"I heard something today."

"From Dad? Because–"

"No. Not from Dad." He gives me a look, like he has questions but he continues on. "I heard you were on campus. Kissing Reid."

"What?" I miss a step, literally almost falling off the curb. Axel grabs me before I can fall, and keeps me upright. "Who told you–"

"Doesn't matter." he shakes his head. "I came to you to ask for the truth. Were you on campus today with Reid?"

I take a breath, looking down at his hands as the wind whips my hair around my face. No scrapes or bruises on his knuckles, which can only mean one thing. He hasn't seen Reid yet–or Reid lied. "Yes. I was on campus. Yes, I saw Reid. Yes, I kissed him on the cheek."

"What the hell, Shelby?"

"It's not a big deal. I saw him talking to that girl–the ex. Darla?" I ask, playing dumb. "I've seen her picture in some socials. He looked uncomfortable, like he needed an escape, and I decided to give him one."

"By kissing him," he accuses.

"*On the cheek.*" I roll my eyes. "And acting like I was his new girl-friend. It was no big deal, I was just trying to be a friend helping him out. Nothing inappropriate."

That is the biggest lie of all lies ever told, because after that Reid took me down to room one-ten and showed me how much he appre-ciated me stepping in to save him. He was very, very appreciative.

Despite the freezing cold, my body is now officially warmed up. I look over at my brother. "Please tell me you didn't do something stupid. Like break his face."

His handsome, gorgeous face.

"No." He sounds bummed about it. "Nadia convinced me to talk to you first."

"Thank god for having a reasonable, smart, girlfriend in your life."

"She's awesome, right?" A grin quirks the side of his mouth. "So what was Darla saying to him?"

"I'm not sure, but he looked pissed. And sad."

"Fuck, I hate her."

"She didn't seem great."

"She's arrogant, and led him on for way too long. They constantly broke up and got back together. It was pretty obvious to all of us that she was going to break his heart, but he couldn't see it." He leads us up the path that goes toward Shotgun. "It sucks, because Reid really struggles with the concept of being good enough, and with Darla, he wasn't. Never could be."

"That's awful." I think on it, then ask, "Why wouldn't he be good enough for her?"

"I think growing up in foster care was rough. In and out of all those homes," he glances over at me, "can you imagine?"

I shake my head. "No."

Our family may not be perfect but we were definitely stable. Predictable, even. It makes me think back to what my father said today about David. Stability is one of the attributes my father sees in him.

"He craves what we had, I think. Two consistent parents. One home. A family that is always there for him. He thought he could have that with Darla, which probably isn't her fault. She's just living her college life and thought Reid would be a fun guy to date. But he got serious–fast–and she played along even though she knew she wasn't going to stick around." He shoves his hands in his pockets and gives me a pointed look. "My boy got played. *Hard.* I worry about him as much as I worry about you."

"Which is why you really don't want the two of us..." I let the sentence linger.

"Exactly." We walk up to the Manor. "You're both awesome, but you're also both going through some shit that needs to be sorted. Nothing good is going to come from the two of you rebounding off the other."

I stop at the bottom step of the porch. "But if we weren't rebounding you'd be fine with it?"

"Oh hell no." He cackles–a belly laugh, really. "Absolutely, positively, hell fucking no."

"Why?"

"Because he's a dirtbag hockey player, Shelly, and we're all scoundrels. Reid's one of my best friends, but if I find out he ever touched you for real, your ass would be on the first plane back to Texas before you could even blink."

"What about him?"

"Oh, I'd kick his ass," he assures me, "but not until after the season is over."

I think for a moment, consider confessing everything, just to blow his mind. But I have no doubt he's serious about the plane. "You're ridiculous, you know that?"

He shrugs.

"Can I ask you something else?"

"Sure."

"How would you feel about me not leaving?"

He leans against the bannister. "You know I like having you around, but Mom isn't going to back off on this."

"Since when do you think someone should do what Mom says?"

He grimaces, but his issues have never been with mom. He and Dad are the ones that haven't ever seen eye to eye. "I think it's good you've broadened your horizons, but if you want this to be a long term thing, then you're going to have to go back and deal with everything. I didn't run away. I made a choice, had a plan, worked my way out of Texas. I'm graduating in a few months which means that even if you could stay, it wouldn't be with me, we'll all be moving out."

He's right, I have no long term plan. No education. No real job experience other than a part time waitress making tips.

"Right, I understand."

"But I'm not kicking you out either. If you need more time, you can stay with me and the guys. It's just–"

"Mom."

He chuckles darkly. "Yep."

I nod, and head up the stairs, trying to pretend the world isn't closing in on me.

"I just have one question," he says, catching up to me. "What were you doing on campus today anyway?"

I sure as heck can't tell him I was meeting Reid for an in between class hook up.

My new ability to think and lie fast astounds me. "I heard a rumor the taco shack on campus has the best nachos in town."

His eyebrow arches. "And?"

"Eh."

"Shitty, right?"

We both laugh, because these people up in the arctic have no clue about real Mexican food. Axel steps ahead of me and opens the door.

The first thing I see is Reid and Jefferson on the couch playing video games. Reid looks up at me, his brown eyes warming. The second? Over on the kitchen table, a giant bouquet of flowers.

"I forgot," Axel says, pulling his hat off his head, making his hair stick up more than normal. "Those came for you."

"For me?" I ask, a hollow feeling spreading in my stomach.

"Secret admirer?" Jefferson calls out.

I have a feeling I know who the flowers are from. They're pink roses, which aren't my favorite, but like my father said. David isn't the most creative.

Everyone is watching, so I pick up the little envelope and open it.

Can't wait to see you this weekend. I know once you're home we'll work this out.

—Love, David

Instead I glance at Axel. The sad smirk tells me he's already guessed.

"So?" Jefferson asks. "Is this the second secret relationship we learned about today?"

"Second?" I ask, shoving the card in my jeans pocket.

"Yeah, Reid's got his new girl." He punches Reid in the arm. "Gigi or something."

"Oh," I say, floundering for words. Reid's expression is carefully crafted into something unreadable. If I hadn't already talked my brother off the ledge about us being together, I'd be more concerned. "Mine isn't really a secret. It's my ex. David."

"He wants you back." Reid suddenly chimes in.

"I guess." He doesn't know about the calls. The pressure I'm under to return home and make things go back to how they were before.

"Makes sense," Jefferson says, turning back to the game. "You're cute as hell. He'd be a fool not to chase you down."

Axel snorts. "I'd love to see David chase anything other than my father so he can kiss his ass."

"Ax!" I admonish, but he's not wrong. "If y'all are done dissecting the love lives of everyone in the house, I'm going to shower, and go to bed. It's been a long day."

Skirting past the TV, I go into my little room and grab everything I need for the shower. Lifting my towel off one of the bike hooks, I pause, thinking of how much I love this crappy, cold porch. A lot of things happened here in a really short time. Most of it because of Reid.

On the way to the stairs, I have to circle around his side of the couch. As I pass I feel the heat of his fingers graze my leg. A shiver rolls along my skin and it lingers until I've got the hot water running, filling the room with steam.

I turn on some music and prop the phone on the little shelf next to the shower. This house is old, but the water pressure is amazing. A strong steady beat. I've just put my head under the stream and grabbed the bottle of shampoo, when I hear a soft click and see a shadow move on the other side of the curtain.

"Ax?" I wouldn't put it past him to invade my privacy.

A hand grips the curtain and I drop the shampoo with a clatter–a scream on the tip of my tongue.

Reid's face appears, eyes hungry and sweeping over my body. "You really should lock the door, GG."

I make a futile, ridiculous, attempt to cover my body. "*You* shouldn't sneak up on people."

"I wanted to see you." His voice is low, and I'm mesmerized by his tongue darting out and licking his bottom lip. "Fuck, you're gorgeous."

My nipples harden just from the way he looks at me—the way he *talks* to me. This isn't a man who is going to send me pink roses and a half-hearted apology. This is the man who is going to do everything in his power to get to me and claim me as his own.

"Where's my brother?" I ask, watching the way his fingers toy with the zipper on his hoodie.

"Video call with Nadia." His hoodie falls to the floor. "I turned on a documentary and shut my bedroom door."

"Jeff?"

The T-shirt goes next, and my fingers curl just wanting to touch him.

"In bed," he says casually, like he's not driving me wild, "probably jacking off to an Ingrid Flockton concert."

"Gross."

The jeans go next, buckle landing with a soft *chink.*

"You asked." He's naked now. Hand dropping to stroke down his thick erection. "And I'd be lying to say that if I couldn't get to you right now, I'd do the same."

I swallow, watching him step inside the shower. "You'd be jerking off to Ingrid Flockton?"

"There's only one woman I fantasize about," he steps under the water, reaching for the bottle of body wash, "and she's right here."

Everything in this moment feels scandalous.

From the slippery heat of the water, to the way our bodies touch in a million different nerve points, to the fact my brother and Jefferson are just outside in their rooms. Reid lathers the blue-green soap into his hands and flattens his palms over my breasts. My back arches, but he slides a hand around my body, drawing me back to him. Leaning down, his mouth claims mine warm, wet, and slick.

I'm most aware of the hard line of his cock pressing into my belly, and I reach down to touch him. "Jesus," he exhales, hand gathering my hair in his fist. "That feels so good."

"Yeah?" I can barely speak. I let my hand do the work, stroking up and down his cock.

"Everything you do feels amazing," he tugs on my hair, "turn around."

I spin, careful not to get our feet tangled up in the small space. Reid's hand glides down my back, cupping my ass. The water rushes between us, and he takes my hands and flattens them against the tile. Twisting, I watch him soap up again, coating his shaft.

His cock settles between my legs, sliding in and out slowly. The tip knocks against my clit, sending a dull ache in my lower belly.

"I'm on the pill." The admission comes out in a rush. He looks surprised. "To regulate my period, so if you want to..."

"Yeah?" His eyebrow arches, but his eyes are glued to my mouth. Tipping my face toward his, he kisses me again. "Because I want to fuck you so bad."

My body melts and part of me knows that this is because we don't have much more time together. I want to experience everything I can with him, every last touch and emotion. I let him take over, nudging my thighs apart with his knee. Grabbing me by the hips and tilting my ass so he gets a better angle. I'm putty in his hands, muscles warmed by the hot water. His hips rock, sliding his cock against my pussy, drawing us into a steady rhythm, until his arm wraps around my waist, dragging me hard into his body. The head of his cock nudges my entrance, and in one swift move, he's inside, groaning in my ear. "You're so goddamn tight."

Despite what he says, there's little resistance, my body ready for him. The angle is different. *Deep.* Unsteady breaths rush from my lungs as he thrusts into me. I find myself wanting more, wanting him deeper, and shift my body to let it happen. Both of his hands land on my hips, giving me what I want, one delirious punch at a time.

The current of energy between us builds and soon I feel the addictive tingle I haven't stopped chasing since Reid gave me my first orgasm. "You close?" he asks in a whispered grunt.

I nod, the water, now running cool, hitting my back. I barely notice a different wave washing over me, one that threatens to carry me under. One that I feel in every bone in my body.

Reid comes a split second after me, our bodies in lockstep. It's different this time, I feel him when he comes, the rush of slick heat making me feel even more full. "Oh god," I moan, the edges of my vision growing blurry. If Reid wasn't holding me up, wasn't keeping me upright, I would have slid to the bottom of the tub.

But he is.

He never lets go of me, not for a moment. Not even after he pulls out and washes us both off with the chilly water. His hands are on me as he bundles me in a towel, wrapping it tight around my body and then pulling me against his chest.

"I know things are weird right now," he tells me, voice still low. With the shower off, all we have is Ingrid's voice covering our own. "That shit is up in the air with your family, and your dumbass ex is sending you flowers. He wants you to come home. Like Jefferson said, he'd be a dumbass to not chase you down."

I tilt my face to look up at him. His hair is wet, water droplets beading at the tips. "Reid, I'm not–"

"I need you to know something," he cuts me off, "I didn't expect you. Not when you showed up on the porch. Not when you crawled in my lap and kissed me. Not the first time you wore my jersey. Not tonight. Not any of it. Ever."

I nod, my throat growing thick with emotion, feeling the same.

"Whatever happens, Shelby Rakestraw, I want you to know that I love you. I want the best for you, even if it's two-thousand miles away."

"Reid–" I try again, but he bends and kisses me. Not hard and passionate. Not desperate and needy. Sweet. Gentle. Understanding.

He pulls back and adds, "I won't beg another girl to stay if it's not the right fit." His jaw locks tight. "You taught me that I'm better than that."

With a towel wrapped around his waist, he exits the bathroom and a moment later I hear his door shut, followed by the click of the lock. I have a million things to say to him, but he's right. If today has taught me anything, I need to figure out my life, before I hurt anyone else.

25

R eid

AFTER SLEEPING LIKE SHIT, I woke up feeling like I'd been run over by a truck. Was I hungover? I wish. This, apparently, is what it feels like to let the best woman I've ever met go–if she wants it or not.

I'm not trying to be a martyr. Or act like this is the product of some miscommunication. I know Shelby is confused. What we agreed on was for me to help her explore a little. Gain some experience. The plan had never been to fall for her.

It's obvious she's being torn in two directions. When I got home and saw the flowers from David, everything slammed into me. Her ex is still very much in the equation. Her time was temporary, break up or not. She got what she needed and I'm glad I could help with that. When I went into the bathroom, I had no clue that would be the last time we had sex. Being in her like that, feeling her tighten around me and take every last drop.

Something in me broke. I confessed my feelings and let her go.

Shitty move? Maybe. But she deserves the truth, and I need to walk away before I get in any deeper. Darla fucked me up. No, my whole goddamn life fucked me up. For once I'm walking away first.

Even though it's early, when I get downstairs, Axel is already down there, pacing, phone in hand. I head straight for the coffee, which thankfully is already brewed and waiting.

"What do you mean you're at the airport?"

I fill my cup and frown, gaze sliding over to the porch. The door is ajar. He walks over to it and opens it wide, making a silent gesture. It's immediately obvious that all of Shelby's things, her suitcase and other belongings, are gone.

The hit to the chest lands harder than taking a direct hit from a puck Reese fires off at ninety-miles an hour.

"She's gone?" I ask, feeling the world tilt. I knew it was coming, I just thought we'd have a few more days. Maybe everything I said last night nudged her to follow her heart.

Or maybe it was telling her that I loved her.

"Okay. Fine. Call me when you land." He hangs up. "Yeah, she's gone."

"When?" I ask, mind spinning. "The middle of the night?"

"Beats me. I got down here and her door was open. I went to check on her and everything was gone. She changed her ticket, deciding to go home a few days early." His gaze flits over to the flowers, just like mine had a minute before. "Fucking David. Messing with her head."

He's not wrong. David's flowers sparked this, but not in the way he thinks. This one is squarely on me. I can't help but think it's for the better–before either of us went deeper than we already had.

"I know you guys think we'll miss it," Jefferson says, ambling down the stairs. His hair sticks up in the back from sleeping too hard, and he rubs his face, "but I'm not going to miss these morning practices."

"You think you're not going to have morning practice in the NHL?" I ask.

"It'll come with a paycheck," he replies, heading straight to the freezer for a bag of frozen fruit for his smoothie. "What are you two doing anyway?"

"Shelby left," Axel says. "Packed up and went home."

"Didn't she have a few days left?"

"Yeah."

He grabs the blender and starts tossing things in. Almond milk, fruit, ice. "What did you do?"

I open my mouth to defend myself but he's looking at Axel.

"Nothing," he says, but there's a hint of defensiveness. "Fine. I went to pick her up from work last night and confronted her about Reid."

I gag on my coffee. "Me? What?"

"Chill out. You got busted hanging out with her on campus yesterday but she told me the truth." He makes a sympathetic face, and says, "Darla," as if that explains everything. "But we also talked about a few other things, like handling everything back home. She wasn't going to be able to run forever. I guess she decided to deal with our mother sooner than later."

"Sucks, because she was cool and made a mean casserole, but we've got to focus on the game tonight." He sets the lid on the blender. "I'm with Reese. Let's lock in the division so we can skip straight to the playoffs."

He slams his finger on the button, the whirring of his smoothie blending filling the air.

Shelby left, I think, and we've got a game to play.

Life moves on.

"I DON'T WANT to see one smile. Not one congratulations. *Not one* celebration." Coach Bryant is seething, his eyeballs bulging in a way that can't be healthy. "Not after the shit show I just witnessed out there!"

The locker room is hot. Sweaty. Not one of us has taken off a pad, a skate, or jersey. I've got an ice pack held against my rib where I got slammed into the boards in the third period about fifteen seconds before I got tossed in the bin.

Sure, we came out of the match up as the victor, but barely. And it was supposed to be an easy win.

"It doesn't matter how many shots Cain or the other forwards get, if the defense isn't doing their job, it's pointless."

The vagueness of his accusation is a joke. There was only one defender fucking it up out there. Number eight, Wilder.

"You show up to the game against Milton on Saturday with that kind of performance, we may as well hand that trophy over right now." I feel the heat of his gaze on me, and I look up, forcing myself to meet it. "What I saw out there tonight wasn't what champions look like. Not even close."

He storms out of the room, and the other coaches and trainers follow, leaving us in silence. There's nothing worse than getting put on blast by the coach, but even worse after a win, because that means we didn't earn it. And that sucks.

Taking a deep breath, I stand up, wincing at the pain in my side. "This one is on me," I say. "That penalty came at a critical point. I was pissed at the hit, but I was slow getting back to the box in the first place. My head wasn't in the game."

It hasn't been anywhere productive in the last few days.

"It's not your fault, dude. McMaster slammed the shit out of you."

"He's lucky they got him off the ice before I got down there," Axel says, obviously still pissed. "That was a bullshit call."

It wasn't and we all know it, but what's done is done. "Anyway, I'll take the heat for that one, and I promise to have my head on straight by Saturday."

Because they're good guys and I have way more good games than bad, they seem to believe me. Still, I wait and let the other guys shower before me, and then I let the spray rain down on me for as long as the water stays warm. My entire body aches, and it's not just from the bruise. I've felt like this for days–ever since she left.

When I come out, thankfully, the locker room is empty. Hopefully the fans will be gone outside too.

The bruise helps make me take my time, the tissue soft and painful. I'm moving slowly down the hall when I hear voices in the training room. Peering in, I see Reese up on the table, while Twyler fusses with his wrist. "See? This is why I don't trust anyone else with your body but me. This wrap is shit."

He laughs with amusement at his overprotective girlfriend, then leans in to steal a kiss. A flicker of jealousy twists in my chest. These two are an odd match, but also perfect in their own weird way. I'm glad they found one another, but I can't help but want that for myself. No games. No pretense. Just true love.

Twyler had pushed up on her toes to return the kiss, but when she drops back down her eyes open and that's when she spots me.

"Reid," she exhales, "Jesus."

Reese shakes his head, probably more annoyed at being interrupted than anything else.

"Sorry" I apologize, not intending to be a voyeur. "I was just heading out. Thought I was the only one left."

As I lean my forearm against the door frame, Twyler tracks my movements.

"Come here," she demands. "Let me check that bruise."

Reese slides off the table, making room for me to hop on. It hurts too fucking much, so I prop my hip against it instead, setting down the ice pack and lift my shirt.

"Yikes," she says, eyeing the spot that has already started to purple. "This is pretty gnarly."

"It's fine."

She rolls her eyes and presses her fingers against the bruising. I wince and tell her, "Coach Green already checked for any broken ribs or other problems. He said to ice it and rest."

She grunts, and turns to her kit, fishing around for something.

"So you want to tell us what's really going on?" Reese asks. "Why the bad attitude and quick temper?"

"Nothing. It's just been a shit week." He doesn't look convinced so I try again. "I think the pressure is getting to me. You know how it is."

I catch Twyler frown, but she just plucks a tube out of the kit and turns back to me.

"Did you end things with the new girl?" Reese asks.

You could say that. All Axel could say is that she got home safe. Otherwise, none of us have heard a word from her. I could reach out to her–should–but I'm the one that told her to go.

"What new girl?" Twyler asks, eyes moving slowly from me to her boyfriend.

"Nah. That wasn't a big deal anyway." I ignore Twyler's question completely. "I'm just busy with classes and the design project for the athletic department. Too much shit coming up all at once."

Reese nods. Twyler holds up the tube, gesturing for my hand, and asks again, "What girl?"

"Some girl he's been hooking up with," Reese answers for me. "No one has met her."

"Is she a secret?" she asks, squirting a dollop of cream into my palm. "Rub that in."

"No," I say quickly. Too quickly, because her eyes narrow in suspicion. "Like I said, it's no big deal."

I busy myself rubbing in the cream, letting the tingling sensation spread. It's a numbing cream, something to dull the pain. "So," she says slowly, "you had a crap week, stopped seeing your mystery girl, and played like ass."

"That about sums it up."

Her arms cross over her chest and her hip pops out. "Reid."

"Twyler." I lift an eyebrow.

We stare at one another, and I'm not exactly sure what is happening between us, but a sheen of sweat coats my neck.

"What is this?" Reese asks, picking up on the strange energy. "What's happening here?"

"Hell if I know," I shoot back.

But I'm starting to think that Twyler knows something she shouldn't. Something that could blow my whole world up. But that's the thing. There's only one person that wants Wittmore to win the championship more than Reese.

His girl.

"I think I know why Reid is playing like shit all of a sudden," she says, tone dripping with accusation.

"Yeah?" Reese asks, looking me over, like he's searching for an injury. I mean, there is, but no one can see a broken heart. "What's wrong?"

"Tell him," she says, lifting her chin. "*Tell him* or I will."

Shit. She knows.

I swallow, realizing there's no way out of this. I look at my buddy and say, "The girl I've been seeing... she's, uh," words fail me, because I feel like the biggest asshole ever. I look at Twyler for help.

"For Christ's sake," she sighs, throwing her hands in the air. "It's Shelby."

"Shelby?" Reese looks shocked. "You've been...Dammit. *God dammit*, Reid. There was one girl you weren't supposed to mess around with and you had to–"

"I knew it!!" Axel shouts from the hallway. A range of emotions cross Axel's face, the final one landing on pure rage. His bag hits the floor, but a second later his body is in the air, diving at me. Before I have time to react, he hits me full force, and we both land on the floor. My bruise screams in pain and I bite off a curse, angling to protect my side. There's no way in hell I'd fight back, even if I could. "I'll murder you!"

His elbow rears back to slam, hand balled into a fist. I brace for it, but Reese gets his hands on him, lessening the blow. I shove him off, kicking him with my foot, but he's not done. He struggles against Reese, shouting, "You lied to me. You both did. Sneaking around under my roof. What the hell, man?!"

"It's not what you think–" I try to work my way to a sitting position and Twyler squats down to help.

"Don't you dare say you didn't fuck her."

"Ax, come on," I start, but I'm barely sitting upright when he escapes Reese and lunges at me again. Twyler yelps, hopping up and out of the fray, and I manage to dodge his fist. "Calm down and let me expla–"

Cold water rains down from above. And we both scream in surprise. The shock allows Reese to get his hands on Axel again, dragging him across the room. I push the soaking wet hair out of my eyes, and look around. Twyler stands over us, a jug of water in her hands.

"Son of a bitch!" Axel shouts, body shuddering.

"Smart move, Sunshine," Reese says, grinning at her, over the top of Axel's drenched head.

"My dad taught me this was the best way to get two dogs separated when they were fighting." She looks down at us, her expression smug. "Works on dumbasses, too."

Axel continues fighting against Reese, but way less effectively now that he looks like a drowned rat. Reese shakes his head and says, "Dude, listen, you can murder him all you want–"

"Reese!" Twyler shouts. "No. Murdering."

"But not until *after* the finals," he concludes.

Twyler opens a storage closet and tosses us both a clean towel. Slowly, with one eye on Axel to make sure he's not going to lose it again, I dry off. Axel takes a deep breath and says, "I asked her specifically if something was going on with you two and she said no."

Reese scoffs and says, "Gee, I wonder why."

"Shut up." Axel runs the towel through his hair, making the blond hair stick up in spikes. "You promised me."

"I know this sounds like bullshit, but I didn't plan on anything happening. She's a cool girl, who just wanted to experience life a little but had no idea how to go about it." The muscle in the back of his jaw tics. "She needed a friend. Someone who wouldn't judge her for being so..."

"Innocent? Virginal? Naive?"

"Oh my god." We both look over at Twyler. "Stop describing your sister in unrealistic, antiquated, sexist, virtuosic terms that you wouldn't be able to adhere to if your life depended on it." She shakes her head. "They like each other, Rakestraw, because they're both awesome people. Shelby could do a lot worse than a guy like Reid, who you know is a fucking good guy who treats women well. And after Darla," she shoots me an apologetic look, "sorry man, but Darla sucked..."

"I know. No offense taken."

She grins. "Shelby was the sweet, unassuming, down to earth girl Reid needed."

Axel scowls, but for once doesn't argue. "So how serious was this thing?"

I look to Reese to see if he thinks this is a trick question, but he nods for me to answer. "It started off pretty innocent. She was overwhelmed by the little bit of college life she had seen, no thanks to your girlfriend by the way," I snort. "She wanted to go home pretty much right away after a night out with the girls. I told her if she stayed and learned to experience life a little, I'd help her."

"You mean, help yourself into her pants."

"*No.*" I glare at him, holding his gaze. "I mean by helping her get more comfortable in her own skin. Taking her shopping, supporting her when she got a job, hanging out with her when she was lonely, and yeah, telling her that I thought her ex was a dipshit who didn't deserve her."

Axel crosses his arms defensively over his chest. "You mean all the shit I didn't do. Except the dipshit part. I said that plenty of times."

I look over at Reese and Twyler. "Can we have a minute?"

Reese raises his eyebrow at Axel. "Are you going to act civilized and promise not to break anything required to play hockey?"

"Yeah, I'm cool," Axel says, sounding like he means it. We'll see.

"We're going," Twyler says, glancing around the room, "and you better clean this up before you go."

"Got it, TG," Axel says, using his nickname for her, 'Trainer Girl.'

When we're alone, I look him in the eye. "You provided Shelby a safe place when she needed it. That's bigger than anything else. I know you know my background, but it's impossible for me to explain how much that means. Sure, Shelby was never at risk of being homeless or without at least part of her family, but leaving home, defying your parents and breaking up with David, it took balls. It was also pretty terrifying. She's brave."

A flicker of understanding crosses his eyes. "She's a Rakestraw."

"Yep." I nod. "She needed a little more support than you could give her, and at the time, I needed something too."

His fist clenches and for a minute I think he may come at me again, but just asks, "You treated her right?"

"You'd have to ask her that, but I didn't pressure her. If anything I let her take the lead as much as possible." He winces, ever the overprotective brother. And I feel like a fool but I add, "The night before she left. I told her I loved her." He looks up, surprised. "I also told her that I knew she had unresolved shit to deal with back home. I may have scared her and run her off. I may have fucked the whole thing up. I don't know, dude."

He grimaces and swears under his breath.

"What?"

"We both may have handled this the wrong way."

"What do you mean?"

"She asked me about staying and I told her that there was no use. My mother wasn't going to back down. Then the flowers came and..."

"And I said what I said," I finish.

We're both quiet for a beat, until I say, "Any idea how to unfuck this?"

"Yeah," he grins, the first one I've seen on him all night, "I think I do."

26

———

S helby

THE GRANDFATHER CLOCK ticks quietly across the room, the sound punctuated by the swish of the pendulum in the dark mahogany case. I'm at a small square table that my father often uses to read his devotion or write his sermons. When we were younger, Axel and I would sometimes do homework here, our books and schoolwork spread across the shiny top. Today the table is clear, save for four cups of tea and a leather bound binder sitting in front of my father. The other chairs are occupied by David's father and then David. It's the first time I've seen David since I returned home, and his first reaction is to dutifully pull out the last seat for me with nothing else but a placid smile on his face. Smoothing my skirt out under my legs, I sit, and brace myself.

It's time for the meeting.

When I'd showed up unexpectedly two days ago, dropped off by a ride-share at the front door, my mother's surprise at both my early arrival and the state of my clothing was evident. She'd looked distastefully at the sweater hanging off my shoulder and the snug jeans. But she just hugged me, told me she knew I'd come back, and sent me to my room to change.

I'd done very little since, other than avoiding my mother by sleeping and scrolling my phone for highlights from the Wittmore game. They'd won, but even I could tell it wasn't pretty. Everyone seemed frustrated when they came off the ice. Reid had taken a major hit during the game and a penalty after. It took everything in me not to text him to see how he was doing, but I'd left for a reason. I'd been way too entangled in Reid Wilder, way too fast.

I needed room to think. A couple thousand miles of room.

I could only hide for so long, and last night before bed I was informed that there would be a meeting with David's family in the morning. Attendance and appropriate clothing was expected. Which is why I'm in one of the below the knee dresses from my closet, pale blue with small flowers, and both of our mothers are in the kitchen preparing lunch for the families. More than anything that says how they expect this meeting to go. That fact does nothing to lighten the tension in the room. Or maybe that's just me.

"Thank you for coming," my father starts, his comments directed toward Reverend Jones and David. "I know this has been a trying time for both families. Your patience is appreciated."

"Of course," Reverend Jones's tone is gracious, "there is nothing we want more than to see this union between our families take place."

"Shelby, I believe the first appropriate thing to do would be to apologize to David and his father."

Apologize? I should've seen this coming.

I take a deep breath. "Running off was immature and disrespectful," I admit, even though I'm not sorry about it one bit. "I was feeling overwhelmed by the engagement plans. It was all moving so fast."

That were being made without any of my input, I don't add, ignoring the way my heart rate quickens.

My father is fully aware that there was no apology in that sentence, but next to me David gives me a small grin.

"That's understandable." Reverend Jones also looks at me kindly. "You wouldn't be the first young bride to get cold-feet, but it's important for you to remember you can rely on David. He'll be the head of your household. It's his duty to support you."

Those little details don't sit well with me, but Reverend Jones seems willing to accept any and all of this if we can just move on.

"I, for one," my father chimes in, "would like to move from the past and prepare for the future." He opens the leather binder, revealing a few sheets of paper. "I suggest we formally sign the paperwork and move on with this."

I stare across the table at the papers but can't read it. "What is that?"

"Just the marriage agreement." His tone is dismissive.

"Whose marriage agreement?"

"The one between you, David, and our families."

That feeling of anxiety creeps up my throat. It's been weeks since I felt it. I take a deep breath. "I haven't seen this before."

"Well, it's not for you to worry about, sweetheart. It's between the Jones' and myself."

The blood pumping in my body reaches my ears, a steady thump, growing louder with each beat. "So you two, set up a marriage agreement for me and David, without speaking to us?"

"There's no need for dramatics. It's similar to a prenuptial but with the values and virtues of our families."

In a feat of sheer willpower, because it takes everything in me not to go off, I turn away from my father and look at David. "Did you know about this?"

David blinks, but his expression is innocent. Confused. He looks to our fathers for assistance. I lean across the table and grab his face.

"Shelby!" my father exclaims.

"David, did you know about this?"

"I, uh, um..." he stammers.

"Oh, for fuck's sake. Did you know or not?"

"That's enough," my father roars, his patience and good demeanor worn thin. "That language will not be tolerated."

"Well, neither will this bullshit!" I snatch the papers off the table and back away as I start reading a section aloud.

"Must live within five miles of Kingdom on approved property.

Must be involved with the church five days a week.

All income and resources must be reported to the business manager of Kingdom.

All future children..."

I stop reading and glare at my father. "You're insane."

"No," my father says, his voice back under control. "I'm being pragmatic. With your brother having fled to live a life of sin and blasphemy, you and David will be the ones to inherit the Kingdom. I'm not just protecting your relationship, but my legacy. I'm aware that you've been on a rebellious streak, but it's time for that to end. Let's talk about this rationally."

"There's nothing rational about any of this!" Something tight in my chest unfurls. "I am an adult. You don't get to sign anything for me. You don't get to choose my husband, or where I live, or how many children I have."

The anxiety that has been building fades out entirely, turning into something else entirely: rage.

"David," Reverend Jones says, his voice obnoxiously calm, "why don't you take Shelby outside for some air. You two talk for a moment."

"Yes," I say, grabbing David by the arm, "I'll go outside with David, but not because anyone told me to, but because we need to talk."

David still hasn't spoken, but he doesn't fight me as I drag him past the table and out the French doors onto the patio. Inside, I can see our fathers trying to figure out what just happened, but I know exactly what just took place.

"What happened to you at Wittmore?"

I spin around and face David and finally take him in. He's still tall, cute, in those pressed khaki pants and blue sweater that brings out his eyes. He looks both confused and annoyed.

"I guess I had a chance to experience life a little." I try to make my voice firm. "And I realized that this isn't what I want."

"This," he repeats carefully.

"Yes. You. Marriage at barely twenty-years-old. A house next door to my father. A lifetime of servitude to him, you and Kingdom."

"This is your brother isn't it?" he asks skeptically, as though none of those thoughts could be my own. "He got in your head."

"Actually no," I can't help but laugh. "Axel is overprotective and a pain in the ass. He loves me, but he'd keep me in a bubble if he could."

"I know it was moving a little fast, but you know how our mom's are. We could probably get them to hold it off for a while." He takes a step toward me. "We're good together, Shelby. We could have a good life."

Good, sure. Boring, definitely. And it may not be fair, but there's no chance I could settle for a man like David after having a man like Reid Wilder.

Other than sending me flowers, which I can't be sure my parents didn't pick out, David hasn't even tried to fight for us. For *me.*

"I'm sorry," I tell him. "I didn't ever want to hurt you, and I don't think you're a bad guy just..." Weak. He's so freaking weak. I can't build a life with a man who doesn't know what he wants and how to take it. I slide my hand into the pocket of the dress and pull out the ring. "Here."

He takes the ring and frowns down at it. "You're serious about this?"

I nod, feeling both sadness and relief. "I'm sure there's another girl out there, probably right here at Kingdom, that will make you a good wife and partner."

I turn and walk back into the house, ready to tell my father to tear up the paperwork. He and Reverend Jones are no longer alone. My mother is there, along with David's mother, Carol. They both look up at me when I walk in the room, but my mother grabs me by the arm and drags me into the hallway.

"I understand you're having an extended tantrum, Shelby, but it's time to get yourself in check. This is your future you're talking about–and the future of Kingdom. David is–"

"Not my problem."

"Excuse me?" She looks aghast.

"The engagement and wedding are off. I've broken up with David and returned the ring."

"Do you know what you've done? How this will look?" She doesn't give me a chance to reply. "It'll seem like your father can't manage his own daughter, or the members of his congregation."

"It will look like he believes in free-will and is letting me choose my own path in life." I cross my arms. "I don't love David. I don't think I ever did. This whole relationship was orchestrated by Daddy and Reverend Jones and was going to continue to be managed by them as well. That isn't what I want."

"Since when do you think you get what you want?" A flicker of pain flashes in her eyes. "That isn't the role of a woman in this world."

"Well, it's going to be mine."

"This is your brother's fault," she rants, twisting the argument. "I never should have let you stay out there with him. Living in a house with four men, allowing you to get a job– in a bar of all places. It's unseemly and inappropriate for a woman your age! Especially when you're promised to get married!" My mother is a small woman, but right now she feels a million feet tall. Her anger and disappointment making her larger than life. For once, I'm not scared.

"Stop blaming other people for my choices, Mother." I want to scream in frustration, but I keep my temper in check. "That's the whole problem here. No one cares what I have to say or think! The decision to go out there was mine, just like the decision to come home and deal with all of this was too. Axel–"

"Did someone say my name?

We both turn to the doorway where my brother stands, hair wild, tattoos and piercings on full display. His tone may be light, but the expression on his face is serious, that jaw locked tight.

I recover first. "What are you doing here?"

"I came to bust up an engagement party, but," he looks between us, clocking the tension, "looks like I may be a little late."

"Not funny," my mother says, but she softens when she sees Axel. My mother may not approve of his lifestyle but he's still her golden boy.

"Are you sure?" he asks, walking over and slings his arm around my shoulder. "So what did I miss?"

I look up at him, feeling steadier just having him nearby. I have a million questions, but they'll have to wait. "Just the falling apart of the Rakestraw-Jones marriage agreement."

He makes a disgusted face. "That sounds terrible."

"Trust me, it was."

"That's enough," my mother says, glaring at me. "I can't believe you're willing to ruin everything over an act of petty rebellion."

"If that's all you think this is, Mother, then I've got nothing else to say."

She's the one that storms out of the room, tossing her hands up in frustration. Axel and I are alone. I take the first deep breath since all of this started and look at him. "Did you really come back to blow up my engagement party?"

"It would've been fun." He shrugs. "But you forgot something and I figured you may want it."

"But you have a game this weekend! The big one." I shake my head. "What could be so important that you came home right before the playoffs–" My jaw drops at the same time my heart surges up my throat. "You didn't."

"Up in your room." He nudges me down the hall. "I'll go distract the parents. Go."

"And you're okay with this?"

"As okay as I'm going to be with you dating anyone." He worries the ring on his bottom lip. "I don't know what's going on with you two, but I know Reid's a good guy. If you're not serious about him, let him down easy, okay?"

I lunge at my brother and he catches me in those big, tattooed arms.

"I love you, Ax."

"Ditto, sis."

He squeezes me once more and sets me on the ground and without another look back, I head up the curving staircase to the second floor. Downstairs, Axel handles the parents and I open the door to my bedroom.

Sure enough, he's here. Reid is standing in my room, among the pile of clothes and boxes. He's studying the books and trinkets on my bookshelf. He turns when I open the door, apprehension written on his face.

"What are you doing here?" I ask first, rushing in and closing the door behind me. I turn the lock.

"Well," he says, setting a figurine of a pig back on the shelf, "I *thought* I was coming here to make a grand gesture by swooping in and stopping your engagement party.

"Oh yeah?"

"Mmhmm. I was going to sweep you off your feet–not literally, because this bruise from the game the other day is about to kill me– but if it wasn't we'd ride away into the sunset on your horse."

"I don't have a horse?"

His forehead furrows. "Really? Isn't this Texas?"

"Yes." I bite back a laugh.

"Doesn't everyone in Texas have a horse."

"No."

"Shit," he rubs the back of his neck anxiously. "I did all of this wrong."

"No. Not all of it." I cross the room, desperate to get close to him. "The good news for you, is that it was already called off, so no need for a horse."

A smile hooks the right side of his mouth. "That *is* good news."

"And this seems like a pretty grand gesture to me. Flying out to

Texas, sneaking into the preacher's daughter's room." We close the gap. "We may not have a horse but Daddy definitely has a gun safe."

"Good to know." He reaches for me, but I catch him wince and mutter a curse under his breath.

Bending over, I push up his shirt. The bruise is awful. "Oh my god. Are you okay?"

"Nothing that won't heal." His arm wraps around me. "And it sure as hell isn't something that can keep me away from you." I look up at him and see his Adam's apple shift. "If that's what you want."

"I'm sorry I ran out like that." This is a man I'm willing to apologize to. "You and Axel were both right. I had stuff to deal with here, and avoiding it any longer wasn't right. It was time to face it head on."

"I assume that since the engagement is over you did that?"

"I did, although no one is happy about it." I take his hand, threading my fingers with him. "And I don't give a shit, which is something I never would have done before." His eyebrow lifts and he's so freaking handsome. "Meeting you opened up something inside of me that I didn't know existed. You showed me parts of a life that had always been either out of my reach, or I was taught to feel ashamed of. You helped me trust in myself, and know what it was like to truly be wanted."

He brushes the hair off my cheek. "I did all of that?"

"You did."

He dips his head down, grazing his nose on mine. "I never wanted you to leave."

"I know."

"And I meant it, I love you." The weight that Reid carries seems heavy on his shoulders. "I've spent my lifetime not being good enough for people and searching for my place. I found that with my adoptive family, and the team. I thought I had it with Darla and I was wrong. I couldn't handle being wrong about you too."

"You're not wrong," I tell him. "You're the best man I know, Reid Wilder. The kind of man I want to build a future with."

"Yeah?"

"I don't care if you're an artist or a hockey player or anything else.

I don't care about all of that. I just want to be with you." I link my arms around his neck. "I love you."

He tilts his head and kisses me. It's the best kind of kiss. The only kind of kiss I ever want to experience again, and I think I knew it the very first day we met.

We part slowly, and he looks around my room. "Your room is a lot messier than I expected."

"That's because I've spent the last two days cleaning and packing."

His eyebrow lifts. "Packing?"

"I didn't just come home to deal with my family and David. I also came to pack up the rest of my belongings." I nod over to the desk where a heavy coat is draped over the chair. "I needed a coat."

"So you're…" he prompts.

"Coming back to Wittmore. I know I can't stay at the Manor permanently, but since Mike said I can come back to work, I figure I can save money to get my own place." He grins down at me. "You know, if you guys are willing to let me stay for a while."

"GG, there is nothing I want more than for you to come back to Wittmore, but I'm not sure about you staying on the porch–"

"Oh. Sure." I interrupt. "I understand."

Axel would probably lose his mind anyway.

He lifts my chin, those brown eyes warming as he looks at me. "If you're coming back to our house you're staying in one place." His hand splays across my lower back, keeping me close. "And that's my bed."

27

—————

R^{eid}

I GREW up in a lot of homes. Nine, ultimately, if you consider the time spent with grandmother before she passed away and I entered the system. Due to that, I was intimately familiar with all kinds of inner family dynamics–especially the dysfunctional ones. I knew both Axel and Shelby had issues at home, but the vibe in the Rakestraw house was like nothing I've ever experienced.

Not only that, but holy shit, they're rich. I knew Axel's father was the head of a megachurch. I knew it was successful and streamed on TV and had a huge following. I'd been stunned when the Uber pulled up in front of the house. I understood better why Axel called it his father's little kingdom.

I'm not sure my NHL money could even compete with this. No wonder the security of coming back here had been a draw for Shelby. It would be hard to give up.

I hadn't thought about what we would do after we got to Shelby.

There was just one goal, getting out here and letting her know how much I want her. It was a risk. She could have made up with David. She could have been in the middle of picking out China patterns. She could have been pissed at what I'd said to her before she left. I didn't have much of a grand gesture planned other than maybe punching David in the face and begging Shelby to be my girl. Turns out, I didn't need one. GG had handled everything by the time I got here.

Not only that, she told me that she loves me and is coming back to Wittmore.

Thank fuck. I could probably do a long distance relationship, and once I get in the NHL we may have to figure that out, but having her close by, snug in my bed, is a win I'll take.

"How do you want to handle this?" I ask Shelby. This is her territory and her family. Things are rocky at the moment and I sure as hell don't want to make things worse.

"I don't want to hide this relationship any more," she assures me as we walk down the sweeping staircase. Axel texted that it was time to come out of hiding for dinner. "But I don't want to put you in the crosshairs. They're going to be upset. Daddy's little plan to keep me barefoot and pregnant while David worked with him in his ministry has been fucked up." I raise an eyebrow and she scowls. "You're a bad influence."

"I love it when you speak your mind."

"Yeah?"

"It's sexy," I say, dipping my mouth to her ear, "as fuck, GG."

She looks up at me and that charged heat between us comes roaring to life. No woman has made me feel the way Shelby does.

"Jesus Christ."

Axel stares up at us from the landing, disgust written on his face. "Mom and the Rev are in a mood so I'd keep the eye fucking to a minimum."

"Is that for their benefit or yours?" Shelby asks when we get to the bottom of the stairs.

"It's for everyone." He pauses and grabs me by the sleeve. "I told them I brought a buddy of mine with me. They think you were upstairs resting after the flight. They'll be on good behavior, because that's what they do, but unless you want shit to hit the fan, keep your goddamn hands to yourself while you're in this house, hear me?"

"Yeah, I hear you," I tell him. Shelby smirks at him, but it's good natured. I think we're both relieved the secret is out, at least with Axel.

Shelby walks off first, but Axel holds me back. "GG," he says, tugging on his eyebrow piercing, "that's the name you had her under on your phone?"

"Yeah."

"What does it stand for?"

I take a deep breath and look at my friend. "You really want to know?"

"No, but you're going to tell me anyway."

"It's my nickname for her. GG, for Good Girl."

A darkness flickers through his eyes and I brace myself thinking he may murder me after all. His jaw clenches and he just turns and stalks down the hall, saying, "You know? That's on me. I shouldn't have asked."

"Nope," I laugh, following him, "you really shouldn't have."

Like Axel said, his parents are all smiles and pleasantries when we walk in the kitchen. The vibe is still there. A current of tension mostly between Reverend Rakestraw and his children, but when it comes to me they're polite and ask me questions about my classes and my family.

"Reid comes from a family with seven kids," Shelby says, over the juiciest brisket I've ever had in my life. Damn, now I know why Shelby is an amazing cook.

"Seven?" The Reverend says. "That's quite a handful."

"It is," I take a sip of my sweet tea, "but they knew what they were getting into. They adopted each of us out of the foster system."

"Well," Mrs. Rakestraw says, clearly impressed, "that's a wonderful example of servitude."

"I think they just like the chaos."

For whatever reason, this topic seems to shift the mood. I suspect everyone is looking for something to talk about that isn't about the feud Axel has with his father or the fact Shelby blew up her engagement, which is why I've become the center of attention.

"Reid is also a talented artist," Shelby continues, reaching for my hand under the table. "The athletic department commissioned him to create the new logo for the hockey team and it'll be on all of the designs for the playoffs."

The Reverend takes a slow chew of brisket, followed by a bite of dinner roll, then he asks, "You're going to the playoffs?"

Axel blinks, realizing his father is speaking to him. "Uh, yeah," he glances at me, "we're a lock for the finals and if we win our game this weekend, we'll advance to the final six in Chicago."

Reverend Rakestraw doesn't say much past that and Mrs. Rakestraw takes over. "So you'll get a degree in graphic design then." I nod, mouthful of food. "I imagine you'll be looking for a job after graduation?"

"Actually, I have one. I've been drafted by New York. Art was a skill I was able to hone and develop no matter where I lived. And if I've learned anything over the last twenty years, it's that it's good to have a backup plan." I squeeze Shelby's hand under the table. "I grew up with a lot of instability and very little control over where or who I lived with. Security is important to me, although my adoptive family, my father in particular, has taught me to also follow my dreams."

The questions fall off there, and the tension returns. Mostly because Shelby's father's eyes ping between me and his daughter, like he's reading a map. It's a relief when dinner is finished. Shelby stands, grabbing plates to take to the kitchen. When she reaches the platter that held the meat, I touch her wrist and say, "I've got it."

"Reid."

I look over at Shelby's father. "Yes, sir?"

"I'd like a word in private, please."

"Sure, let me take this in the kitchen first."

"I'll be in the library."

I carry in the plates, and set them on the counter by the sink.

When I turn, Axel and Shelby are both in the kitchen doorway. He rolls his eyes. "I told you to cut out the eye-fucking."

"We weren't eye–" she swallows the word. "Shut up."

"Yeah, you were, and now that I know about it, it's all I can see." He looks at me. "The Rev probably just wants to save your soul or something. No matter what, tell him you're baptized. I don't want to go out to the creek tonight."

My eyes widen at that one but Shelby says, "Ignore him. Daddy isn't going to try to baptize you." Her nose wrinkles. "At least I don't think he will."

By the time I walk down the hallway toward the Reverend's office, I have no idea what to expect. I tap on the open door and when he calls for me to enter, I get a good look. He's sitting in a leather arm chair by the fireplace.

He points to the one next to him and says, "Take a seat."

I sit across from him, feeling the weight of his attention. "Thank you for having me for dinner," I say, ready to get to it–whatever 'it' is. "And I appreciate you letting me stay overnight."

"You seem to be a good friend of Axel's."

"He's one of my best friends," I tell him. "He's always got my back, on and off the ice."

He nods, "And my daughter?"

Ah, so not a baptism. I fight the urge to run my sweaty palms down the front of my jeans. "What about her?"

"Although I believe in miracles and divine intervention, I don't subscribe to coincidences." He pins me with a look, his eyes blue like his kids. "You showing up on the day that my daughter breaks off her relationship and announces she's moving back East seems a little timely."

"Your daughter has a mind of her own. You should be aware of that."

"She didn't used to," he says firmly. "Not until she ran away."

"Reverend Rakestraw," I lean forward, "would you like the truth?"

"Always."

I decide it's time to come clean. Well, clean-ish. I haven't forgotten the warning from Shelby that her father has a gun safe.

"I'd never met your daughter before she showed up in Wittmore, scared and overwhelmed. She was looking for somewhere to get a little solace and to think about her future, which is something that was never afforded for her before. Axel didn't hesitate for a second and neither did the rest of us that live in the house. He is very protective of her."

"I'm aware that my daughter feels like decisions were being made without her. She's correct. Some things are too important to be left up to the decision of the young, but even with her tantrum, I don't believe for a minute Shelby wouldn't have returned home and followed through with her plans if something hadn't changed."

"She's the one that changed."

He shakes his head. "Then why does she look at you like you hung the moon?"

I guess we really do suck at that eye-fucking thing. I could answer this and tell him that I gave Shelby the opportunity to explore life, that I supported her desire for experience and adventure. But those things are between me and her, not for someone else to exploit. I look Reverend Rakestraw in the eye and say, "Your daughter deserves a man that will fight for her. That'll help her realize her dreams. That'll give her a say in her life and future. She's more than a bargaining chip for your legacy. She, and anyone else that meets her, knows that."

"And what? A man with a troubled past and an unpredictable future playing sports is going to be able to support her and give her what she needs?"

"Shelby will give herself what she needs because she is a strong, capable, independent woman." I stand, signalling that I'm done with this discussion. "If I'm lucky, I'll get to spend my life with her, but that will be her choice. Not mine or anyone else's."

I exit the room, both nervous and feeling like I'd done the right thing. Also thinking I should probably go pack my bags because there's no way I'm welcome in this house for much longer. I start for the direction I think the stairs are in when I run smack into Shelby.

"Sorry." I steady her by grabbing her upper arms.

"You okay?" she asks.

"Yeah." I glance over my shoulder. "I'm okay."

"I heard what you said."

"You did?"

"Yeah, I'm a master of eavesdropping on my father in that room." Her arms wind around my waist. "Thank you for saying all of that. It's the first time anyone, other than Axel, has defended me when it comes to making decisions about my life and future."

"I hope I didn't overstep." This all feels new to me. I know we said we loved each other but we've never even been on a date. I don't want to screw this up. "I meant it, what you decide to do with your life is your choice."

"Good." She slides her hand up around my neck and tugs my face toward hers, saying, "Because I choose you, Reid Wilder," before brushing her lips over mine.

Every touch from her, every kiss, feels like I'm stepping into something new. I thought I was the one teaching Shelby how to experience a bigger life, while she taught me that sometimes the best things in life just show up at your door.

You just have to let them inside.

EPILOGUE

S helby

THE CROWD outside the arena is so jammed that it makes it hard to navigate. Thousands of fans are here for the final game of the season against Milton. I can't imagine what the Frozen Four in Chicago will be like in a few weeks.

Nadia said she and Twyler would wait for me by the side door, but I'm squished between the opposing red and black jerseys and I'm pretty sure I'll never make it.

"Shelby! Over here!"

I push up on my toes, looking over the bushy haired teenager more interested in his phone than anything else.

"Hey!" I shout, waving when I see Nadia jumping up and down trying to get my attention.

It's a struggle, but I manage to squeeze my way through the swarm and reach them.

"Sorry I'm late." Nadia gives me a hug. "The plane sat on the tarmac for thirty minutes and wouldn't let us off."

"I'm just glad you made it," she says. "Are you excited about your first game?"

"I am, actually." Since Mike had already prepared for me not to be at work tonight, I could actually come. I look over my shoulder at the massive crowd. "Seems like I picked a good one."

"It's going to be intense." Twyler already looks like her head is in the game. "But as long as no one acts like a dumbass I think they can take it."

"All I know is that Axel gave me an update of everything that went down in Texas," Nadia says, eyes rolling, "but I need a first hand account. He's not a reliable narrator when it comes to gossip."

"Can we do it inside?" Twyler asks, edging toward the building.

"No complaints from me. I already miss the warmer weather in Texas."

"Tell me about it," Nadia agrees. She's from Florida, where it's even warmer all year round.

"Here's your wristband." Twyler pulls the strip of waxy paper out of her pocket.

Reid told me that he'd leave me a ticket to the game, and I just needed to meet up with the girls to get it. I stretch out my arm and push back my sleeve, so that she can secure it for me.

"He also sent this."

Nadia hands me a shirt. A Wittmore jersey. I hold it up. It's one of the new designs and when I turn it around I see his name on the back. My belly flutters knowing that he wants me to wear this. Like he told me when we first met, how if he was my man, he wouldn't be shy about claiming me.

"They're revealing the new line of spirit wear tonight as a boost for the finals," Twyler says. "They're still moving forward even if they lose tonight, but they'll get to skip to the top six if they win and the athletic department wants to capitalize on it."

Twyler takes us to a side entrance where she knows the security guard.

"Twyler, come to see our boy pull off a win?" the guard asks.

"He better." She holds out her arm and he scans her in. Nadia and I follow.

"I have no doubt they'll pull through."

"Thanks, Stan," she says, giving him a wave.

"Do you know everyone on campus?" I ask, following her down the hallway. She's always taking us in and out of back doors and no-access tunnels.

"The security guards work all of the games. The basketball games, too. But I know Stan from my time here. He's cool."

"We're inside," Nadia elbows me, "spill. What happened in Texas? With you and Reid."

"I was shocked he came," I admit. "Like, totally surprised."

"But a good surprise?" She grins.

"Yeah, a really good one."

As we walk down the long hallway, I give them the update. How I'd gone back to end the relationship once and for all and to tell my parents I was moving back East. How no one was happy about it, but then Axel showed up, and unbeknownst to me, Reid was waiting up in my room.

"I told him I love him. And he told me he wanted me to come back and stay at the Manor."

"I bet he did." Nadia is beaming. "Did you fuck him? In your parents house? I bet they would lose their minds."

"Jesus, Nad!" Twyer glares at her friend. "You can't just ask people things like that!"

I give a shrug, but there's no hiding the smile threatening to expose me. I'd snuck into the guest room after everyone was asleep and Reid and I definitely made up.

"Oh yeah," Nadia grins and holds up her hand for a high five, "you totally fucked him."

I roll my eyes but slap her hand, marveling at this new life where we go to hockey games to support our boyfriends, wear their jerseys, and laugh and talk about sex, like it's no big deal.

That's what all of my new friends have taught me, Reid too. Sex isn't something to be ashamed of, or kept secret. But it is still a *big* deal, because of the way he makes me feel. I didn't know that love and sex could be so intense until he showed me.

Uninterested in my love life and singularly focused on the game, Twyler surges forward leading us to an entrance to the lower level. The lights, the crowd, the energy is instantly overwhelming, and I take it all in as we climb a few rows to get to our seats.

Before I sit, I peel off my jacket and pull the oversized jersey over my head. The person behind me grins. "I love your jersey."

"Thanks."

That's when I look around and take in the fans around me. Dotting through the crowd are pieces of the new, Reid created, swag.

"Holy crap, guys," I poke Nadia in the shoulder, "look."

Since we came in through Twyler's side entrance, we didn't see the merch being sold. But what I'm seeing goes far beyond a few T-shirts and jerseys. Reid's design is on everything, hats, scarves, patches and bags. They've branded everything with his sassy retro badger, or the new font, including the little guy stitched onto a neck-tie, and the pattern of a button down shirt.

"This is amazing," Twyler says. "I had no idea they were going to do this."

Reid didn't just design a T-shirt or something for a one time use, he's created a new brand altogether.

A motion catches my eye, I look over and see Reid's sister, Veronica waving at me. His parents are next to her, and two other young adults I recognize from photos Reid's shown me. His family. Ronnie shouts my name, "Shelby!"

"Hi, Ronnie!"

She grins when I see her, and I also wave to his parents, which is a whole other can of worms I haven't even processed. Do they know? What will they think?

That answer comes a little sooner than I expect. I've barely sat down, when I hear a shriek. We all turn around and see Ronnie with her eyes bugged, leaning over to one of her siblings and pointing. At me. It's no secret that they're discussing me and the jersey.

"Busted." Nadia smirks. "Guess that's one way to announce your relationship to his family."

My cheeks burn red, but the pleased expressions on his parent's faces tell me all I need to know. They approve.

Taking a deep breath I focus on the ice, where both teams are zipping back and forth. I'm a lot faster at finding the players now. My brother, covered head to toe in pads, hunched in the goal. Reese, with his captain's badge, commanding the players. Jefferson skating around the ice with unnatural grace, like his massive six-five frame and broad shoulders weigh nothing.

And then Reid. Number eight, seemingly focused on the ice, snaps his eyes up to the stands, directly at me. Adjusting his helmet, he lifts his chin and gives me a wink, before skating off to join his team.

And even though no one around me can tell, I swoon. Flat out swoon, because this man is the best thing that ever happened to me.

WITTMORE DOESN'T JUST WIN—THEY dominate.

I've watched the games on TV at the Badger Den and came to the family event a few weeks ago, but nothing matches the exhilaration of watching the sport in action. The guys are fast. Rough. Sweaty. I can't keep my eyes off of Reid as he skillfully commands the ice.

"I think I lost my voice."

Twyler looks exhausted, like she played the game herself. Her high pitch scream is still rattling in my ears, even after the final buzzer and I think my arm is bruised from where Nadia's fingers squeezed me in a death grip every time the puck got near Axel.

"You picked a doozy for the first game," Nadia tells me as we start up the stairs. "The guys are going to be wild tonight."

"What do you mean 'wild'?"

"All that adrenaline running through them..." The girls share a look. "Just prepare yourself."

I have no idea what that means, but we dispatch to the Badger

Den to wait for the guys. Apparently, after a game like this there will be extra press and time with the coach. The fans are already lined up behind the arena, waiting for the players to come out.

"Shouldn't we wait?" I ask.

"Nah," Twyler fluffs her hair, "we'll save them a table, then order some food and beer."

The Badger Den is wild when we get there, stuffed with fans from all over. Mike and Josie give me a quick wave as they manage the crowd near the bar.

"Saved you the long table in the back," Josie says on her way to a table carrying a tray of drinks.

"Thank you." I shrug off my jacket.

She notices the jersey, grins and says, "Nice."

The compliment hits me in a weird way, and I mull it over as I walk to the table. There's a sign marking it reserved. Once we sit, Nadia asks, "What's that look about?"

"I'm just thinking how no one ever talked to me like that about my promise ring from David. I mean, I got congratulations from church ladies and stuff like that, but no one ever looked…" I search for the word, "impressed."

"David is a dud," she says with authority, although she's never met him. "I'm sure there's some girl out there for him, but Reid Wilder? He's a catch. Darla was a fucking fool to let him go–"

"Thank god, tho, right?" Twyler adds, opening her menu.

"For real." Nadia looks at me. "You bagged yourself a future NHL star who is also an amazing artist, and is also the biggest, sweetest, Teddy bear, who–"

"Gives amazing orgasms," I blurt. A second later my face burns hot. "Oh my God, I can't believe I said that."

Both girls lean toward me. "How amazing?" Nadia asks, but Twyler definitely also looks interested in the answer.

I grin, thinking about how weird and wonderful and exciting my life is now that I'm not bound with the rules and expectations I grew up with. Still, some things are just between me and Reid, so I just reply, "Pretty fucking amazing."

My truth bomb shocks them as much as it does me, but thankfully there's a diversion. I don't even have to look to see that the guys have arrived. The cheers and shouts are deafening. My heart hammers just knowing he's here. I haven't spoken to him since I got on the plane from Texas. By the time he, and the others, work their way to the table they have drinks in their hands and wide smiles on their mouths. Then it hits me. It's the first time we've been out together as a couple, and I have no idea how to do that.

They converge on the table, my brother making a beeline to Nadia and Reese pressing a slow kiss on Twyler's temple. I feel that panicky heat until Reid's eyes land on me, and the sweetest, sexiest smile curves his mouth.

"Hey." He skims a hand down my throat, resting it at the base. "Have a good time?"

"It was incredible. You were incredible. You guys killed it."

"It helped having you there." His thumb rubs the neckline of the jersey. "Just knowing you were back and sitting in those stands made me able to focus."

Wow.

Josie and the other waiter start delivering the massive amount of food we'd ordered. Wings, fries, cheese sticks and beer, of course. Nadia had been right. The energy put off by these guys is amazing. They're obviously tired. A few of them bruised, but they're all running on endorphins and adrenaline, replaying the game and strategizing for the next.

The entire time, Reid has me as close as he can get me.

"Anything else?" Josie asks, while picking up empty bottles and baskets.

"Let me help," I say, grabbing a few.

"You're off the clock."

"Yeah, well I can carry a few bottles on my way to the bathroom, right?" I look back at Reid. "I'll be right back."

I toss the bottles into the recycling bin and notice that the container behind the bar is almost out of napkins. I figure I can grab a new package from the storeroom.

I push past a couple making out in the back hallway and step into the supply closet. I've barely stepped inside when someone comes in behind me, shuts the door and wraps their arms around my body.

Reid.

"Thought you could get away, GG?"

"I was just being helpful." I lean into him, feeling the hard line of his erection against my backside. Craning my neck I look up at him. "You need me to help you get a handle on that?"

He pushes the hair off my neck and sucks a kiss into my skin. "I wanted to fuck you so bad the last time we were in here." He licks a hot trail up to my ear. "You weren't ready then. Not the way you are now."

He's the one that taught me how to love and make love. How to be adventurous, chase what I want.

"It's worse now. Ever since I saw you up in the stands." His hand pushes up under my shirt, palm flattening over my belly as it skims upward, until he reaches my breast. My nipples harden instantly, and he squeezes. "I can't wait until we get home, GG."

That's the thing. Neither can I.

Lifting my chin, his mouth meets mine, and he kisses me in that sweet but urgent way that sets my skin on fire. "Fuck me, Reid," I demand, wanting him to know I need it as much as he does.

He groans, breath hot and hands moving, pushing down my pants. "You wet for me?"

Spearing his fingers between my legs, he grunts in approval at the slick heat already building. All those touches and looks back in the bar got me warmed up, and feeling his desire for me only made it more intense. Unbuttoning his pants, I reach for him, wrapping my hand around the smooth velvet of his erection, stroking upward until I feel the pearl of fluid at the tip, and spread it over the head. He rocks into me, thickening at my touch.

"I'm going to fuck you here, GG, then I'm going to take you home and do it again in my bed." He lifts me with his strong arms, positioning me in the way he wants. I let him take charge, I like it that way, I like him bold and forceful. There's no hesitation, he just thrusts into me, thick and hard. I gasp at the welcome invasion, clinging to him as he takes me. Even like this, his fingers dip to touch my clit, rubbing delicious circles with every rock of his hips.

It's fast and dirty, something I never thought I'd enjoy–truthfully, something I'd never even thought about until this man entered my life. The build up, the short, quick, breaths drag me into a headiness that consumes me. One that only breaks as the orgasm shatters over me, I know the second before he comes, because Reid's teeth bare down on my shoulder and he thrusts into me one last time, cock twitching as I tighten around him.

"I love you, Shelby," he says, holding onto me.

I look at him, feeling him inside and out. "I love you, too."

TRUE TO HIS WORD, as soon as we get home from the game, and the after party at the Badger Den, Reid moves me into his bedroom.

And as expected, my brother isn't a fan of this arrangement.

At first we tried being discreet, keeping our PDA to a bare minimum, but everything, every touch, look, glance... it all sets him off.

"I can't sleep knowing you're in there... together," he declares after we return home from the bar. Reid has already carried both of my suitcases upstairs. The boxes being shipped will have to get sorted later.

"Then stop thinking about it, dude," Reid says, wrapping his arm around my waist. "You're the one being weird."

"It's not weird," my brother argues. To be fair. He's a little drunk. Hell, we all are. "How would you feel if it was your little sister?"

"My little sister is fourteen, so we'd have bigger issues." Reid pulls me close. I'll admit, it is weird to be so out in the open with our affection. It wasn't something I did with David and this is all new for me and Reid. Still, I like having my man's hands on me, even if it makes my brother crazy.

"Babe," Nadia says, "Do you want Shelby to think about what *we're* doing?"

"No!" His hand thrusts in his hair. "Why would you say that?"

"You're an idiot, you know that?" She sighs and sits on the arm of the couch.

I open my mouth to tell him to chill out, that I'll go back to the porch, but Reid must sense what I'm about to do and shakes his head. "This isn't our problem, GG."

Finally Axel looks at his girlfriend and says. "Fine. Get your stuff."

Nadia rests her hands on her hips. "Where are we going?"

"To the Teal House where I can pretend none of this is happening."

"Whatever." Walking past me for her bag and coat, Nadia rolls her eyes at me, and pushes Axel out of the house.

"Thank god," Reid says, pulling me against his body. "I thought he'd never leave."

"I feel bad."

"Don't." He takes my chin in his fingers and lifts my face to his. "I have no interest in being quiet."

Reese clears his throat and I realize he and Twyler are still here. Jefferson, too.

"Yeah," Twyler says, grabbing Reese's hand, "we may head down to the other house too."

"Have fun!" Reid calls, watching them scurry out of the house. He then sets his eyes on Jefferson, who is sprawled on the couch, staring at his phone. "What about you?"

"Oh, I don't give a shit about your sex sounds." Jefferson grins, the dimple appearing in his cheek. That little divot gives him a touch of innocence that is false advertising. "I'm here for it."

"Why aren't you at some sorority house or shacked up with a puck bunny?" I ask. After a big win like tonight, I'd think Jefferson would be ready to party.

"Didn't you hear?" he looks up from his phone. "Ingrid Flockton tickets go on sale tonight. She added a surprise show here in two weeks. Right before we head to Chicago for the playoffs."

"Ooooh!" I perk up. "Get me one too!"

"What's your deal with this girl?" Reid asks. "You can't tell me you're really into her music."

"Dude," he says, tone a little hurt, "you know she's my number one."

"Number one?" I ask, looking between them.

"Jefferson has a list of people he wants to hook up with." He cuts his friend an look. "An actual, physical list. Ingrid Flockton is number one."

"She's held that spot since I was thirteen," he says proudly. "I didn't lose my virginity to her, but I did lose it to one of her songs. This may be my chance."

The look Reid gives him is nothing less than incredulous. "You think you'll go to her concert and somehow end up hooking up with her?"

Jefferson's shoulders rise, meeting the blond fringe on the back of his neck. "You gotta shoot your shot, bro, you know that."

"Alright, we're done," Reid says, lifting me in his arms. "Have fun with all that."

"No, you guys have fun." He grins and then goes back to his phone. "And be as loud as you want. No judgment."

Even more than holding hands and kissing in public, it's strange going into Reid's room knowing it's no longer a secret. But it's also nice not to sneak around. He must feel the same because the minute the door is closed he has me pressed against the back of it, hands pushing up my shirt.

"You've been driving me crazy wearing my shirt all night."

"I liked wearing it at the game. People noticed."

His lips are back on my neck. "Yeah?"

"*People* like your family."

"Ah." He straightens up, but doesn't move away, keeping our bodies close. "They told me after the game. Ronnie loves your hair and told my other siblings every detail she knew about you. My mom remembers you as Axel's sister and the nice girl she talked to at family day, and was a little pissed I didn't introduce you that day."

"You in trouble?"

"Nope." His thumb presses into my hip. "They want you to come to the house once the season is over, so that you can meet everyone."

"Is that what you want?"

"They're my family. Of course I want you to meet them. But," his eyes sweep over me and his tongue darts out to lick his bottom lip, "right now I'm too distracted by you in that shirt."

"You want me to keep it on?"

"Fuck no, it'll look even better on the floor."

He wastes no time, stripping both of us down to nothing in a heartbeat, and tossing me on the bed. To my surprise he doesn't make a move, instead, winding our bodies together, more content to just be close than anything else. Poor Jefferson may not get the show he was hoping for.

"You know," he says suddenly, "I never thanked you."

I crane my neck to look at him. "For what?"

"For walking in that door on Valentine's Day and kissing me."

I laugh at the memory because oh my god what had I been thinking? "Well, I want to thank you for giving me the courage to be more than a housewife in Texas."

I run my finger over his tattoo, tracing over the number eight.

"I'm going to need to update that."

"Yeah?"

He looks down at me, and if I ever thought I knew what love looked like before I met Reid, I was wrong. "I thought that when the Wilder's adopted me, that was it. That was the definition of family. That they would be my final home," his fingers skim over my chin, lifting my face to his, "but then you came along and I realized that it's not about the location. It's about the person."

With everything coming our way; my new life. Reid's career. The uncertainty and upheaval, of the two of us finding our path. He's right. I feel it in my bones. It doesn't matter where we live, or whatever we do, as long as we have one another we'll both be home.

AFTERWORD

Want a little extra of our Wittmore U couples? Don't miss out on the bonus you can download straight to your device! You can find it HERE.

~

Jefferson Parks finally meets, not only his crush, but his match, Ingrid Flockton, in *Enchanting the Enforcer,* book 4 in the *Wittmore U: Hockey series.*

~

For special editions of the Wittmore U series please check my TikTok shop at @angellawsonauthor

ACKNOWLEDGMENTS

Some books are harder than others and for some reason Daring the Defender was one of those. The year I wrote this book life was more than a little chaotic. Mr. Lawson had multiple complications that sent him to the hospital, the Dukes kickstarter was a huge undertaking. I felt torn in many directions but writing these guys is always my safe space. It never fails that I feel a little sturdier when I complete a Wittmore U book.

Special thanks to everyone that supported me writing and releasing this book! Anna, my long time PA with @theindieacademy, then Chelsey who handled the backend of the KS that allowed me to focus on the writing. Cat Banks for proofreading, Lisa for being an on the spot beta reader, Mariana for catching all the loose ends. I always say it takes a village to release an Angel Lawson book, so thank you for that!

I also want to shout out to everyone who read the other two books in the series, posted about them on the socials, ordered special editions and spread the love. You guys are rockstars!

Angel